The Serpent and the Eagle

Book One in the Tenochtitlan Trilogy

Edward Rickford

Praise for The Serpent and the Eagle

"A captivating, well-plotted, bicultural dramatization of the months prior to Motecuhzoma's meeting with Cortés, deftly transporting the reader 500 years back into the eyes and intimate relationships of key participants—Mesoamerican and European, emperor and counselor, conqueror and slave."
—Andrew Rowen, author of *Encounters Unforeseen: 1492 Retold*

"The Serpent and the Eagle is a finely crafted story that will captivate anyone interested in history… a lively and entertaining look at people and the greed that drives them."
—Keith Julius, Readers' Favorite

"A wonderful premier novel."
—N.D. Jones, USA today bestselling author

"When two cultures collide, there are always multiple versions of history. A brave and expansive look into the bygone era of exploration by the Spaniards into Aztec lands. A thinking person's novel. Fascinating!"
—Chanticleer Reviews

"The story weaves a rich tapestry of Spanish conquistadors and native Mexica—commonly known as the Aztecs—as well as the neighboring native tribes, that transports readers to the lush jungles and grand cities of pre-Hispanic Mexico. The writing is clear and easy to read, with just enough Spanish and Nahuatl to add deep flavors without slowing the pace."
—Casey Robb, author of *The Devil's Grip*

"Beautifully written."
—Jeyran Main, book blogger for Review Tales

"The Serpent and the Eagle is expertly written and painstakingly researched.... Rickford has captured a fascinating historical moment and turned it into an absorbing story that makes the history come alive."
—Jim White, author of *Borders in Paradise*

"In The Serpent and the Eagle, Edward Rickford has achieved wonderful world-building/scene-setting to the extent that even if you aren't familiar with the history surrounding the novel, you can pick this book up and enjoy it regardless."
—Aaron Booth, author of *Life Eternal*

"The Serpent and the Eagle is another literary text that may offer the reader exits out of the colonial wound of indignity and entrances into the enunciative reclamation of silenced historical, social, and cultural spaces."
—C.T. Mexica, Ph. D, Arizona State University

"I was damn near astonished at the novel's craftsmanship, structure, integrity and accessibility... I've read a great deal of historical fiction—Shaara, Rutherford, Margaret George—and I would stand this work in their company."
—Greg Fields, Acquisitions Editor at Koehler Books and author of *Arc of the Comet*

"Told through multiple points of view, Rickford's words flow from the page like silk, engrossing the reader in insatiable Spanish hunger for gold and the anxiety Cortez's conquest brings to the native Mexica."
—K.M. Pohlkamp, author of *Apricots and Wolfsbane*

Glossary

Mexica: the most powerful people in pre-Hispanic Mexico. Also known as the Aztec, an erroneous demonym popularized by 19th century historians.

Great Speaker: term that refers to the highest-ranking political figure in the Mexica Confederacy. Known as *Huey Tlatoani* in Nahuatl.

Totonacs: disgruntled vassals of the Mexica.

Pilli: the upper class in Mexica society.

Motecuhzoma: leader of the Mexica Confederacy. The Anglicized version of his name is Montezuma and the Hispanicized version of his name is Moctezuma.

Cempoala: capital of the Totonac Confederacy. Sometimes referred to as Cempoallan.

Spanish League: about 3 miles.

Tezoc: High-ranking general in Mexica Confederacy.

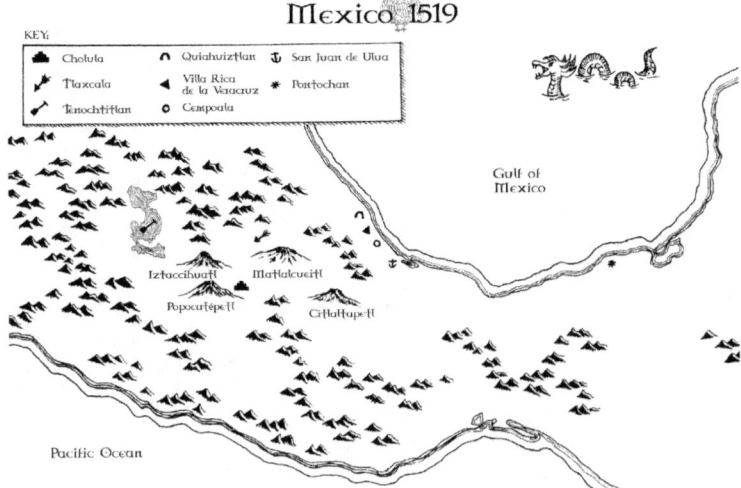

Mexico 1519

Gulf of
Mexico

Iztaccihuatl   Matlalcueitl

Popocatepetl   Citlaltapetl

Pacific Ocean

Chapter 1

Aguilar licked his lips, relishing the briny taste imparted by the tangy ocean breeze. Nearby, a one-armed slave struggled with a bucket of hot tar and a fleet-footed boy scurried up the main mast, but neither kept his attention long. His gaze drifted to the soldiers practicing drills, the pilots taking measurements, the loose sails that flapped with a rhythm not so different from his heart.

Aguilar let out a contented sigh. The *Santa María de la Concepción* exuded so much purpose and activity that a part of him wondered if he was looking at a living organism rather than a technological marvel.

"Has your return to Christendom been all you imagined?"

Aguilar jumped at the sound of Captain Cortés' voice and whipped his head toward him.

Cortés' broad shoulders and scarred knuckles seldom failed to grab Aguilar's attention, but most striking was his posture. With a hand never far from the crucifix hilt of his sword and knees slightly bowed, Cortés appeared poised to strike whether in casual conversation or heated argument. A mere glance from him could check the ruffians.

If Aguilar stared at a crew member, he received disgusted sneers. Perhaps it was his unkempt hair or his fidgety eyes, but neither expedition veterans nor hardened sailors cared to hold his gaze. Aguilar studied his hands. Once soft and gentle, they were now calloused and raggedy. A man could only spend so long in the wilderness before he became something else.

"Lost your hearing?" Cortés asked. His voice came across light and piercing, a rapier in the hands of an expert fencer.

Aguilar apologized in Yoko Ochoko, and then remembered he was supposed to speak Spanish. Eight years had passed since he had spoken the language of his countrymen, and he struggled to remember the right words. In stiff and halting Spanish, he said, "The beauty of our surroundings is overpowering. Can cause a man to forget his wits."

"Is that why you give your back to the real beauty, then?" Cortés gestured to the mainland with a grand wave.

Aguilar turned toward it. He could understand why others might find it pleasing. The endless expanse of verdant jungle offered a bonanza of natural goods ripe for exploitation and the glimmering, deep-water harbors would be ideal for permanent trading outposts. A wave of melancholy rolled over Aguilar as he took in the stunning sight. The mainland used to beckon like light at the end of a cave. Now, he could not look upon it without thinking of all the outrages he had endured the past eight years.

"I prefer the coastline of our home," Aguilar said.

"I love Spain with all my heart, but the natural wonders of the New World cannot be found in all of Christendom. Has your time with the Indians left you so jaded that you can no longer appreciate splendor? Does this garden of Eden not please the eye?"

Aguilar forced a laugh. "I was counting on the beautiful sights to save me. I knew more Spaniards would come one day to..." He searched for the right words.

"Behold the sights? I assure you I intend to do much more than just that." Cortés laughed. Still chuckling, he sat next to Aguilar. "Are we near to where you first landed?"

Aguilar stiffened as the memories came rushing back. The elation when he stumbled out of the poorly-provisioned longboat onto the deserted beach with his delirious countrymen; the apprehension when the Indians emerged from cover; the horror of watching the Indians sacrifice the strongest Spaniards to their cruel gods; the numbness when he learned he would be spared death so that he could toil away as a slave. "We landed elsewhere," he said in a quiet voice.

"You must speak with the cartographers soon. Precious few Christians have mapped these lands. Your insights would be most valuable."

Aguilar nodded and wiped away the sweat beading on his forehead. He adjusted the hem of his shirt, wishing the midday sun wouldn't bear down with so much intensity. But the heat was a constant in this part of the world, as fixed and imposing as the Pyrenees of home.

"It must have been difficult, being a slave for so many years," Cortés added.

Aguilar winced as he recalled the sensation of a switch on his bare back. "I suffered no more than Joseph. I was fortunate, compared to others. I survived. It took many years, but I earned the trust of the Indians, and they granted me freedom."

Cortés huffed. "Surely you did not find your predicament agreeable?"

"I wronged if I suggested such blasphemy! Every day—" Aguilar stopped. Hot tears spilled from his eyes, and he shook with a burning rage confined for years. "I counted the days in my head to track passage of time, I recited what I could remember of Psalms, and I prayed every day so that God would hear me and know I had not lost my faith."

Aguilar succumbed to silent sobs, but he stilled once Cortés placed a hand on his shoulder.

"It's that faith which places you here now," Cortés whispered. "God has raised you from bondage for a reason. Here, do you see that slave?"

Cortés pointed to a nearby slave laboring on hands and knees. He had a complexion that reminded Aguilar of cocoa beans and wore a forlorn expression that spoke to a terrible burden and a long memory. Aguilar watched him pound a length of oakum into the ship planking with mallet and chisel, wondering if the two toes missing from his left foot had been removed with the same tools. He shuddered and chided himself for thinking on it. A free man was not supposed to concern himself with the travails of a slave.

"What about him?" Aguilar asked.

"Do you not notice the resignation etched into his face? These slaves come from all over—the Moorish lands, the Guinea lands, the West Indies—and have little in common other than their condition, but you will find that expression on all their faces. Put a Christian in the same lamentable condition, and you will never find resignation. Our strength is too great to suffer so meekly, and the only indignities we suffer are temporary. Whenever thoughts of the past weaken you, remember the strength our good Lord gave you, and know that He has not taken it away."

Aguilar felt a sharp pang of guilt. He came to the New World as a priest, but he did not know if he could still call himself a believer. His dreams were filled with all his most terrible memories—the torment of being adrift at sea in a leaky longboat, the agony of watching the Indians tear out the still-beating hearts of his countrymen, the revulsion of watching them feast on human flesh—and his faith had been shaken by the unrelenting onslaught.

"Father Aguilar, do you doubt Providence had a hand in our fates?" Cortés asked, his tone earnest and gentle. "How else would you have found me if not for His will?

God guided us to Cozumel Island so that we could find you there. It is by God's grace that you have learned the Indian tongue, and you can have faith that knowledge will be a boon to this blessed expedition."

Aguilar tried to agree, but the words caught in his throat like a jagged bone. He swallowed. That only made the pain worse. "I fear God has not blessed me with a spirit as great as yours."

Cortés stared at him askance. "Do you fear the Indians now?"

"Some of them." He wanted to add that he feared any Indian he did not know, but he knew better than to be so honest.

Cortés shook his head. "I cannot have my translator balk at the mere sight of an Indian. Rest, my friend. We need you to be strong."

Aguilar's strength had left him years before, and he prayed that Cortés might lend him some. "I've never seen another Christian do what you have done."

Cortés arched his brow.

"You traded and bargained with the Indians of Cozumel as if they were your own countrymen," Aguilar said. "I lived with them for years and never had that. I know you don't come to the New World for trade or sights; you have too many soldiers for that. But seeing how you... interacted with them, I would have never known you had anything but peaceable intentions."

The corners of Cortés' lips curved upwards as if pulled by tiny hooks. "The man who can wear only one face can only play one role."

Aguilar wondered which face Cortés was currently wearing. "You intend to make conquest, don't you?"

"I mean to find gold and have no thought but to serve God and king."

Aguilar whispered, "I hope you do. I am at your service no matter the cause."

5

Cortés unsheathed a knife and ran a whetstone along the edge. "Good."

Aguilar fixed his gaze upon the crusty red ring that had collected near the knife guard. More likely Indian blood than Christian blood, but he knew it could be the latter. If the stories were to be believed, the captain was not one to shy from a duel. "Tell me of Spain," Aguilar said.

"Gladly." Cortés held up the knife to check its gleam. "Our home country fares well. His Excellency Don Carlos I is our king now, and he is heir to all the great monarchies in Europe. Germanic lands and Sicilian lands are his by birthright. There is talk of Europe being united the way it was during the time of the Romans."

Aguilar furrowed his brow. "Europe unified—under one power? Could it really happen?"

Cortés waved dismissively. "First Don Carlos would have to get all his subjects to call him the same name. He goes by Charles the Fifth in some lands, Karel in others. I will lose no sleep over it. I love Spain far more than I love Europe."

Aguilar lowered his voice. "I hear the Moors mean to reclaim their holdings in Spain."

Cortés' face soured as if he had consumed curdled milk. "Our people will never have to fear the Moors again. They have learned their place and from now on, they will grovel before us."

Aguilar said no more. He would save his other questions for other men. He could not risk earning the ire of his commander. He bid Cortés farewell and took his leave.

"Make acquaintance with the other translators," Cortés called out. "They are Indian, but they will do you no harm. It is high time you stopped fearing the Indians."

Or perhaps, Aguilar thought, *it is time you learned to fear them.*

Chapter 2

Tezoc waited with the other counselors for Motecuhzoma and watched Chimalli, his vice general, run a finger along the lip of a golden goblet. Chimalli had been fascinated by gold for as long as Tezoc could remember, but the substance was by no means a novelty to either of them—few in the One World were unfamiliar with its charming glint.

Tezoc might have shared the interest if it had some practical value, but gold could not provide nourishment or good health. Sure, the soft metal could be molded into interesting shapes or melted into a nice finish, but Tezoc cared little for such trivialities. Nonetheless, Chimalli marveled over the substance like it was green jade.

Tezoc shook his head and wondered what made him so drawn to Chimalli. *Perhaps it is because he is a mystery... or perhaps it is because he is loyal and discreet.* Memories of his last tryst with Chimalli rushed back to him, but Tezoc dismissed them as quick as they came. It would not do to think about such things in Motecuhzoma's palace. If the true depth of his relationship with Chimalli was ever discovered, censure was almost a certainty. As the Cutter of Men, Tezoc was one of the most distinguished generals in the nation, but that afforded him little protection from royal wrath.

His focus drifted to the others seated at the council chamber's table. Fellow generals Chimalli, Itzli, and Cuitlahuac were members of the Shorn Order so they had shaved their scalps save for one braid tucked behind the left ear. Only a handful of warriors were allowed the honorific braid, and Tezoc gave thanks to the gods every day he had been deemed worthy. Merely defending ground in the face of imminent death was not enough to gain entry into the Shorn Order; one had to take a minimum of six captives on the battlefield.

Milintica, the only counselor present who did not command field troops, had no such braid, but he kept his hair short anyway. His position as political advisor to Motecuhzoma ensured his inclusion in high-level discussions and what he lacked in military honors, he made up for with expensive trinkets. Both his wrists were encased in thick, gold bracelets, and he had plugs of green jade for his nose as well as his ears.

A servant entered the chamber and yelled, "Great Speaker Motecuhzoma Xocoyotzin of the Triple Alliance approaches."

Tezoc sprang to his feet and bowed his head so low he had only the floor to behold. To stare at the Great Speaker when he first entered the room was a high offense.

"I would look upon the faces of my counselors," Motecuhzoma said in a voice thick with regality.

Tezoc lifted his head slowly and took a seat. His neck ached, but he dared not complain. Besides, the pain was mild. Sometimes Motecuhzoma had them bow their heads for what felt like hours.

Tezoc's gaze flitted over Motecuhzoma, snagging momentarily on the deep furrows in his brow. Motecuhzoma's fine visage spoke to his distinguished lineage, but his features looked as if they had been crafted by two different artists. The first, a master of his trade, had spent ages polishing Motecuhzoma's swarthy complexion, hewing his chiseled nose and piercing eyes; the second was little more than a vandal and had carelessly etched lines into Motecuhzoma's forehead out of spite.

"How goes the campaign against Tlaxcala?" Motecuhzoma asked.

8

Tezoc studied the other generals, hoping one of them would speak up. Not one did. Milintica, however, actually looked eager to answer the question. Tezoc was not surprised. Milintica was responsible for giving advice to the Great Speaker and managing the affairs of the capital city, but he was not responsible for carrying out the campaign against Tlaxcala. And that made him a very lucky man.

"The trade sanctions have not broken Tlaxcala yet," Tezoc said. "The Choluteca leadership continues to abide by our sanctions, as do our other allies, but they are keen to resume trade with Tlaxcala. They will soon send an envoy to remind you of such."

"Another, so soon?" Motecuhzoma asked.

Tezoc nodded. "The longer these sanctions persist, the more frequent these envoys will become."

"Perhaps now is the time to send Tlaxcala the shield and the arrow," Cuitlahuac said. "Steering traders away from Tlaxcala has not been enough. Let's see if they still refuse to bend the knee when our warriors are at their walls."

Cuitlahuac was brother to Motecuhzoma, but the two were little alike. Cuitlahuac was always ready to pounce, and even a fool knew to tread lightly around him. Motecuhzoma, however, had a knack for putting his enemies at ease—and striking once they let their guard down.

Motecuhzoma rapped his fingers on the table. "Cuitlahuac, I look forward to the day when a political crisis arises, and you counsel against military action." He turned his gaze toward Milintica. "How does our capital city fare?"

"Tenochtitlan thrives," Milintica replied. "Our citizens enjoy unprecedented wealth, and our subjects are safe from all aggressors. The Republic has never been so strong. All glory to you of course."

"Do the Givers still press for more sacrifices?" Motecuhzoma asked.

"Of course. I cannot recall a time when they believed we were offering too many sacrifices. But we do what we must to keep favor with the gods."

Everybody nodded in agreement. Except for Motecuhzoma.

"Perhaps I ought to better educate the Givers on the military situation in the outer provinces," Motecuhzoma said. "Maybe they can let the gods know it is most difficult to keep favor with our vassals when we insist upon more tribute."

A few in the room laughed quietly. Motecuhzoma offered only a pained smile himself whereas Tezoc stared into his cup. The Givers could rip the hearts out of a hundred tributes and still feel like the gods had not been offered enough. No amount of blood would satiate the gods, and the Givers seemed quite similar in that respect. Tezoc's fellow warriors were no different and not so long ago, he was captive to the same bloodlust. He wondered if he could have earned his braid without it.

"Is there still talk that the lower-class children lack food?" Motecuhzoma asked.

Milintica shifted in his chair. "A handful of teachers claim that hungry students are causing classroom disruptions, but it is no urgent matter."

"Our future warriors come from those classrooms," Chimalli said. "It's probably best if they are properly nourished."

Milintica narrowed his eyes. Tezoc sipped his cup to hide a grin.

"One can dig a little in this world," Milintica said. "We can't do much to help the lower class if they won't put away extra food for hard times. Fortunately, our best warriors come from the *pilli* class. There will be many fine, strong warriors when we need them."

"What do the *pilli* suggest?" Motecuhzoma asked.

"They suggest a strong-handed approach. They fear the lower class may forget their place otherwise."

Tezoc glared at Milintica. "I doubt that such a consensus has been etched in stone. Great Speaker, you have courted favor with the *pilli* ever since you were elected. You have earned their gratitude and more. Now would be a good time to make an overture to the lower class."

Milintica opened his mouth to respond, but the Great Speaker silenced him with a wave. "I will think on it and make a decision. We have other issues to discuss. The pale people weigh heavily on my mind."

Tezoc sucked in a breath. Looking around the room, he could see he was not the only one surprised by the turn in conversation.

Itzli cleared his throat and cast his gaze toward Cuitlahuac. Technically, Itzli was successor general to Cuitlahuac, but the title was a formality. He was far better known as Cuitlahuac's Parrot. "They have not returned from beyond the mists," Itzli said. "There have been no recent sightings of them anywhere in the One World. Some say they have left."

An uncomfortable silence settled over the room. Leaving the One World was unimaginable, but nothing about the pale people kept within convention. Some reports indicated that they started landing in the far reaches of the One World nearly ten years ago. They arrived and departed without ceremony, traveling in impossibly large water-houses that moved with incredible speed. Sometimes they sailed by the coastal settlements peaceably; sometimes they established friendly relations with the locals; sometimes they plundered the coastal settlements; sometimes they retreated to their water-houses just to avoid a skirmish. If there was some pattern to the madness, Tezoc could not see it.

"Who in the city speaks of them?" Motecuhzoma asked.

"Only those who are supposed to," Milintica said. "It has been a long time since there was a fresh appearance so talk has died down."

Motecuhzoma looked genuinely pleased. For a moment.

"Great Speaker, why do you worry so much about the pale people?" Chimalli asked.

Tezoc's stare slowly drifted to Motecuhzoma. He had asked himself the same question many times.

"These pale people augur misfortune," Motecuhzoma said. Just thinking about the people seemed to deepen the furrows in his forehead. "Some time ago, a rather unusual merchant came to Tenochtitlan. He brought goods to trade like all his ilk, but he also brought an item he had no wish to part with. Who here remembers that item?"

"A chunk of dark copper, Great Speaker," Tezoc said.

Motecuhzoma pursed his lips. "Well, that is what our artisans tell me, but there is nothing about this chunk of copper that keeps with convention. No furnace generates enough heat to melt it, and no tool can split it. But somehow it must break because this chunk was cleaved from a larger, more fulsome whole. Tell me, what force can break material that an axe can't?"

No one had an answer.

"And the shape is most unnatural," Motecuhzoma continued. "It is smooth and curved on the bottom and artisans tell me that if I found more of this dark copper, I would have an item that looked like a perfectly round melon. None can recreate the object, and I am told there is no duplicate in all the One World."

"Perhaps the merchant was gifted with the dark copper by the gods," Itzli said.

"Then I will suffer terribly, for I have seized the gift and keep it by my bedside." Motecuhzoma flashed a

12

mirthless smile. "However, the story of the merchant gives me cause to believe that I have not offended the gods."

"What story does he tell?" Chimalli asked.

"He claims the pale people brought the dark copper to the One World." Distaste dripped from his every word. "He says the pale people possess a terrible, booming weapon that can fling a volley of dark copper rocks with a force that shakes the thirteen skies."

"A volley of rocks shook the thirteen skies?" Cuitlahuac asked, his voice laced with scorn and disbelief.

Motecuhzoma stared fixedly at his brother. "Others make similar claims. Many Potonchan villagers fell victim to these weapons when the pale people attacked their settlement last year. The body of one child was maimed so terribly she looked as if she had been savaged by a jaguar." He sighed and shook his head. "When I think about the power these pale people command, I shudder to think of the destruction they could unleash on our lands."

"Great Speaker," Milintica cried out in shock. "I have seen you cave in a man's head with just a wooden club. You were the greatest warrior in all your time, and you are the greatest Speaker of all time. What have you to fear?"

Motecuhzoma nodded, but his expression did not lighten. "I am the Great Speaker of all the Triple Alliance, and it is my duty to fear. I have to fear for our precious Tenochtitlan, as well as every other *altepetl* aligned with the Triple Alliance. We must not let our guard down. The pale people do not share our sense of decency. They have no ceremony or ritual for death and take life with the most terrible of weapons. These are not people we want in our lands, yet they are here all the same."

Tezoc studied the glittering golden sculptures scattered throughout the room, the jade-studded mosaic discs, the crystalline face masks, and wondered if it was even possible to prevent the pale people from taking an interest in Tenochtitlan's splendor. An acute thirst struck him, and he reached for his glass of water to ease the pain.

"Great Speaker, some in Tenochtitlan claim that the pale people do not come from the One World. If they do not come from here, then where are they from?" Tezoc asked.

"Not from the One World!" Itzli shouted. "Foolish drivel. There are no other worlds to come from except the world of the gods, and the pale people are not brethren to Huitzilopochtli."

"Be calm," Motecuhzoma said. "The rumors may be true for once. These people do not come from any place we know, but they are not gods. Reports from the village people indicate the pale people suffered mightily to reach our lands. The ones who came two years prior lost many to battle, and those who came last year lost many to disease. The gods know not of death, but the pale people know it same as us. They are not so different from us, even if they come from a foreign land."

"No land I have ever heard of," Milintica said. "It seems the One World is much larger than we ever dreamed."

"Or they come from another world entirely," Tezoc added.

"If we know so little of these people, what can be the proper course of action?" asked Chimalli, his voice heavy and his countenance dark.

Tezoc could not remember the last time he had seen Chimalli so worried. But Tezoc also saw something familiar in his expression: a grim determination to do exactly as commanded.

"Defend the Triple Alliance," said Motecuhzoma. "The pale people crawl along the coastline because they are searching for something. That search must never bring them here. If it does, our own kin may learn for themselves that a volley of rocks can shake the skies."

Chapter 3

Vitale braced himself against the corridor railing as the ship made an unexpected dip and clenched his teeth in frustration. He took a deep breath and laid a hand on his roiling stomach, begging it not to eject dinner onto the floor.

A minute passed before Vitale finally let go of the railing and resumed his march through the fusty innards of the ship. He shook his head and cursed his weak bearing. After weeks of sailing on the *Santa María de la Concepción,* the pitch and roll of the open sea still unsettled his stomach.

Plenty of the men who had joined Cortés' fleet also suffered from seasickness, but he doubted the others suffered as much as him. Not that his suffering mattered to anyone important. Cortés alone would decide when the crew made landfall again, and Vitale had long since accepted that he would have no say in the matter. Just like the rest of the crew, he could no more leave the expedition than he could strike a fortune in Spain. However, unlike them, he would be spending his night attending to a Moorish slave beaten senseless earlier in the day.

Vitale hadn't tried to hide his shock when ordered to attend to the Moor. No one tried to stop Bernal Díaz when he beat the slave in full view of the crew, so Vitale couldn't understand why some *hidalgo* would take such an interest in the Moor's well-being now. It wasn't until he saw the fiendish grin of the *hidalgo* that he realized he was being goaded into an act of senseless defiance.

He almost wished he'd let himself get carried away. Instead, he surprised everyone by agreeing to carry out the task. The *hidalgo*, once he recovered his composure, muttered something about scum looking after scum before dismissing him. Disappointing his would-be tormentor was supposed to feel good, but Vitale felt exhausted more than anything. He was tired of groveling for companionship, bending his knee for men of better station, not having anything to his name.

The ship lurched again, and Vitale careened into a deckhand. The man gave him a gruff push and continued on his way, cursing under his breath.

"Know where the Moor is?" Vitale shouted. If the deckhand gave an answer before disappearing into the half-lit corridor, he did not hear it. Vitale resumed his fruitless search, running his hand along the grimy wall for support.

Something scampered over his feet. A rat, and a large one at that. Everything about the ship was disgusting. The sweet words Cortés had sung in Cuba seemed a cruel joke now. Had he known the privations involved, he would not have joined the expedition. Probably. His squalor in Cuba was no fond memory, and his company on the island left much to be desired. To think he once believed that settlers would not care about his heritage.

The ship rolled again, and Vitale lost his footing. He fell to his knees, and his head collided with something cold and metallic. Pain crashed down on him like a giant plume of ocean water. He waited on his knees for the pain to recede, gingerly rubbing his forehead.

He wanted nothing more than to abandon his search and return above deck. The *hidalgo* probably didn't know where to find the Moor. He wouldn't know if Vitale lied about attending to him. But if the Moor's condition worsened during the night, Díaz wouldn't be the one held responsible.

His head cleared, and a quiet groaning filled his ears. A ship at sea groaned more than a soldier at death's door, but the sound was always in a state of flux, like a choir that couldn't hold the same note. The ship could not have made the noise he heard. The pitch was all wrong. It was too steady, too mournful.

Vitale stood slowly. His head swam, but he could still hear the groaning when he focused. He noticed the faint outline of a doorframe ahead and moved toward it. The sound grew louder.

The ship pitched forward again, and he was thrown against the door frame. He barely caught it and took a moment to steady himself before peering into the tiny room before him.

An overturned chamber pot rolled across the floor. Other than that, little in the room seemed to have any life. Especially not the small prostrate figure lying on straw bedding fit only for an animal. That figure, he realized, was the Moor. He had never seen one so dark-skinned before. It was like seeing a five-legged cat for the first time.

"Have you come… to end my suffering?" the Moor asked in a weak voice.

"Yeah, I guess I have." Vitale paused before stepping into the cramped room.

A shaft of moonlight crept up the Moor and revealed his ruined features. His upper back was crisscrossed with angry welts and ragged cuts, but his face was much worse. It was horribly swollen and misshapen, like an overcooked sausage. Every cut wept blood. Vitale felt a twinge of pity. "Want some water?" he asked.

"Water would be a fine way to end my suffering. Let the sea take me. It's as good a death as any."

Vitale knelt next to the Moor. "Afraid I can't do that. Got orders to take care of you. Drink some water. It'll help."

He pulled out a canteen from under his waistband and swirled it around. He expected the slosh of water to

18

prompt a reaction, but the Moor did not stir from his bedding.

"You really fixin' for an end?" Vitale asked.

"More than you can imagine."

Another twinge. Vitale cleared his throat. "You gotta die another day 'cause I need you to still be around in the morning." He offered the canteen again and set his jaw in a hard grimace. "I'll make you drink it, if I have to."

The Moor stared at him. "Turn me on my side. and I'll drink your damn water."

Vitale pursed his lips. Taking orders from a slave wasn't much better than taking orders from a *hidalgo*.

"I see why Díaz worked you over," Vitale muttered. He tucked the canteen away and, before the Moor could protest, pulled him onto his side in one swift motion. The Moor gasped and sputtered like a man saved from drowning. Once his breathing calmed, Vitale guided the bottle to his lips and tilted it back.

The Moor took long, greedy gulps. He had every excuse, but the water was simply too precious to give it all away. Vitale pulled the canteen away, and the Moor offered only token resistance.

The Moor sighed. "I would show you the way to Timbuktu just for a blanket and some warm food."

Vitale arched an eyebrow. He had never heard of Timbuktu, but the Moor referenced the place so casually it seemed like everyone knew about it.

"You got a name?" Vitale asked.

Pain clouded the Moor's features. "My people call me Suleiman, but I believe you would pronounce it Solomon."

"I hear you come from Granada."

Solomon laughed weakly. "You must not have explored the ocean much if you think that makes me some kind of novelty."

"I hear you lived in Granada before it belonged to Spain," Vitale clarified. "Before it fell to the Christians."

Solomon's gaze drifted somewhere far away. "I consider myself fortunate to have lived in the Emirate of Granada when it was the last stronghold of Al-Andalus. When it was a shining beacon for the world to behold. When it was a home to people who recognize Muhammad and those that put stock in Jesus or Moses."

Vitale laughed and took a swig from his canteen. "You know, not everyone living in Granada is Christian these days."

"I lived in Granada when it was independent, and I lived there after the Christians seized it. It was a very different city from then on."

The finality of his tone made it clear he no longer wanted to talk about the past. Vitale considered leaving. He had already spent more time below deck than he had intended, and he couldn't do much for the Moor by staying. But instead of walking away, he sat next to Solomon. He had heard so much about the magical emirate that it seemed foolish not to stay and hear more. After all, he could not go to his Christian countrymen for answers.

"What was Granada like? When it was your home and you were free, I mean."

A curious look came over Solomon's face. He quietly came alert, like a mastiff sensing something amiss. He pushed himself up and turned toward Vitale. For the first time, Vitale was able to see all of the Moor's face and knew with a sad certainty Solomon was half blind. One eye was little more than a slit. The other eye was so swollen it seemed to pop out of the socket, like a cork on the verge of release.

"I owe you thanks for the water, and I would like to sing your praises to Allah. What is your name again?" Solomon asked.

Vitale smiled thinly and put away the canteen. "I go by Vitale."

"With a name like that, you could be a New Christian."

Vitale's eyes widened in surprise. He leaned in close and whispered, "Accusations like that could get you beat."

"No need for threats. It bothers me none if your family once put stock in the Torah. You can trust that I am not an Inquisitor. I'm just inquisitive."

Vitale stared at him. "No New Christian admits to being one."

"Very true," Solomon said. "The Inquisitors have made many lost souls think twice about converting to the Christian faith. And I used to think the Church couldn't sink any lower than the Avignon Papacy."

Vitale laughed more than he meant to.

"Did your family convert at the point of a sword?" Solomon asked.

Vitale pursed his lips and studied the slave. "We saw the sense in converting. That's all that matters."

Solomon smirked and shook his head. "I wonder if there is any sense in converting to something you don't believe in your heart. I am surprised you keep company with Old Christians. The Edict of Expulsion was issued not so long ago."

"Can't always choose our company," Vitale said.

"Couldn't agree more. I suppose that sharp sword of yours keeps the worst at bay, though."

Vitale chuckled and tried to forget all those times where his sword had not been enough. "You know, I used to live near Granada. Back when I couldn't even grow scruff on my chin. Nobody called it the Emirate then. Just Granada."

"None too surprising. You are just a boy, after all. The Emirate probably fell before you were even born."

"Almost half a decade before."

"You are even younger than I thought. It seems there will never be a shortage of boys who jump on board a ship just to escape."

"Well, truth be told, I thought there would be a few more women on board." A smile split Vitale's face. "My ma sailed to Granada when she was hardly any older than me."

"Where did she begin her journey?"

"Amsterdam. She met my father in port and came back with him to Granada. She could hardly speak the same language as him at first. Faith was really all they shared then."

Vitale sighed. His parents had built quite the life together. But that life did not last long because the Emirate fell, and the Christians took over. And the fools they were, they stayed long after the Edict of Expulsion was issued.

"You're a Spanish-speaking Dutchman with a Sephardic name?" Solomon spat out Dutchman like it was something rancid. "Now that is very unusual."

Vitale shrugged. "I speak Spanish the same as everyone else."

Solomon stared at him like he was an animal.

"Dutchman sounds like an insult, the way you say it," Vitale said.

"Well, it's certainly no great accomplishment to be one." Solomon's face twisted with rage. "My people established kingdoms that lasted centuries; we made contributions to philosophy, art, and science that will endure for all the ages. And what have the Dutch ever done? Nothing. But my current condition in life would be immeasurably improved if I were a Dutchman instead of a Moor, would it not?" Solomon stopped and caught his breath. He sniffled and added in a quiet voice, "Perhaps if my people had confronted the distant horizons less with our minds and more with our swords, we would still have our homes and I would not be here, ruminating on a better station."

Vitale huffed. "Keep your head down around Díaz and you won't get beat so much. Probably easier to ruminate when you're not bloody and sore."

"He beat me because I wouldn't say *Reconquista*," Solomon grumbled. "If I want to avoid beatings in the future, I will have to renounce my Moorish heritage."

Vitale mulled over what to say next. Judging by the hard gleam in Solomon's eye, he had resigned himself to many more beatings. "Well, why wouldn't you?"

Solomon wrinkled his nose. "Because I refuse to glorify the campaign they waged against my home and my people. I would sooner suffer a hundred beatings before I did that."

Vitale doubted Solomon could survive a hundred more beatings, though he was certain that Solomon would suffer many more if other members of the crew overheard him. Talk of the Moorish wars often brought out the worst in his countrymen.

"Granada was home to me all my life, home to my father before me, and his father before him." His voice broke as he said the last few words. He took a deep breath before continuing. "Now it's gone. They want me to think it never existed. That it always belonged to them and that everything before doesn't matter."

"I hear you fought at Granada. That true?"

Solomon laughed. "Your friends, the Old Christians, have taken everything from my old life. All I have left are my memories, and I won't give them away to some Dutchman I hardly know."

For some reason, Vitale felt confident that Solomon would tell him some other day. Part of him rebelled at the idea of seeing him again, but another part welcomed it.

"Abusing me won't convince me that you love your home," Vitale said.

"Loved. I have a home no longer. My people lost Granada because we were too weak to hold it, and the good things in life belong only to the strong. Ask your *caudillo* if you don't believe me."

"I don't serve any *caudillo*."

"You serve Cortés, don't you? He hopes to take a piece of the New World for himself, and he just may be strong enough to do it."

Vitale blinked and wondered if he had heard wrong. The Moor did not seem the slightest bit concerned that leveling such an accusation could get him beaten or worse. Had a priest said the same thing when they were still in Cuba, even Cortés would have drawn his sword.

"We didn't come to conquer," Vitale said. "We came here to trade and explore."

Solomon scoffed. "Boy, if you've come looking for adventure, you're on the wrong ship. Look around the fleet. Tally up all the slaves and sailors. There are hundreds in number, and they are still not as numerous as the soldiers."

"Soldiers? You mean the ragtag lotta' men armed with shoddy swords and rusty armor that Cortés scraped together for protection? We're sailing for dangerous lands. You forget what happened to the men that sailed here with Grijalva and Córdoba?"

"I did not," replied Solomon. "They were invaders without an army. Cortés has learned from their mistakes. Otherwise, he would not have built one of the biggest private armies in all the West Indies. Over half a thousand soldiers answer to him now."

Vitale shook his head. "I'm part of Cortés' fighting force and I tell you now, I didn't come to conquer anything. I came to protect a trading mission from Indians. Governor Velázquez is only letting us trade—"

"You think Cortés will be reined in by mere parchment? You saw the way he commanded and

24

charmed on Cozumel just as I did. He has been making designs for power all his life, and he will wage war to have his power. You are his tool and a gullible one at that. At least the other soldiers have some understanding of their role."

Vitale narrowed his eyes. "Watch your tongue. We did nothing but trade with the Cozumel Indians."

"Trade we did. We gave them our glass beads for their gold, the little they had. But when I look around the ship, I do not see that many glass beads. I see muskets, falconets, lombards, crossbows, swords, armor, and cavalry gear, but not much in the way of glass beads. Tell me, do you know a single settler in the West Indies that trades weapons for Indian goods? I can't say I know any. But I know many willing to aim those weapons at Indians so that they will be more forthcoming."

Vitale's gut tightened. The New World could often be unsafe for explorers, but it was downright dangerous for conquistadors. "I should get going. Been gone too long." He made his way to the door.

"Your naïveté will cause you more misery yet," Solomon called out.

"Keep counting on that tongue and that wit to save you. See the good that come of it."

Vitale stopped in the doorway. The Moor had been kind in his own way. It felt wrong to just leave him lying in the room in his own filth. He walked back to Solomon and held out the canteen for him.

"Take it," he commanded. "Trade it with another slave for balms. God knows your body needs them."

Solomon pushed the canteen away. "I do not want your pity."

"Are you daft?"

"You are a Dutchman, and I am a Moor. It should be me offering you aid, and you lying here feeling grateful.

Please, no more of your charity. The world is turned upside down enough as it is."

Vitale stuffed the canteen away and stormed out of the room, struggling to remember the last time he had ever felt so slighted.

Chapter 4

Aguilar stared at the foul combination of bile and half-digested food floating behind the longboat. Giant mangroves shrouded the river in shadow, and the opaque water contrasted sharply with the bright contents of his stomach. His gorge rose up again, but there was nothing left to purge. He forced himself back into an upright position with all the grace of a drunk.

The Potonchan Indians were gathering all along the riverbank and made little effort to hide their presence. Or their weapons. *Not Indians—Potons. You've been here long enough to learn the names.* His gut twisted, and he grabbed at his midsection in pain. He took deep, ragged breaths and turned his eyes away from the riverbank.

Cortés' piercing eyes bored into Aguilar and made him feel like retching again. He was tempted to apologize for his weak stomach, but he knew the words would fall on deaf ears.

He cast his gaze upward, hoping he could find some comfort in the heavens. No such luck. Above he saw only a tangled canopy of branches and leaves, thicker than the walls of a castle. Some shafts of sunlight had pierced the foliage, but a tomb half-lit was still frightening.

Not being able to see the sky made Aguilar feel cut off from the rest of the world. They had not traveled under the canopy long, but he already missed the soft blue expanse. It was certainly more comforting than the sights in his immediate vicinity. The Potons were studying his every move like he was some exotic animal. Or invader.

He wished he had been brave enough to refuse when asked to join the exploratory party. Now, he was in a pitiful longboat heading toward some settlement called Potonchan. For company he had Cortés, twenty Spanish soldiers, and the dozens, if not hundreds, of Potons aiming their weapons at them from just a few boat lengths away.

"Father Aguilar, you do not seem well," Cortés said.

Aguilar wiped away the last of the vomit from his lips. "I fear you may have expected too much of me."

Cortés grunted and treated him to a withering glare. "Father Aguilar, why did the Indians grant you freedom?"

Aguilar bit his tongue to keep from answering. He yearned to say that the Indians freed him because they knew he was weak and broken, but he knew he could only expect scorn if he said as much. Judging by the hard-set expressions of the rowers, he was not likely to get much sympathy from them either.

He was sure, however, Cortés would take great offense if he did not respond, so he cleared his throat and said, "There was a *halach winik*—that's what they call the chiefs around here sometimes—named Ah Kin Kutz. Despite being unknown to the tenets of our great faith, the *halach winik* knew me to be a man of virtue. In order to test my resolve, he sent a woman who urged me to violate my vows. Please understand I had known nothing but hardship for years and this woman... the women here are not like other women. You'll never meet a single one with odor. They grow hair only on their scalps and their..."

Aguilar trailed off, searching his memory for an appropriate euphemism. Plenty of Yoko Ochoko ones came to mind, but he could think of no helpful Spanish turns of phrase. *Am I even a Spaniard?* He shook his head and continued. "The woman Ah Kin Kutz sent was absolutely beautiful, and she was determined to have my honor. She told me of her deep longings to give me her innocence, and she swore that our love would be a secret. Oh, the temptations she gave me when she disrobed! I

28

would speak of them, but I could not in good conscience ruin a fellow Christian ear. Even now, she troubles my sleep!"

Cortés chuckled, and the soldiers shared knowing smiles.

"Father Aguilar, there is no need to be bashful," Cortés said. "God forgive my transgressions, for they are many. Beautiful women are the bane of good Christian men everywhere."

They both laughed.

"How did you do it, Father?" Cortés asked. "Resisting women who desire my affections has never been my strong suit."

"I wish I could say I have some great strength, but I abstained for reasons far less noble. She thought that disrobing would make it impossible for me to resist temptation, but it just made it impossible for me to stop staring. I swear by God I cannot remember a single word she said once I saw her naked figure. Couldn't do anything besides stand in place because I was so stunned. She left wondering if I had any sense of hearing, and it was only after she left that I realized that my gaping had driven her away. Ah Kin Kutz was so impressed by my abstinence he granted me freedom."

Cortés tutted and shook his head. "I fear your solution will never work for me. I am not one to let an opportunity pass."

Aguilar mulled over Cortés' words. He doubted any in the expedition considered it a fault. "How are you so calm right now?" he asked. "The Indians might spear us as soon as we step foot on land, but you don't seem the slightest bit worried."

The nearby rowers shot Cortés furtive glances, and Aguilar cursed himself for being so direct.

"Don't think about how many there are," Cortés said, an edge to his voice. "A fall off Seville Cathedral is just as deadly as a fall off El Tajo, and worrying about the height won't change anything. Besides, we have been in range of their weapons for at least twenty-five strokes now. They would have fired already if they intended to kill us."

Aguilar gulped and turned away from Cortés. He hunched forward when he saw a Poton notch an arrow. "They may just want to take us prisoner."

"Every swordhand here knows how to fight in formation so that would be no easy undertaking." Cortés waited a moment for the hurrahing to die down. "But should they succeed in taking us prisoner, I pray God will have mercy on them. Pedro de Alvarado will not, unless I am there to rein him in. That man hunts with more fervor than a mastiff, and he would not let mere jungle hide us from him."

Aguilar had heard rumors of Pedro's brutality. Having them confirmed provided an odd sense of comfort. He stared into the pockmarked, dirty faces of the soldiers and wondered if he had been wrong to feel worried.

~ ~ ~

Caamal pulled back on the bow, ignoring the ache in his shoulder that told him not to. The ache was as familiar to him as his own name.

He could hardly remember a time in his life when he lacked the strength to use the weapon. These days, that strength defined him. His respect, his standing—all of it came from his abilities with the bow. And today, for the first time, he might be able to use it on the pale people.

Had it not been for the water-houses downriver, Caamal and the nearby archers would have already fired on the pale people rowing upriver in their odd boat. He rubbed his thumb along the bow string. He wanted nothing more than to release his arrow, to watch the shaft bury deep into muscle and marrow, but the memory of their terrible weapons stayed his arm. If the pale people in the water-houses possessed the same weapons as those who had attacked Potonchan the year before, firing on the approaching men could prompt a terrible retaliation. He shuddered as he remembered the devastation wrought by the booming volley.

One shard of dark copper had grazed his skin, leaving behind a jagged scar that stretched from shoulder to shoulder. To this day, the wound still pained him. His brother was not so fortunate. A shard of dark copper struck his brother in the throat, and he died choking on his own blood. Caamal had no wish to face those booming weapons again, but if the pale people could only be ejected by means of force, Caamal would face them a hundred times over. He took heart knowing that Tabscoob, leader of Potonchan, would also stand alongside him in battle.

The pale people continued to advance, and their faces became clearer as they approached. Of the twenty-two, only two were not rowing. Caamal focused his attention on them.

One had a subdued look in his eyes; the other had a dead stare like a python. Both had hair growing out of their faces, and Caamal had to wonder if he had ever met Potons with half as much facial hair as the pale people.

"Do not come closer," Tabscoob shouted at the pale people. Undaunted, they continued to row upriver. Tabscoob motioned to a nearby archer, and an arrow went flying out from behind cover.

The arrow buried deep into an oar and the pale man who had not been rowing shouted at the others. Finally, the boat came to a stop and the loud man who had not been rowing said something to the other pale man who had not been rowing.

The pale man with the subdued expression stood and almost fell over when the boat rocked to the right. His arms shot out for balance, and it seemed an eternity before

31

he lowered them. "We come in peace," he said, surprising them all by speaking Yoko Ochoko. "We are part of a search mission and wish to trade goods for food and water"

Caamal looked to Tabscoob. He was half a bowshot away, but Caamal could still make out his fierce visage. Tabscoob looked as if he could stare down a jaguar whereas the pale man speaking to them looked as if he might flee from a pup.

"Do not attempt to land," Tabscoob shouted.

"We are short on food and water—"

"Make no landing!"

The pale people conferred amongst each other. "We want to trade," the standing pale man yelled. "We have gold. Do you have gold?"

Caamal's pulse quickened. First, the pale people asked for food and water. Now they had somehow leaped to gold. The ways of these strange foreigners made no sense.

"Advance beyond the line of the palm trees and we will attack," Tabscoob said.

The pale man who could speak their tongue translated for the other one. The boat ebbed innocently in the water. The pale people made no move to advance or retreat and the pale man with the dead eyes studied Caamal and all his countrymen as if he were sizing them up for slaughter.

Chapter 5

Cortés looked over the expedition officers assembled in the cabin. Almost a dozen of them—some born to higher station, some more skilled with steel—and they all answered to him. In theory.

Cortés had his doubts. He'd lost count of all the lengthy family histories he had suffered, all the petty squabbles he mediated, all to earn their goodwill. Nevertheless, many of them answered only to themselves, to God, or, even worse, to Governor Velázquez. If the situation in Potonchan did not soon improve, he knew some of them would, once again, re-evaluate their loyalties. Had he any confidence that a hanging would bind some of the weak-hearted men more firmly to the mission, he would have fetched the rope himself.

"The Potons rebuffed our every attempt at dialogue," Cortés said bitterly. "We may as well have been unfurling sails in a doldrum."

"Perhaps instead of pretending we need food and water, we should just tell the Indians we want their gold." Pedro's suggestion prompted a chorus of laughter. "Along with all their other valuables," he added.

"One swallow does not make a spring," Cortés said in a stern voice. "We still have use for subterfuge, even if it did not work with the Indians this time."

"So, what's the plan now?" Pedro asked. "More subterfuge?"

Cortés snorted. "War, actually."

Silence settled over the group. Escalante, usually too occupied with his chapped lips to take an active role in discussions, froze. Lugo, often content to gaze off into the distance with glassy eyes, regarded Cortés as if he had blasphemed. Puertocarrero paled and stared at his boots.

Of all the officers, Pedro handled the news the best. Whereas many looked to be in the grips of panic or alarm or both, Pedro's expression reflected only mild confusion. His bushy eyebrows furrowed as if he were trying to work out a riddle, and he rubbed his hand through his fiery blond hair.

"Cortés," Escalante said in a hushed voice, "didn't you say the Indians number almost twenty-five hundred?"

"I did."

Puertocarrero gasped. "That means the soldiers would be outnumbered five to one!"

"I said the settlement numbered twenty-five hundred. I did not say they had an army of twenty-five hundred. They will leave their women, their elderly, and their children out of this fight."

"So, perhaps we will only be outnumbered two to one," Escalante demurred. "Those are not good odds."

Cortés turned toward Pedro. "When you landed on Cozumel Island and chased away the Indians, how many men did you have?"

Pedro stiffened. Not only had Cortés publicly censured him for his unauthorized raid against the Cozumel Indians, he had even punished Pedro's main subordinates with time in the brig.

"Just the few aboard my ship," Pedro said.

"But still you managed to gain the village center without a single casualty," said Cortés. "With the few aboard your ship, you made all the Indians too terrified to trade or converse, correct?"

Pedro shifted in his seat. "Yes."

"Only a fraction of the fighting men sailed with Pedro. Remember how few we took Cuba with? They were thousands in number, and we had barely five hundred fighting men, but we crushed them like eggs underfoot." Cortés ground his fist into his palm. "These Indians don't know war like we do. Of all the Indians I came across today, none of them had armor strong enough to stop even a dull sword."

"The ones on Cozumel were helpless lambs," Puertocarrero objected. "These Indians could have real weapons."

Cortés tutted and wagged his finger. "They don't have a single weapon more sophisticated than a bow. We have armor made of Toledo steel. Their numerical superiority will gain them little."

The officers mulled over the information. Many of them were veterans from former New World expeditions, but they had grown accustomed to following timid and meek men. Cortés hoped there had once been a time when they'd dreamt of leading an army to victory for the king. Now they probably just worried about currying favor with some petty lord.

Lugo scratched his chin. "What do we gain by attacking them?"

Cortés stared at him askance. "Their riches, of course."

"And if they lack riches?" Lugo asked.

"Information," replied Cortés. "The Potons may not be willing to dialogue with us now, but they will once we force them to sue for peace. From them, we will learn the lay of the land and, most importantly, where we can find gold."

Pedro huffed and swatted at a mosquito. "I am all for killing Indians, but I also remember what happened to Córdoba's expedition. Makes no sense to attack a large, well-defended settlement without a proper strategy. If we travelled in longboats as you did today, even if we came at night, we would not be safe from the Indians. They could probably shoot a thousand arrows at us before we could row a league upriver. Trying to paddle while arrows are zipping past your face is hard enough, but our troubles wouldn't end once we reached the village."

Pedro shook his head. "Every man would have to unload from the longboats in their cumbersome armor, and then charge up the riverbank. I have not had the chance to study the Potonchan settlement, but I know riverbanks are often muddy. Hundreds of harried men running up a slick slope in armor makes for a risky charge."

"Aye, your way would be quite dangerous," Cortés said. "But there's a better way."

Lugo furrowed his brow. "What is the other way?"

"The Indians have requested my presence in the town center at noon tomorrow for further talks," Cortés said. "Judging by their intransigence, it is either a trap or a waste of time. Either way, little will be achieved if I go alone. But I can bring the soldiers with me when I accept their invitation. The Indians may even be foolish enough to let me stride into the town center with them."

The men laughed.

"Why would they let you sail to the town center with an army?" Pedro asked.

"The way they see it, we're sailing into a trap," Cortés said. "They outnumber us and they have never done battle with our kind so they think they can best us. Nobody wants to spring a trap early so they'll let us sail quite far upriver. Chances are they'll tell us to stop at a line of palm trees near the town center. And by the time we get there, we'll be close enough to the town center to make a rush. Then they will have to engage us with their short-range weapons."

"So, their darts and arrows will be less useful," Puertocarrero said. "They must have other weapons."

"Only spears and clubs," Cortés replied. A few grim faces brightened. It was hard to fear an enemy with no knowledge of gunpowder or swords. "The Indians here don't fight like us," he continued. "Instead of trying to kill us, they will try to capture us alive since it goes against their ways to kill an enemy on the battlefield. Much better to take him prisoner and sacrifice him to false idols later."

"Who tells you this?" Puertocarrero asked.

"Aguilar. He has lived among them for years and knows their ways. He even knows their names. He says they are called Potons."

"Impossible to tell these damned savages apart," Lugo cursed.

"Aye." Cortés nodded. "I struggle too, but I struggle even more to think of reasons why we should not be confident in our abilities. Pray tell, does anyone think that Toledo steel will fare poorly against wooden clubs? Boiled leather would suffice as armor against most of their edged weapons."

Laughter filled the tent again, but it seemed less feigned to Cortés.

"The plan is just a simple brute charge then?" Puertocarrero asked, a hint of worry in his voice. Puertocarrero may not have been Cortés' most valuable soldier, but he was invaluable as an officer on account of his familial relations with the Count of Medellin.

"Pedro has already done me the kindness of pointing out my great affection for subterfuge. The charge past the palm trees will be our main thrust, but it will not be the only card we have at play. Once the charge begins, a second contingent will flank the Indians. These men will have to take position well ahead of the main thrust, but the staggered approach will yield dividends."

"When will you have the flanking contingent take their position?" Escalante asked.

"Tonight."

A pained silence took root among the men.

37

After a long pause, Puertocarrero asked "Who will lead it?"

Judging by the grim expressions of his officers, none wished to leave the safety of the ship to traipse through the jungle in the dead of night in order to set up an ambush that would not engage the enemy until morning.

"Pedro de Alvarado, of course," Cortés said. "I think we can all agree that he has a keen eye for military matters."

All the officers turned to face Pedro. An uncomfortable silence settled over the group like a cold mist. Some of the men fidgeted in their seats, others coughed. Cortés cared little for their discomfort. His gaze was fixed on Pedro so intensely that if the Holy Ghost graced the room with His presence, Cortés would not have noticed.

Pedro laughed, and the tension dissipated. "Couldn't agree with your determination more."

Cortés slapped his knee enthusiastically. "Then it's settled. Tomorrow, we teach the Indians a thing or two about killing."

~ ~ ~

Motecuhzoma stared out at the setting sun from the pyramid's summit, studying the sky's dazzling crimson spectrum the same way a general would study a battlefield. In some places, only a faint red. In other places, an overwhelming flood. But no matter where Great Speaker Motecuhzoma looked, there was always red. Huitzilopochtli, the god of war, had made his desires clear.

The deep resonance of a drum brought Motecuhzoma's focus back to the sacrifice ceremony. He turned from the beautiful view toward the grand mass of Mexica subjects gathered at the base of Tenochtitlan's Great Pyramid.

His subjects were a proud lot, but they never failed to humble themselves before the gods. It was both the sensible and pious thing to do. The gods had given life to all the One World, and the gift had a price. To satisfy this debt, the Mexica offered the ultimate sacrifice every evening without fail. To do otherwise would be tantamount to collective suicide. Huitzilopochtli would not return with the sun without his blood debt, and Motecuhzoma was honored to participate in a ceremony of such immense consequence.

The Givers hauled the first tribute, a captive seized in a long-ago raid, up the stairs to the sacred block. Barely large enough to place both feet upon, round like the sun and inlaid with beautiful carvings, the sacred block had played a key role in thousands of deaths.

The Givers paused before it. Like everything else in the ritual, this was hallowed tradition. The tribute always had the choice of walking to the sacred block free of any compulsion, so it was customary that the Givers pause to let him exercise that right. The tribute refused to do so and tried to slip their grip once the Givers halted. Two Givers then grabbed him by his ankles while two grabbed him under the arms. Together, they lifted him off the ground with the same ease that an eagle swoops up prey.

Despite the tribute's kicking and struggling, the Givers were gentle as they laid him atop the slender block. They stretched him spread-eagle across it, the man's bones and joints cracking in protest. A fifth Giver stepped forward to secure his head. No amount of squirming or struggling would help him now.

As the man succumbed to his sobs, the Giver that would serve as the conductor for the sacrifice stepped forward to address the throng of Mexica gathered at the base of the pyramid. Motecuhzoma paid little attention to the words of the conductor. They were the same every time, even when the Giver was different.

He focused his attention on the cheering crowd. Looking down on them from the pyramid summit, Motecuhzoma should have felt powerful. Yet when he looked at the tens of thousands gathered for the ceremony, a mere fraction of his nation, it inspired within him awe, humility, and fear. He was just a lonely figure standing before a massive horde. If that horde ever turned on him, he would be powerless against it. No man could boast the might to stop that kind of human wave.

He pondered the rumors circulating among his people. They must have been wondering why the offerings were so numerous this ceremony. Ever since he had been elected Great Speaker, he had done his utmost to rein in the sacrifices, but five would happen today. Perhaps they assumed it was some sort of ploy to keep favor with the gods, but Motecuhzoma suspected the astute knew that the increase was just a ploy to mollify *pilli* who did not approve of his religious politicking.

The tribute's shrill scream pierced his concentration. As if to match the increased noise from the captive, the entire ceremony picked up in volume. The syncopated drum beat became more rhythmic, the chanting Givers more mesmerizing, the conductor's bellowing voice more spellbinding, and the cheering crowd even wilder. A scream that had been so terror-inducing only moments before was reciprocated with a wave of festivity that reaffirmed the true theme of the event.

The conductor lifted the flint blade into the air as the sounds of the crowd washed over him. He paused to deliver the final words and then plunged the blade into the small cavity between the tribute's chest and stomach. The knife entered swiftly and easily but had no time to rest. With a feverish gusto, the conductor sawed through sinew and flesh to create a slit large enough for his hand. Warm red blood poured out of the wound and mixed with the white paint that had been slathered over the tribute.

Not a twinge of discomfort flashed across the conductor's face as he carried out the work.

Motecuhzoma watched as the tribute that had been so vocal before was overcome by agony so great he could only blubber in protest. He convulsed weakly, but did little else to fight his fate. Within seconds, his chest cavity was opened to the world, and the conductor went searching inside for the great treasure. His deft hands wasted no time finding it, and he severed the man's life source with nothing more than a strong tug.

The conductor sauntered forward with prize in hand and presented it to the Mexica people. Steam wafted upwards from the displaced organ, and blood dribbled down the conductor's arm, tracing a path along his very own veins. Triumphant and unperturbed, the conductor strode toward the row of receptacles. Each one took on the form of a different stone animal. Some were jaguars while others were eagles. The conductor would decide which was most worthy of the offering. Today, he chose the bird of prey. He gingerly laid the beating heart on the hot coals that filled the basin of the receptacle, and the smell of roasting flesh wafted toward Motecuhzoma.

The crowd cheered, and the conductor beckoned with his knife to the sections of the crowd that were not being loud enough. Behind him, the other Givers removed the body from the stone and carried it toward the steps. The conductor recognized the signal and turned his back on the fawning spectators so he could prepare for the next sacrifice. The Givers who had taken such pains earlier to handle the tribute gently now cast the lifeless body down the long procession of stairs.

There was no denying it was all a grisly affair, but it was necessary to curry favor with the gods. Huitzilopochtli, god of the sun and god of war, had led the Mexica Confederacy to its great heights and they would need his strength to preserve that prosperity.

Huitzilopochtli, however, could lend no strength to the Mexica if he had none himself, so it was vital that the sacrifices continue.

Prosperity was never recognized for its fragility until it was too late. Motecuhzoma worried that the pale people could upend that frail prosperity by returning, but he knew that the growing power of rival nations did not bode well for stability. Tlaxcala remained insubordinate and resources were becoming scarce. Peace had only come to the One World a short time ago, and already it seemed to have overstayed its welcome.

Motecuhzoma turned away from his dear people. The last tribute had yet to reach the top of the pyramid, and Motecuhzoma approached the edge to watch him ascend the hallowed steps.

The tribute walked free of assistance and appeared as if he were preparing for a simple chore. He must have sensed he was being watched because he turned his gaze toward Motecuhzoma. There was something intriguing about his bold stare, his methodical advance.

Many of the tributes climbed the steps unassisted—the warriors most often—but this tribute was different. He had eyes that danced like a moth before a flame and seemed more eager than anxious. Motecuhzoma could not remember the last time he had seen a tribute approach with such a sense of purpose. In their last year of life, many tributes were treated like gods. They were given women, riches, and all they could desire—except more time on Earth. A lavish life was never without cost.

The tribute crested the last stair, and Motecuhzoma stepped aside to let him pass. He was within reaching distance of Motecuhzoma, but he paid his Great Speaker little heed. Instead, he immediately proceeded to the block he would be offered upon. He stroked it tenderly but did not take his rightful place. Instead, he approached the edge of the pyramid. The Givers instinctively stepped forward. At this height, the tribute would die if he jumped. A death like that would give no nourishment to the gods, but it would spare the man a painful ordeal. Perhaps the thought did not occur to him, or perhaps he did not want that death, because he made no move to jump. Rather, he looked upon the crowd as if to evaluate his spectators. He beheld them, and they beheld him in a strange symbiosis. The distinction between spectator and victim blurred.

The conductor tapped the tribute on the shoulder and motioned to the block. The tribute nodded and left his place at the edge, without even a backwards glance at the people who had been singing and dancing in celebration of his impending death. Life falteringly returned to the crowd.

The tribute laid himself atop the sacrificial block and extended his arms. For the briefest of moments, the Givers could not hide their surprise. Motecuhzoma was proud to see, however, that they did not allow themselves the luxury of hesitation.

They secured the tribute in place, and the conductor continued with the usual incantations as if nothing spectacular had happened. When the conductor finally finished, he advanced upon the trembling tribute.

Few tributes were immune to the tremors that stole over people in their final moments, but Motecuhzoma suspected he was seeing a reaction born from excitement rather than fear. He wondered if this tribute had been given the high treatment. If so, Motecuhzoma doubted it had made the man forget the fate that would befall him atop the Great Pyramid. It had probably been a painful reminder more than anything else, and no amount of pampering would have made him forget that he was a prisoner. The confines of life had been the true agony for this man and this was his glorious release.

The conductor raised the knife. Before he could make the final stroke, the man looked him in the eyes and uttered his heartfelt thanks. Fleeting as the moment was, Motecuhzoma was sure he would remember it as long as he lived. The simple words were so powerful, he almost thought he had imagined them. Even the conductor seemed awestruck, and it looked for a moment as if he considered sparing the man.

But that would be no mercy. This tribute was being privileged with a death that would give sustenance to the gods as well as his fellow mortals. Thousands would remember his death, and he would never have to suffer the anonymous, quiet death typical of the unprivileged.

It would be cruel to take that away, so the conductor slashed with the knife. Motecuhzoma thought upon the good death they were giving the man, the good kill the man was giving them, the good sacrifice they were giving the gods, and he knew he was not the only one who felt satisfied.

Chapter 6

Vitale sat in the middle of the longboat, his stomach tightening with every oar dip that pulled the boat closer to the Potonchan settlement. He glanced at his fellow soldiers, wondered if they felt the same numbing fear. Some men made the cross, others muttered prayers, and a few whispered dark jokes.

He exhaled slowly, thinking of all the reasons he should feel safe. Almost every man in the company had been trained in arms from youth; the company leaders had decades of fighting experience between them. He knew he should feel safe. But he didn't.

Reports indicated the village was home to thousands. Vitale had no interest in waging an offensive against an enemy vastly more numerous, especially since he didn't understand why it was necessary to attack. But his confusion mattered little to high command, so he readied for battle like everyone else.

Some great military genius had decided to split the army into separate contingents and decreed they would not initiate battle at the same time. The flanking contingent was given strict orders not to attack until the first contingent had engaged the enemy. If there was some logic to the tactic, he could not see it. Dividing forces when outnumbered seemed a fool's gamble to him. Consolidating forces seemed far more sensible. Or just not attacking. Not that it mattered what he thought since high command gave the orders. All Vitale could do was grumble and be grateful he was not assigned to the flanking contingent that marched into the jungle in the dead of night to take up position. Nonetheless, that gratitude was tempered by the knowledge that his company would lead the attack on Potonchan. He woke up hoping it had all been some elaborate jape. Much to his dismay, he was told to prepare for battle with the other men.

Vitale clenched his fist, counted to three, and opened his hand. Doing so did little to calm his frayed nerves, no matter how many times he repeated the routine. He had spent much of the night searching for a way out of his current predicament yet every "solution" he thought of worsened his situation. First, he considered injuring himself to get out of fighting. If he knew he could avoid the severe punishments inflicted on self-injuring soldiers, he would have.

When he realized he couldn't, he considered fleeing to the jungle. Deserting, however, was far more frightening than facing the Indians in battle. He was in foreign lands and would be lucky to last a day. He knew nothing of surviving in the wilderness and if the stories about the Indians were true, he would have to avoid them at all costs. While he almost fooled himself into thinking he could hail a friendly ship, he knew it could be months or years before he came across other Spaniards. He had no interest in ending up like that Aguilar fellow.

A rustling nearby grabbed his attention. It might have been a small animal. Or it could have been an Indian who would be their enemy as soon as they passed the Point of the Palm Trees—wherever that was. All he knew was that it was somewhere along the river and close to the town center of Potonchan.

He looked behind him and saw many of the longboats were now drifting toward the riverbank. It was a deliberate maneuver. Starting with the rear, all the rowers had been instructed to swing toward the shore in a line that would gradually compress as they neared the Point of the Palm Trees. He understood the benefit of the tactic, but he never would have thought of the maneuver on his own. What he didn't understand was how they managed to row so far up river without incident. He had yet to see a single Indian, and he wondered if they were hiding behind cover.

He tapped the man nearest him on the shoulder. It was hard to know if the man noticed anything since almost all of his upper body was encased in forged steel. Vitale had nothing more than a rusty helmet, ill-fitting chain mail, and a wooden shield; it had been all he could afford and, in some cases, steal.

The man turned toward Vitale. "Yes?"

"Don't it seem odd the Indians let us get this far upriver?"

"No," he said. "Why would it?"

"Well, Cortés said they demanded we leave. If they demanding we leave, why they letting us sail to their town center in force?"

"These supposed to be the friendly Indians, remember?"

"Then why we attacking them?"

"Because Cortés said they demanded we leave," the man said and continued rowing. Vitale pinched the bridge of his nose in exasperation, but he stopped when he noticed the tremble in his hand.

Up ahead, the lead longboats came to a stop. Meanwhile, the swing toward the shore continued. The line was constricting much more visibly now, and the men tasked with rowing were now tucking away the oars. He hoped the Indians were so focused on the head of the column that they hadn't noticed how much the rest of the column had contorted.

"The lead longboats at the Point of the Palm Trees," somebody whispered.

Vitale scoured the river ahead. He found it odd such unassuming trees would serve as such important markers.

Cortés, situated at the head of the column, yelled, "On the part of the King, Don Carlos, subduer of the Barbarous Nations, we their servants notify and make known to you, as best we can, that the Lord our God, living and eternal, created the heaven and the earth—"

He paused, and a new voice began speaking in a foreign language Vitale could not understand. Nonetheless, he could tell the speaker's voice was faltering, stammering, and bereft of conviction.

"Who that talkin'?" somebody asked.

"New translator. Name is Melchior and he's an Indian so he's translating for the other 'uns," a man said in a hushed voice.

"What happened to the old one? Named Aguilar or something like."

"Got sick—"

"Refused to come—"

"Supposed to be useless—"

"What's Cortés talkin' 'bout?" Vitale interrupted.

Jeers of laughter broke out. "Greenhorn so wet behind the ears he don't know *Requerimiento*!"

More laughter. A man behind him shook his shoulder hard and whispered, "It's the speech we're supposed to say to the Indians before we attack 'em. Haven't you ever done battle here?"

"Only training," Vitale said. "Most of the conquesting was already done by the time I got to Cuba."

The soldier looked at him askance. "You mean this your first battling outside the Old World?"

Vitale nodded. It didn't seem prudent to admit that he had never done battle anywhere. He was supposed to fight in the Battle of La Motta, but he caught a fever that almost killed him instead.

"Good luck to you then." The soldier straightened in his seat, his polished armor gleaming like a diamond. He was the perfect model of a conquistador. It was clear to Vitale that this man belonged here and that he did not. He had the sinking feeling the soldier felt the same way. The man looked at him like he was a corpse already. Vitale put a hand on the hilt of his sword and tightened his grip on his shield.

He heard a strange sound, a single tiny *punk*, and looked up to see a thick cluster of dark shafts arcing through the air.

"Arrow volley!" yelled a nearby man.

Every man in every longboat took cover behind their shields and then flung themselves into the river once the onslaught lessened. Vitale attempted to do the same, but he lacked the speed of others. With nobody left in the longboat to balance the weight, it rocked as he leapt out and he crashed into the shallow water face first with an ungainly splash.

He sank to the bottom in seconds and was overcome by a strange sense of serenity. Then he heard the *punk* sound again, felt it this time. A spear had hit his helmet.

His legs and his arms started moving on their own volition, and he pushed himself back above the surface. On his feet again, the water reached no higher than his hip. He gasped as he took in a world full of fighting and chaos.

The sounds of the battle hit him first. He heard cries of anger, agony, even laughter. It was so sickening that he was tempted to submerge himself underneath the water again just to find peace.

The sights of the battle hit him next. The Indians weren't just shooting arrows—they were actually rushing down the riverbank into the water to fight the Spaniards hand to hand. He would find no reprieve underwater, perhaps not even above it, but at least he could find safety by joining rank with his fellow soldiers.

Flailing and struggling, he waded into the shallows until he found firmer footing and then charged forward. Somebody running past him gave him such a hard shoulder he almost lost his balance. He felt like he was in a stampede, and everything was such a blur of motion he almost did not notice the Indian sprinting toward him.

His slippery hands groped for his sword hilt. No time to pull the blade out. Vitale covered himself with the shield and vaulted forward with a tremendous surge right into the Indian. As they made contact, Vitale swung his arm outward with so much force he carried the warrior off his feet. He heard something crack deep inside the Indian and knew the man would pose a threat no longer.

His lungs were burning by the time he reached solid ground, but he charged up the embankment without even pausing to catch his breath. He slashed at a nearby Indian who had his back turned. Bone and flesh instantly became visible.

A Testudo square began to take shape among some of the soldiers, and he rushed to join it. The fighting continued to rage on, but once he joined rank with his countrymen, the pounding in his chest subsided. In the square formation, he had the security that came with numbers and organization. It was impossible for any enemy to attack his rear unless the entire backline fell, and a frontal attack would collide head on with a shield wall. The Testudo square even provided protection from falling projectiles since the men in the center used their shields to create a makeshift canopy.

"Stay tight!" somebody yelled. The call was echoed throughout the formation. As they tightened, Vitale took a position in the shield wall on the outside of the square. As the call echoed, he noticed how small the square was. Only two dozen had joined so far. Still, they were formidable, and the warriors who rushed the formation learned this with their lives.

"Part!" a haggard voice screamed behind him. Vitale obeyed without question. He only moved half a handspan before a crossbow arrow whizzed past him and buried itself in the skull of a distracted Indian.

"Advance!" the square screamed and the soldiers obeyed. Step by step, the unit moved forward in choppy bursts. The rain of projectiles—rocks, arrows, spears—hissed and whizzed all around them. It felt like he was advancing on a hornet's nest. Determined to defend the hive, more Indians poured forth in a new wave. The flood of warriors became so thick that he could make out nothing more than an indecipherable tangle of limbs and combat.

The squad ground to a halt as the route forward became impassable. Vitale staggered back as a spear was thrust into his shield, and he responded by thrusting his sword into something soft.

He realized too late he should huddle closer to his countrymen. Three warriors latched onto his shield and pulled him forward. He let go of the shield and was pleased to see the unexpected maneuver unbalanced his enemies. Vitale drove his foot into someone's groin, slashed outward with his sword to sever a hand, and dived for the shield. He grabbed the handle and rolled over just as a fallen warrior crashed down on top of him. A sharp pain in his wrist made him cry out, and he struggled to push the dead weight off.

A warrior raised his club high in the air and Vitale realized with a sickening certainty his head was the intended target. The world seemed to slow as Vitale watched the club descend and then shatter as a loud explosion ripped the air. The bewildered Indian turned in the direction of the cannon volley and fell to the ground after a well-aimed falconet took him in the chest. The confidence of the remaining Indians broke as Pedro's flanking contingent rumbled to life with more gunpowder weapons, and the town defenders ran for the dark thicket of mangrove forests. The retreat could not have lasted any more than a few moments, but it seemed a lifetime before Vitale could stagger to a knee and purge his stomach of all contents. The immediate threat was gone, but a deep sadness took hold of him, and he wondered if the menace was truly gone.

~ ~ ~

The first and second sword slashes were deep, but Solomon only felt the pain with the third slash. His hand touched his chest. He reminded himself Cortés had drawn the sword not against his flesh, but the flesh of a defenseless tree. Nevertheless, Solomon still felt a lingering and distinct pain as if he had suffered the injury.

He studied the faces nearest him to see if he was alone in his pain. Around him he saw only enraptured faces and idolizing eyes, all of which were focused on Captain Cortés. If the crowd was any indicator, salvation had taken human form.

Much as Solomon hated it, he had to concede that Cortés deserved some praise. He half-hoped the Christians would be repulsed by the locals, or at least suffer heavy losses. Neither had occurred. Instead, Cortés had managed to capture Potonchan after a few hours of fighting. It was over so quickly they were able to transport all of camp into the town center while there was still daylight.

"Men, look around," Cortés shouted. "This morning, this town center belonged to the Indians. Over two thousand Indians lived here. Now they are all gone, save the ones we have in captivity. We fell upon this village with merely five hundred, and here we stand victorious. It can only be the work of God."

Solomon scoffed. Fortunately, the Spaniards nearby did not notice.

"With the royal notary Goday at my side, I hereby proclaim this village conquered and take possession of this land in his Majesty's name. For God and King!"

He raised his sword and was met with a joyful chorus glorifying his majesty the king. It was easy to think Cortés was being praised as his majesty rather than Don Carlos. Solomon did notice, however, that some men grumbled about Velázquez not getting his due.

Cortés returned to his duties, and the crowd eventually dispersed. Solomon hobbled toward a stump to take a seat.

Walking was difficult as he was still recovering from his savage beating, and he took a deep breath once he could finally sit down. He laughed at his sad state. Sweat began beading on his forehead, but he wiped it away before it became noticeable. He learned long ago to never let weakness show.

He took a closer look at his surroundings, and his eyes settled on the stump he had used as a seat. In the morning, it had been a mighty barricade erected by the Indians to stanch an advance. Now it was no more than an unsightly block hacked to pieces by the soldiers. He was surprised the town had not been razed, but he suspected it wouldn't be long before every trace of Potonchan was erased. If Cortés' men didn't do it, some other band of conquistadors would. He had lived with the Christians long enough in the West Indies to learn their conduct by now.

He tore his eyes away from the Potonchan settlement and focused instead on his captors. It was a habit of caution. An idle slave always had to keep an eye out for an idle whip. Slaves were not allowed to sit for long, so he took it upon himself to look busy. Wincing, he reached forward to grab a helmet and a rag carelessly tossed aside.

He rubbed the rusty helmet with the rag and returned his gaze to the new world he had been plunged into. The Indian lands were unimaginably vast by some accounts, and he felt like a flea at the base of a mountain. He knew he was standing amid something far greater than himself, but he had only the vaguest sense as to how small he really was. It frightened him to think that a world so large could be hidden for so long just because of ocean. Had he traveled here as a free man, it might have been humbling. Coming here as a slave, it was another grim reminder that the world he once lived in was far outside his reach.

His chest tightened. He almost gave in to despair, but a strange substance on the helmet distracted him. It was dried blood. Could be Christian blood, could be Indian blood. No way of knowing.

He rubbed more vigorously, and the flakes peeled off. His blurry vision soon cleared. Bondage had long ago dammed the tears.

He stopped to observe his progress. Most of the caked blood had been removed, but some discoloration remained. In some ways, that was comforting. Bloodstains hidden were bloodstains forgotten.

A soldier plopped down next to him. Solomon tensed, expecting to be chastised. The Spaniard, however, did not utter a word and moved little after taking off his helmet for a drink.

Solomon continued to polish the helmet, but he kept the soldier in his periphery. He looked familiar. His features were soft, his eyes doe-like, and his brown hair was rather short. Whereas many Spaniards prided themselves on their copious hair, this one seemed ashamed to have hair. Solomon turned toward the soldier to see more of his face, and he realized he was looking at Vitale, the Dutchman who had offered the canteen.

Vitale turned toward him. Surprise flickered across his face as he took in Solomon's presence.

"Mighty conquistador, you look thirsty," Solomon said.

The soldier pinched the bridge of his nose. "Not so tired I can't still lift my sword arm."

"Then who would tell you stories of the Emirate?" Solomon asked.

Vitale grunted. "I still can't believe how fast it all happened. Before we even got to the point of the palm trees, they was attacking us. Must have been over a thousand of them."

"Tomorrow they will say thousands," Solomon said with a wry smile. He reached for a new piece of armor to clean. "They really had nothing better than bows?"

"Nothing... but there were so many."

"I suppose that is a weapon of sorts. The islanders rarely had that advantage."

Vitale did not seem to hear him. "Cortés saved us all."

"Ah, so now you are enraptured with him too?"

"They were so many. A mob!" His voice quieted. "We only survived 'cause Cortés' tactics. He set up the flank that broke them."

"May he live a thousand years," Solomon said. "Don't forget how much your steel helped."

Vitale lifted his arm and cocked his head to study his chain mail. Solomon wondered if he had forgotten he was wearing armor. That happened to men who warred enough. He hoped that wouldn't happen with Vitale.

"Still can't believe we here."

"Believe it," said Solomon. "The Indians won't soon let you forget."

"Cortés will keep us safe."

"You're placing a lot of faith in him."

"Deserved faith."

"Seems you find your commander invincible after only one battle."

55

"We won even though we were outnumbered two to one, if not three to one," Vitale reminded. "I don't think a single soldier died. Some of us wounded, nothing serious, though. Cortés lost his boot charging up the muck, and that's one of our worst losses. Our enemies lost more than a hundred fighters and their entire settlement."

"All impressive, I admit. Don't fool yourself into thinking you were doing battle with the Sultan's finest troops, though. Your enemy today had no cannons, no guns, no crossbows. You also had surprise on your side today. That may not be true next time."

Vitale glowered and fixed his gaze on Solomon. He opened his mouth as if to let loose a string of invectives, but he stopped himself before uttering a word. He sighed and hung his head. "No need to remind me that I oughta keep my guard up. And you don't got to convince me to hate being here either."

Solomon pursed his lips. "Maybe you really are different than the others."

Vitale smiled. "Feels like I've stumbled into some kind of hell, being here and all. It's intolerably hot and the air—my god, I feel like I'm breathing in steam. Don't help that I got such poor company either. All the Indians want to kill us, and the crew can't talk about anything other than God, gold, and glory. Not that we got any riches coming our way so far. Seems like the only thing we got coming is a whole lot of hate."

"I suppose your esteemed leader will fix all that."

"Maybe. There's nobody I want leadin' us more than Cortés. He saved us from the mob. A lot of us would be dead if it weren't for Cortés."

"A lot of Indians are dead because of Cortés." Solomon shook his head ruefully. "But how do you fare? Are you injured?"

Vitale rubbed his neck. "I got some bruises and some sore spots. Nothing more." He cracked his back. "You go by Solomon, right?"

"Indeed. And your name is Vitale, correct?"

He nodded and stared into space, taciturn as a mute. Solomon had seen it in other men before. Their tongues grew as heavy as their arms when a battle was done.

"This was your first battle, wasn't it?" Solomon asked.

Vitale gave a curt nod. "Went off to some places where there was battle before but never got a taste anywhere. Guess my luck finally ran out."

"Well you are still here, so maybe not quite yet."

Vitale stiffened. "You feel lucky just cause you not dead?"

The bitterness in his voice was just as startling as the question. Solomon was at a loss for words. The soldier did not wait for an answer. He shoved the helmet back onto his head with a grunt and disappeared into the teeming mass of invaders.

It was only later Solomon realized Vitale had left his canteen. Solomon was tempted to leave the canteen where it was, but that felt too callous. Vitale would never get it back since a light hand would be sure to lift it. For all he knew, the boy may have deliberately left it for him. Solomon grabbed it up, feeling like a thief himself, and hid it away for safekeeping. Next time he saw Vitale, he would have an answer for him.

Chapter 7

The events of the day weighed heavy on Cortés, and his body ached as if he had been stretched out on the rack. Just a few hours before, he strutted through camp, reveling in the glory of victory. Then he learned that Melchior had escaped.

The wind went out of his sails after that, and it became harder to ignore the stench of the dead, to block out the lamentations of the Indians taken prisoner. He took to checking in on the wounded men and while he was heartened to know that few men had been seriously injured, it was not enough to revive his spirits. Now, standing outside a physician's tent, he marveled at his carelessness and wondered if he had the energy to meet with any more wounded men.

He doubted any of the men could understand his gloom. Most were overjoyed that Potonchan had been won with so little effort and did not seem to care that reprisal would surely come on the morrow. They only cared the town center had been gained in less than an hour of fighting, and that no company man had been killed in battle, though a great many had been injured. Some knew that Melchior had escaped, but it appeared to Cortés no one else shared his melancholy. Success, it seemed, made for a heady brew that could rob men of their senses. Any thinking man had to recognize that Melchior's treachery could doom the enterprise. Without an effective translator, victory could be achieved, but conquest could not.

Since Melchior had yet to be recovered, Cortés would have to rely on Aguilar once more, the wild man who could not function without constant reassurance.

Cortés took a deep breath and focused on his most immediate tasks. Once he finished visiting with the wounded soldiers, he would have to confer with the officers about sending out scouting parties and improving defenses around Potonchan. He had no idea how long he had been standing outside the physician's tent, but it seemed pointless to wait any longer. Rest was not enough to make this exhaustion go away. Pausing one last moment to rub away the sweat brought on by the infernal humidity, he brushed aside the tent flap and entered.

He was surprised to see the physician had only one patient. The physician was busy tending to the ugly gash on the patient's thigh, and the patient was busy watching, so neither noticed his entry. Cortés considered leaving. The man's wound did not look life threatening, and he doubted his words would help. Kind sentiments could not close a wound.

Cortés scrutinized the soldier. Most would lie down when receiving treatment from a physician, but the soldier had propped himself up on his elbow and watched with a blank face as the physician pushed the needle through toughened skin to stitch the bloody wound close. As Cortés studied his features, he recognized the soldier as the one who had disciplined the Moor.

"What's your name?" Cortés asked.

The soldier turned in his direction, and his eyes widened in surprise. He did a hasty salute and sat up. The physician remonstrated him for his sudden movements, but the man did not seem to care overmuch.

"Bernal Díaz del Castillo," he said, his voice brimming with pride.

"I came here to thank you for your services, but I don't want to disturb you in your current state. Should I visit another time?"

"There is no need to fret; you can visit now. I will be on my feet again in a matter of days, sir."

Cortés smiled. "Men like you are the reason the *Reconquista* was won."

The soldier beamed like an adolescent boy.

"Is this your first expedition, Díaz?"

"My third. I sailed with Córdoba and Grijalva."

"Quite the accomplished man. I pray this search expedition will be more successful than your previous ones."

"It already is. Neither Grijalva nor Córdoba had the strength to fight the Indians and win. Many Christians died because of them. But today, we faced an enemy force thrice our own, and not a single Christian died. I've never been led by such an able commander. It's an honor to be at your service."

Cortés put a hand over his heart. "Please, you flatter me too much. The honor is mine. All I lost today was a shoe, and it has already been replaced. You've lost blood for the cause."

Díaz nodded and furrowed his brow. "The cause," he whispered under his breath as he stared at his wound. Cortés wondered if he had misspoken. "So, there is a cause?" he asked. "We are not just here to trade and search?"

"If you joined out of a deep and abiding love for exploration, I think you might be alone. Your fellow men are here for the gold. Trade will not be enough to bring the promised riches. There will be more battles along the way."

Díaz pursed his lips.

"Is this troubling?" Cortés asked.

"A soldier ought not question his commander, especially one so able." Díaz paused and took a deep breath. Cortés looked at him expectantly, and Díaz cleared his throat. "There are rumors we have only been commissioned to search for gold and to trade with Indians. Many say we have run afoul of Velázquez. They're saying you are a renegade."

"Are we not exploring now? And trust, in a few days the Indians will come to the trading table with gold. This renegade business, it's just idle talk."

"The men will be glad to hear it."

"Any men in particular?"

Díaz stiffened. "It is not my place to talk of these things."

Cortés flashed him a smile as wide as the Grijalva river. "Where do you stand, Díaz?"

"With you. I will follow wherever you lead us."

"And if the riches are slow in coming?"

"I did not come for the riches."

Cortés chuckled. "Have you ever heard of a man named Alonso Quintero?"

"I have not."

"No surprise. He was an undistinguished, lowborn captain. I only know him because he brought me to the West Indies. No memorable qualities other than an astonishing capacity for cupidity. I traveled westward in a fleet, and my captain was a devil among angels. He had no thought other than getting the leg up on his competition, so Quintero was adamant we arrive in the West Indies before the rest of the fleet."

Díaz shook his head. "He certainly wouldn't be the first captain that tried to corner the market."

"Very true, but he could put any other captain to shame. When we stopped in the Canary Islands, we hardly had time to restock our essentials. We were off again so soon that some of us didn't have time to stand on dry land. It wasn't long before we put the fleet far behind and while fortune may favor the bold, I'm less sure it favors the unscrupulous. A storm hit our ship shortly after we left port, and we were forced to return to the Canary Islands following a terrible dismasting."

"That dismasting could have been a death sentence if your captain had sailed farther out," Díaz said.

"It absolutely would have, so we were all grateful to make it back to port. Much to our surprise, the rest of the fleet was still there and stayed docked until we were ready to leave. Their kindness was little appreciated by Quintero. We all left port together, but once we neared the West Indies, he tried to steal ahead in the dead of night. It worked at first. We put ourselves many leagues ahead of the fleet before the storms hit us. We lost our reckoning, and we drifted for days at sea, completely lost. Wasn't until a dove landed on our ship that we learned salvation was at hand. When we arrived in port, we were so thankful we kissed the ground. Quintero's scheming had nearly killed us, yet not one of us begrudged the man. Can you guess why?"

Díaz scratched his head. "I would embarrass myself if I tried to."

"Our captain was a nefarious schemer with little honor, but deep down we knew we weren't much different. The lure of fortune is what brings men across the Atlantic. My pilot was the lowest of the low, yet that did not stop me from feeling that we shared a common creed. But you feel no such kinship, correct? Because you did not come here for gold?"

Díaz straightened. "I came here for glory."

"You have come here for reasons far better than most of your countrymen then."

"Perhaps. But I am just as thankful as the other men to have you as my leader."

"You are not just a mere soldier. You are a conquistador."

Díaz's eyes glittered with dreams of splendor. "For God and King."

"I'm glad to have made your acquaintance. Follow me, and you will regale posterity with glorious tales of conquest all your own."

Before leaving, Cortés ordered the physician to provide Díaz with everything he needed, and the physician informed him he had already given the conquistador generous helpings of alcohol. Realizing Díaz might only remember snippets of their conversation tomorrow, Cortés laughed and slipped out of the tent. The talk with Díaz had put the skip back in his step. If all his men had similar mettle, they would be returning with gold and glory aplenty by the end of the month.

Chapter 8

Pedro stared into the rushing river as he marched with the rest of his company through virgin territory. Onboard the ship, he had traveled hundreds of leagues in a matter of days. Now that he was on land, he could barely cover a league without encountering difficulties.

The meandering river before him was more than just a difficulty. It was damn impossible. Cortés had given him orders to scout the interior for resources, and Pedro worried he would be forced to return to camp without any actionable scouting information, all because the river lacked a ford.

If Pedro had been the only officer tasked with exploring the countryside, it might not have been embarrassing to return empty-handed. However, Cortés also saw fit to send Lugo on a scouting mission, and Lugo would not hesitate to show him up. Any officer would do the same. Unfortunately, Pedro's need to find a way across did not make a route materialize. And he knew Cortés would be no more sympathetic than the river.

Pedro trudged forward with the rest of his company, scanning the hilly clearing for provisions. Most of the men were too awestruck by their surroundings to study it with a military eye. He could hardly blame them. Everything about this land was alien. Even the sun seemed to shine differently here. It was natural they'd be more enraptured with the exotic wildlife than the depth of the river. Less than a league ago, they were traipsing through endless jungle. Now they were wandering through a clearing as vast as the sea, and the jungle was only a distant memory.

He wiped the sweat trickling down his cheek and scoured the terrain for a ford. The river was still impassable, and no amount of wishing could change that. Still, he could not tear his gaze from the river to admire the land like the rest of the men. They were enraptured with the colorful birds and the towering plants, but he found himself unmoved by it all. Too long had he lived without gold to love so unconditionally.

Now he could only look upon the land in terms of personal value, and he saw nothing he wished to possess. All he saw was a river that refused to yield itself to fording. He grumbled to himself that the Indians had probably never even built a bridge. He doubted they had the capacity.

A distant pop made him pause. It sounded as if there had been a gunshot. The popping increased in intensity. Lugo and his men were nearby—it had to be them. And there was only one reason they would be using their firearms.

Pedro charged forward with newfound energy. "Spaniards are under attack!"

Paces disappeared beneath his voracious feet as he charged up a nearby incline. The acrid smell of gunpowder filled his nostrils, and his eyes watered. Blood pounded so hard in his ears he struggled to distinguish the wild Indian whoops from the heartrending cries of his countrymen.

As he drew closer, the twang of freshly released bows came into focus. His spirits lifted a fraction. An enemy that lacked firearms was more worthy of scorn than fear.

At least that's what he thought before he crested the hill and saw the disparity between the Indian force and Lugo's force. The Indians outnumbered Lugo's men by a factor of four to one, and the Indian archers were sending so many arrow shafts into the sky that some of the Spaniards could do nothing other than cower behind their shields. Pedro charged ahead regardless, but deep down he wondered if Lugo might not be the only officer to lose a battalion today.

~ ~ ~

"Are the Potons willing to sue for peace?" Aguilar asked the kneeling prisoners in Yoko Ochoko.

The three Potons said nothing. Aguilar swallowed down his anger and wondered why he ever let these poor creatures scare him witless. He knew they were warriors—they had been captured by Pedro's soldiers during the rescue of Lugo's battalion—but they looked pitiful more than fearsome.

The engagement had not gone well for the Spaniards, Lugo was forced to make an ignominious retreat as Pedro's forces provided cover, but the capture of the Poton warriors could help them win the next battle.

If Aguilar could get them to talk.

Cortés considered the interrogation of the captives to be of such great importance he insisted it happen in his own tent.

"What will it take for the warriors to lay down their weapons?" Aguilar asked a different Poton in a more forceful tone.

Once again, no response. They were all chained together to form a messy line, and Aguilar doubted he would get answers from any of them.

"Do they understand you?" Cortés' voice was full of accusation and contempt. Much as Aguilar wanted to attribute it to the events of the day, he suspected it was due more to his performance as translator.

"They understand. They just aren't replying," Aguilar said.

"Ask again."

Aguilar ordered them to answer his question. Once again, he was answered with silence. Nevertheless, he did notice something new this time. When he asked the Poton on the far left a question, his eyes darted to the Poton in the middle.

Aguilar moved to the Poton in the middle and asked the same question, all the while keeping his eyes on the Poton to the far right. Just like the other one, his eyes darted toward the middle prisoner as soon as Aguilar started speaking.

Aguilar stepped back and studied the middle prisoner. He didn't look like the other two Potons. His body paint was different, his hair was different, even his proud composure was different. Not to mention he had a jagged scar that stretched across his chest from shoulder to shoulder.

"The one in the middle is a leader of some kind," Aguilar said.

"What makes you say that?"

"Whenever they hear a question, they always look to him first. It's as if they are asking approval." Aguilar cocked his head to the side. "And his appearance."

Cortés rose to his full height with the grace of a black mamba. He advanced on the Poton leader, staring right into his eyes. The Poton held his gaze without flinching.

"Ask him his name," Cortés commanded.

Aguilar did as he was told, but the Poton remained mute. Cortés nodded his head slowly, weighing the new development. Quick as lightning, he slapped him across the face. The Poton seethed with anger, and his fellow captives shouted curses. Cortés raised his hand high, but the Poton continued to hold his stare.

"Cortés, would you allow me to step in for a moment?"

Aguilar turned to see which officer had spoken. Pedro de Alvarado, the one with the fiery hair. Everything about his appearance made him seem a born leader. He was tall, imposing, and handsome, in a rugged sort of way. Aguilar wondered how Cortés had come to be the leader when Pedro seemed the natural fit, but then he remembered

Cortés' gift with words. Few others could boast the same talent.

A smile played at Pedro's lips as he pulled out his knife and advanced toward the Potons. He did not bother to brandish the weapon; he simply tapped it against his leg as if it were an innocent plaything.

In a sudden flash of movement, Pedro seized the hand of the Poton leader and pulled him forward. The others, still chained to him, shouted and fell forward in a tangled mess. Pedro silenced them with a fierce glare and held up the knife to let the Poton leader admire the blade. Chained and splayed out on the ground face down, he was in no position to defend himself. The Poton tried to resist staring, but his eyes inevitably drifted to the jagged edge.

Apparently satisfied, Pedro plunged the knife into the prisoner's hand. A terrible scream rent the air, but Pedro grinned as if greeting a longtime friend. He twisted the knife and let his anger shine through for a brief moment. Aguilar blanched, but his disgust soon gave way to an unexpected interest. It was nice to see the tables turned.

"Ask him about the warriors again," Cortés said, his voice still calm and level.

Aguilar did as he was told. The prisoner's eyes darted back and forth between Aguilar, Pedro, and Cortés. Aguilar had never seen a more confused creature in his life. It occurred to him torture might not be a customary interrogation technique like it was in Europe.

Pedro twisted the knife once again. The prisoner shrieked, and Pedro ripped the knife out. His sudden ferocity vanished, and he reverted to his calm self.

He laid the knife against an unprotected pinkie, but he did it so gently it looked like he had not an ounce of malice in his body. He was anything but gentle when he began pushing the knife down.

"Make it stop!" the prisoner screamed.

"We need to know about the next attack," Aguilar said.

Bone split with a sickening crunch. The prisoner's screams reached a pitch that no longer seemed human. "Stop!"

Torn between pity and approval, Aguilar looked on as Pedro sliced through the finger. The Poton shook as if he were having a seizure. His legs kicked, his arms jerked, but his desperate squirming helped him little. Aguilar was sure of few things in life, but he knew that Pedro would finish this task regardless of how the Poton protested. And complete it he did.

He held the man's severed finger up afterward, and the screaming gradually lapsed into whimpering. Pedro laughed and took a seat next to the Poton, wiping perspiration off the man's brow and brushing his sweat plastered hair back.

"Will the warriors sue for peace?" Aguilar asked.

"No," the Poton whimpered, his face buried in the ground.

Aguilar translated for his fellow countrymen. Pedro looked pleased by the Poton's response, perhaps because it meant more battle.

"Ask him how many warriors will fight for the Potons," Cortés commanded.

Aguilar did as instructed, but the Poton said no more. He sobbed as if his life were ending. Pedro sighed and cleaned his knife against his britches. For a moment, it looked as if he might put the knife away. Instead, he plunged the knife once more into the prisoner's outstretched hand.

The Poton became hysterical. Over and over, he screamed twenty-five thousand as if he knew no other words. Aguilar went dizzy as he put meaning to answer. He staggered into the nearest seat and buried his head in his hands.

"What did he say?"

He looked up from his hands, tried to swallow though his mouth was parched as a desert. "He said there are twenty-five thousand warriors."

Pedro and Cortés exchanged a glance. Pedro sneered while Cortés smiled blithely. Aguilar wondered if there was some joke he had not been made privy to, but he felt too stunned to inquire.

Twenty-five thousand... that was almost fifty times their fighting force. He doubted the Spartans had been that outnumbered at Thermopylae. *This place is not meant for us.* So deeply did he ruminate on the menace that was the Poton army, he did not notice as Cortés knelt down to unlock the manacles binding the Potons. The click of the releasing locks, however, pulled him out of his reverie.

"Tell them they can return to their people," Cortés said. "We want peace and wish to trade. Make sure they know that."

Aguilar desperately wanted to ask why they were releasing them, but he knew better than to question his commander. He translated the statement and watched as the Potons stumbled out of the tent, the leader being helped along by the other two.

"Once the other Potons see what we have done," Aguilar whispered, "they will want revenge."

"Indeed, they will," said Cortés. "Shame they don't have an army equal to the task. The Potonchan settlement is only twenty-five hundred and it's the largest in the area. The Potons could barely field a thousand men before we landed and they have lost hundreds of fighters to our forces. The Indian must have been mad to think we would believe a bluff like twenty-five thousand."

Pedro must have agreed because he looked just as untroubled as Cortés. He wiped a bloody hand through his hair and studied Aguilar closely, as if challenging him for blanching earlier. Aguilar tried to project some of the same confidence as his countrymen. All he managed was a choked laugh.

"How long until the Indians pass on the message you think?" Pedro asked Cortés.

"Before the end of the night."

"Well, I'm glad to have done my part," Pedro said, wicking blood off his knife with a quick snap of his wrist.

"As am I. You have proven yourself today. You saved Lugo's men and got those Indians talking. I won't soon forget it."

Pedro smiled and put away his knife.

"One last thing, Pedro: see if the hounds can't pick up the scent of our bleeding friend. We ought to know where their great army is hiding. Would save us weeks of trouble if we can hit them while they are still a unified body."

Pedro nodded and took his leave.

"What do we do now?" Aguilar asked. "The Indians may expect some sort of peace overture come morning."

The grin that split Cortés' face stretched from ear to ear. He answered as if it were obvious: "Now we ready for battle."

Chapter 9

A series of explosions split the air, and Caamal threw himself against a tree for cover. He gulped air through clenched teeth, wincing as the stub of his pinky brushed against bark. Tears sprang to his eyes, and he gritted his teeth.

The throbbing in his maimed hand intensified, and he swore to get vengeance against the people who had the temerity to seize his home, take him captive, torture him for information, and attack the last remnants of the Poton army.

He breathed in through his nose and peered out from behind the mossy tree to assess the danger posed by the thumping weapons. The grass-covered embankment thirty paces ahead provided ample protection, but it also hid the battle from view.

A new round of explosions commenced, and a startled lizard fell out of the tree to land on his shoulder. He chided himself for flinching. The thumping weapons of the pale people were undeniably dangerous, but they posed no direct threat to him while he was behind the embankment.

Many of his countrymen were not so fortunate, if the agonized screaming was any indication. Guilt and despair welled in his stomach. Only a coward would hide in the forest while friends risked their lives to attack the pale people in the open field.

Caamal took a deep breath to calm himself. Like the other archers, he needed to stay in cover. Otherwise, the trap would fail. He glanced at the eight archers nearby, saw only hard-set faces and hateful glares. He hoped they also understood the need to stay in cover. Most of all, he hoped the warriors dying in the field understood their sacrifice would be rewarded.

A snapping branch grabbed his attention, and Caamal whipped his head in the direction of the sound. Seeing nothing, he let his gaze drift upward. Bright sunlight streamed through the leafy branches, and he had to shade his eyes to see the young one that had climbed into the tree for a better firing position. Caamal would have done the same, if not for his hand. A part of him wondered whether he would do more harm than good in the battle on account of his hand, but he dismissed those thoughts. The Poton army had been too devastated by the battles with the pale people to exempt any man from fighting.

Caamal's hand throbbed with a newfound intensity, and he loosened the bloody poultice wrapped around his pinky stub. His vision swam, and he focused on the battle to clear his head. Soon, he would have his vengeance. Once the field forces knew all the archers were in position, the signal would be given for a feigned retreat to the embankment.

If all went as planned, the pale people would give chase, and the Poton archers would pummel them with a devastating arrow volley once they started down the slope of the embankment. It wasn't a perfect plan, but the pale people had a standing formation far too formidable for a head on attack. Their armor was too strong, their weapons too powerful against massed bunches.

Caamal retrieved a stone-tipped arrow from his quiver. He closed his eyes and strained his ears. Once he heard the signal, he would draw the bow. Then he would finally be able to repay the pale people in kind.

The wind carried a distant jangling to his ear. His brow furrowed. The signal for the feigned retreat was supposed to be a spider monkey howl, not a jangling. He wondered if his ears were deceiving him, but the sound seemed to be growing louder.

"What's that noise?" asked a nearby archer.

Caamal opened his eyes and looked to the other archers for explanation. The one nearest blanched, and the others muttered amongst each other. The jingling gave way to a new sound, a pounding that reminded Caamal of stampeding deer. But it couldn't be that. The stampede he was hearing sounded heavy... and ominous. Caamal's gut twisted in knots, and sweat beaded on his brow.

He looked up at the boy that had climbed up in the tree. "What do you see?" Caamal shouted.

If the boy heard him, he gave no indication of it. A wave of screaming erupted on the other side of the embankment. Caamal swore and rushed out of cover. He wasn't going to hide anymore. His friends needed him. He sprinted up the slope and paused at the top to take in the battle field.

The sight that confronted him was unlike any he had ever seen. The pale people were riding giant, hornless stags so heavy they kicked up clods of dirt and grass with every step. Any Poton unfortunate enough to be caught in front of one of these charging creatures was brutally shoved aside.

Caamal's mouth went dry. The smallest creature was at least a head taller than him, a size he would not have thought possible for any beast with four legs. To even conceive of such a beast seemed ridiculous, but to ride one seemed absolutely preposterous. Yet the pale people were not only riding them—they were attacking the Poton warriors from atop these terrible beasts.

Caamal watched in dismay as the Poton army disintegrated under the assault, scattering like leaves captured in a strong gust. The bulk of the Poton army fled the open field for the embankment. They would need to cover almost a hundred paces just to reach it, and then fifty more to reach the forest.

A ragged cheer rose from the ranks of the pale people as the Potons made a panicked retreat. Instead of giving chase to the Poton warriors, they let the riders cull them into a bunched mass and felled them with targeted volleys.

He winced as he saw one of the riders veer toward a group of fleeing Potons and trample them down like stalks of corn. Caamal rushed down the embankment and focused on the nearest rider. He stopped once he came within forty paces, knelt to gather a handful of grass and dirt. He trickled the debris between his fingers to take measure of the wind and took a deep breath to steady his arm as he took aim at the rider.

His maimed hand burned like fire as he notched his arrow, and his poultice fluttered to the ground. A tear spilled out of his eye, and he wiped his face on his shoulder to clear his vision. Caamal drew the bowstring, but he froze at the sound of a familiar voice. He turned in the direction of the sound. He would recognize the voice anywhere; it belonged to the leader of the pale people.

Hatred refined his senses with a startling precision, and he turned toward his new target, angling the bow above his head to account for the range. His target was sixty paces out and moving laterally. Even an experienced archer with two whole hands would struggle to down that kind of mark. Caamal trained his bow to the movements of his target, thought of all the hours he had spent refining his skills as an archer, the terrible cruelty he had suffered at the hands of the pale people, and prayed the gods would guide his arrow true as he let it fly.

The arrow arced downward with a grace and beauty that would rival an eagle in descent. For a few precious moments, he forgot about the throbbing in his hand and could think of nothing besides the trajectory of the arrow.

His heart stopped as he watched the stone-tipped arrow strike the pale man right in the side of the head and bounce harmlessly off his metal armor.

The rider whipped his head toward Caamal and urged his mount in Caamal's direction. In a matter of seconds, the creature crossed a distance that no man could cover with thrice as much time. The beast had hooves the size of his palm, a body almost twice as long as his bow, and a mass that made the earth tremble. Caamal had no idea what to call the creature, but he was certain he could not kill it with any weapon he possessed.

He opened his mouth to call out for help but thought better of it. Nobody could help him now. The only Potons nearby were fleeing the pale people and would pay no more regard to him than a beetle underfoot. Caamal could join them in their panicked flight, would maybe even make it to the forest if he was lucky. It would be easy to hide amongst the trees and the undergrowth.

Caamal squared his feet. He was done hiding and running. He had given his back to the pale people before, and he would not do it again. He bent down to pick up a discarded club and wrapped his good hand around the handle. Only a few more moments before the rider reached him. He let his eyes rove over the landscape—the towering trees that he had climbed in when he was still whole, the grassy clearings he had raced through when his friends were still alive—and basked in the warmth of late morning sun, wishing only that his arrowhead had been strong enough to pierce the armor.

The beast made a terrible snorting sound as it came within striking distance, and Caamal swung his club outward in a vicious arc. His wooden club connected with the long, bladed weapon of the rider and snapped at the haft like a dry twig. A bitter smile crossed his lips as he felt something cold and sharp cut into his neck.

~ ~ ~

The slave girl eyed the pale people cautiously. For days, her Poton captors could talk only of the monstrous pale people. They did not look dangerous. Strange, but not menacing. Yet if the whispers were true, the pale people had killed hundreds of Potons and did battle from atop giant hornless stags. The Potons were mighty warriors, but they were unprepared for this type of fighting and had no choice but to surrender.

Other stories about the pale people were even more incredible. They were said to command the power of thunder and lightning and wore armor that made them invulnerable. Much of it seemed too wild to be true, but the slave girl knew better than to dismiss it all. The Potons would not be sending peace envoys to the pale people if they weren't powerful. Moreover, they would not be handing over twenty slave women, herself included, to them.

While the pale people did not appear frightening, there was something unsettling about them. Their clothing was odd, their language indecipherable, and their beasts unlike anything she had ever seen. Most noticeable was their stench. She never knew people could smell so foul! They smelled as if they never showered or bathed, but no people could be that barbaric. She did not want to serve any of the pale people, but she was a slave, so her opinion mattered none.

Once, long ago, she had no master. Her eyes misted as the memories came back too strong. She focused again on the pale people lined up before her. They seem fixated on the gold and paid hardly any attention to the girls huddling together. Their utter fascination with the gold was beyond comprehension. The shiny metal was pleasing to the eye but had little value otherwise.

Two of the pale people approached her, and panic seized her. She fought the urge to flee. If she ran into the jungle, the Potons would catch her. If she hid behind her old masters, they would beat her, and hand her over.

She took a deep breath and readied herself for her new fate. If the pale people were merciful, it might be a Flowery Death. But deep down, she rebelled at being made a sacrifice. For some strange reason, despite how cruel life had been, there was a small part of her that fought to survive.

The pale people stopped in front of her and stared expectantly. They did not need to beckon for her to understand their intentions, and she stepped forward after taking a moment to calm her breathing.

They guided her to a man surrounded by guards, and she saw for the first time the one who led these strange people. Dark, bushy hair obscured his chin and upper lip, but skin as white as a maguey bud peeked out from underneath. The leader looked her over. His eyes lingered on her breasts and lips before moving up to her eyes.

Her breath caught. It felt like poisonous fangs had stabbed into her heart. He smiled, and it almost looked as if he was pleased with her. Pain gave way to dismay. She had hoped the pale people would not be captive to those same urges as other men.

He placed a hand against her upper back. His hand was startlingly cold, and she jumped. He looked at her askance. She hardly noticed. His cold touch had unearthed a memory of the other life, when she was a carefree little girl hearing of ice for the first time, that cold substance that somehow numbed sensation. She pushed the memory down. The touch of ice seemed far preferable to the touch of these pale people.

Their leader strode forward and gently guided her toward a pale man with ugly dimples and crooked teeth. Crooked Teeth looked pleased with her appearance, but she noticed a touch of apathy in his stare. The leader of the pale people joined their two hands together and smiled again. He motioned to a pale man dressed in black. The leader kept a firm grip on their hands as Black Robe ambled over.

She tried to hide her confusion. Black Robe placed a desiccated hand atop the knot of hands. For some reason she did not understand, the leader withdrew from the knot, and Black Robe was now the one that made her hold hands with Crooked Teeth.

Unlike many of the other pale people, Black Robe wore no jewelry except for a necklace with small wooden beads. She noticed an odd item hanging from the bottom of the necklace. Two perpendicular lines formed the item's shape, the horizontal line being noticeably shorter. While the design was rather simple, the significance of the foreign item was lost on her.

Black Robe placed two fingers on her forehead before placing them on her stomach. He then moved those same two fingers up to her chest and tapped her twice near each shoulder. Some word, Kristun, was repeated over and over. It almost seemed as if Kristun was being used in reference to her. She wondered what a Kristun was.

Her wondering ceased as Crooked Teeth pulled her forward with a brusque tug. The leader diverted his attention elsewhere, and Black Robe turned away from her. The two pale people that had been so fixated with her now busied themselves with more important matters.

She realized she now belonged to the man she was holding hands with. She looked him over. Crooked Teeth had hair that sprouted from his ears as well as his cheeks. She did not want to think where else he had hair and was grateful he did not return her gaze.

If she was lucky, his loose grip on her hand meant he did not have much interest in her. All the same, she suspected he would interest himself in her body the same way her old Poton masters had. She had learned long ago that men did not need to have much interest in a girl to do that. She tried to swallow the dread down. It almost worked.

She saw a new girl step forward. For a moment, she thought the girl had done so on her own accord. She soon realized she was simply doing as commanded. The pale people were bidding her to come forward with hand gestures and whistles, like one would with a dog.

The ceremony was soon over, and each slave girl was joined with a stranger. There were hundreds of pale people present, but only twenty had been granted slave girls. She realized her master must be an important man, but that mattered little to her. Men of great stature could be just as cruel as men of poor stature.

Her new master led her toward a collection of flimsy shelters supported by beams and stakes. A material not so different from deer skin formed the walls of the structure, and she wondered if it would provide any protection from the elements.

As she was led away, she heard the pale person who could speak Yoko Ochoko ask about gold. He said they came here searching for gold and wanted to know where more could be found. The Potons answered by pointing northwest and saying Mexico over and over.

The translator whispered to the leader. Nothing about the translator looked special yet he had the ear of the leader because he could speak the Yoko Ochoko tongue. She wondered what it would be like to have that kind of power, all because of one simple skill.

The leader nodded and spoke to the translator once again. The translator announced that the pale people would like to go to Mexico and asked for more information. The slave girl froze out of sheer shock. Crooked Teeth did not look pleased by her insolence, but she was too stunned to care. The pale people were going to Mexico, and they were taking her also.

Her new master tugged hard on her arm, and she remembered her place. They resumed their walk, but her mind was aflame. She was returning to the land that had reared her, rejected her, prostituted her, and shamed her.

She wondered if the pale people would ravage Mexico the same way they did Potonchan. If so, her return would be far different than her departure. But Mexico might not notice at all. The land was no stranger to bloodshed.

Chapter 10

Standing in the ship's slave hold, Vitale found it difficult not to think about his station in life. He never had much to his name and had joined this expedition to change that. But even a poor man could feel rich when walking amongst slaves. Once he left he would go back to being a heathen waif with limited prospects, but he was somebody worth fearing when he was in this room.

He tended to avoid the slave hold. The heady mix of sweat, waste, and sickness that hung over the room like a funeral pall was reason enough to avoid the place. The furtive stares were even worse than the noxious odor, though. He had never owned a slave, but that didn't matter once he stepped into the room. It seemed as if every slave would shoot a cautious glance his way, eyeing him like he was some vicious beast that would pounce at the slightest provocation.

The looks used to bother him. Now it was a perverse reminder of the power he had gained since joining Cortés' crew. With sailing begun anew, for some place called Mexico this time, he wondered how high he would be allowed to climb—and if he was safe from falling.

He shivered and rubbed his necklace pendant. The necklace was his only trinket to remember his mother by, and he never took it off. Looking at the slaves, he had to wonder if any of them had trinkets to remember home by. He tucked his necklace away and raised his lamp higher.

He knew Solomon was in the hold, but he could not pick him out amongst all the other dozing laborers. Even with the lamp raised above his head he couldn't see all the slaves, and he had no interest in walking down each row just to find one.

He sighed and knelt down in front of the nearest slave. The slave clenched his eyes shut and moved back a fraction. Inspiring such abject fear may have been humbling in different circumstances.

"Where Solomon at?" Vitale whispered.

The slave said nothing, but his frantic intake of breath made it clear he was not asleep.

"Sol-o-mon," Vitale said through gritted teeth.

The slave slowly opened his eyes and fixed his gaze on Vitale's sword. Without saying a word, he lifted up his arm and pointed across the room. Vitale thanked him and went on his way.

Even knowing where to look, it seemed an eternity before Vitale found Solomon. When he finally found him, he was more exasperated than relieved. His exasperation, however, soon gave way to pity as he took a closer look at Solomon.

Owing to the chains and fetters, Solomon slept on his side, curled up like a wounded animal. Most of his face had healed and only a few thin scars bore testimony to the beating he had suffered only a few weeks before.

Vitale set the lamp down on the grimy floorboards and sat down next to Solomon. Vitale gave him a gentle shake. Rather than rousing from sleep, Solomon muttered incoherently. Vitale shook him harder and Solomon's chains jingled. Vitale winced at the sound.

"It's me," Vitale whispered.

Solomon chortled weakly. "Are you eternal and everlasting truth?"

He furrowed his brow in confusion. "No."

"Well, then go away because I don't want to be woken by anyone else."

Vitale's expression lightened. "Come on, up now. Need to talk to you."

Solomon groaned and sat up. He hunched forward on account of his restraints and sucked in his lips. He didn't say anything. He just jingled the chains a bit and motioned to him. Vitale shook his head. Disappointment flashed across Solomon's face, and he fingered the keyhole in his fetters.

Vitale hesitated. He wondered if his knife could force the catch on Solomon's chains. He dismissed the thought and chided himself for being ridiculous.

"Did you wake me because you are tired of waiting for my answer?" Solomon asked.

Vitale stared in confusion. "Answer to what?"

Solomon looked taken back. "You don't remember? Last time we saw each other, you asked me if I felt grateful to be alive. That wretched question has tormented me for days now."

"Oh. I don't remember asking that." He looked down. The canteen seemed less important now. "I came here because I wanted to know if you seen my canteen."

Solomon huffed and stretched his back. He did not look in Vitale's direction. Instead, he carefully studied each slave as if checking to see if any were awake. "I don't think there is anything less important you could have woken me up for."

"Last time I remember having it, we was still on land. It was just after Potonchan. You seen it around at all?"

Solomon donned a half-smirk and looked him in the face. "I have a proposition for you."

"What?"

"A proposition. An agreement—"

"Thought you was too good for my help."

"I am. However, I would sully myself none if I entered into a mutually beneficial exchange with you."

Vitale glared at the cheeky slave. "I asked if you seen my canteen. You seen it or not?"

"I have your canteen," said Solomon.

Vitale stared at him in disbelief. "Well, I'm needing it back."

"I would be happy to give you back the canteen. But I would ask that you do me a favor as recompense."

Vitale pulled out his knife. The blade glimmered and winked as it caught the light of the lamp. He pressed the blade to the skin underneath Solomon's good eye. He used his other hand to grab Solomon by the back of his head. All Vitale had to do was dig the knife in a little deeper, and he could finally put an end to the impudence.

"I don't got a lot of patience for disrespect," he said. "You wanna lose the other eye?"

Solomon laughed. "I'm a slave. What does it matter what I want?"

Vitale pressed the knife down harder, and Solomon's smile fell away.

"Spending time with the Old Christians has changed you," Solomon said.

Vitale slackened his grip and cocked his head. "What you mean?"

"You ever threaten to cut out a man's eye before joining this expedition?" Solomon asked.

Vitale rotated his shoulder to ease some of the stiffness. "Sounds like you saying Christians aren't too civilized." Speaking the words aloud unnerved him. The crew was not without zealots.

"Of course, I don't think that about all Christians!" Solomon protested. "Yes, there are some rotten ones, and I wish the good ones would bring them to heel, but I certainly don't think they are all violent brutes. However, I must say, the Christians taking part in this expedition have to be some of the worst around."

Vitale withdrew the knife. "What makes Cortés and his lot so bad?"

Solomon stared at him in disbelief. He shot a furtive glance toward the other slaves before leaning in. "Don't you remember what he did to the slave girls?"

Vitale looked at him quizzically. "He didn't do nothing to them. He married the slave women to the officers. Nothing strange about that. Except that I guess he didn't take them all for himself."

Vitale's ribald smile withered under Solomon's withering stare.

"Didn't it strike you as odd that Cortés baptized the girls but didn't free them?" Solomon asked.

"No, why would it?"

Solomon shook his head and sucked in a deep breath. "Perhaps as a free man, you cannot understand the harm that bondage does to the soul, but surely you free people understand the concept of kinship. I understand why Cortés married the slave women to his officers, but I don't understand why he baptized them first. He must know that masters often abuse their slaves. Does he believe abuse is more permissible when master and slave share the same faith? If your countrymen can make slaves of people who share their faith, I shudder to think of the horrors they will unleash on this New World."

Vitale brooded in silence. He didn't even take a woman and Solomon was making him feel like he had committed some monstrous crime. He let go of Solomon and pushed him back.

"You know they don't see things same as you," he said meekly. "They're just following the code of chivalry. When you defeat a man, you take his woman. That's the way it's always been. And besides, can you blame the men for thinking that God smiles on our expedition? Just think of all the times we beat the Indians when they outnumbered us."

"Victory tends to favor the better organized, the better armed, and the better trained; the cause matters less,"

Solomon countered. "Allah does not pick sides in battle any more than he picks a side in the daily lives of people. The Christians know it, too, even if they say otherwise— unless of course they believe that Allah guided my people to victory in Anatolia, in Iberia, in the blessed Holy Land. Allah leaves us to our own devices here on Earth, have no doubt of that."

Vitale stretched out his legs. He noticed he still had the knife out and sheathed it. "You said you had a favor to ask me."

"Many thanks for reminding me—"

"I will listen to what you got to say, but not because you've been kind to me. You haven't at all really. But your people have been very kind to my people in the past, so I will hear you out."

"Many thanks. You know people of my faith are not supposed to eat swine, correct?"

"I do, but I can't say I know much else about your people," Vitale admitted.

"Onboard these ships, there's not much besides bread and pork. Unfortunately, I cannot subsist on bread alone. Now even a pious man would choose pork over starvation, but I'd prefer not having to make such a choice."

"Go on."

"Once we are back on land, there will be game you can hunt and produce you can pick. Since I am a slave—and even worse, a Moor—I cannot stray from the camp, not even for food. But you are a soldier. You can leave camp and can return with all the food you want. I'd like you to bring back food for me. Anything will suffice."

"Almost sounds like you putting yourself at my mercy," Vitale said with a smile.

"Please, I have too much pride to put myself at anybody's mercy."

"I hear pride a sin."

"Well, if I've already earned God's ire, then I definitely want to stay away from the swine."

Vitale chewed the inside of his cheek. "So, after I spare you from starving, I get my canteen back? Feels like I could do a whole lot of waiting while I am providing for you and all."

Solomon straightened himself up as much as he could and began rolling up the sleeve on his trousers. Vitale huffed. The canteen he once thought was gone forever was wrapped around Solomon's calf with a bit of twine.

"You could have traded it to anybody," Vitale said. "I wouldn't have even known you had taken it."

Solomon handed him the canteen. "I didn't take it. I kept it safe for you. And now I'm giving it back to you with the hope you can find mercy in your heart. Whenever you have food you can spare, wrap it in whatever you have at hand and bury it under the sand at the beach. Place three large rocks on top and I will find it."

"I will do what I can," Vitale grunted as he leaned forward to grab the lamp and take his leave. He pushed himself onto his knee and stared at Solomon. "You didn't tell me your answer by the way. About whether you feel lucky to be alive."

Solomon's good eye clouded. "I don't know. And it scares me."

~ ~ ~

Aguilar studied the half-naked slave girls the way an equestrian would horses. Most were scared to look him in the eye and huddled together as if they had been corralled into some invisible enclosure.

Some were bruised from beatings, but most appeared to be in good condition. It was good they weren't too battered—he wasn't sure he'd be able to get information from them if they were in a poor state.

"Can everyone understand me?" Aguilar asked in Yoko Ochoko.

The majority of them nodded, some more enthusiastically than others, while a small handful paid him no heed at all.

Aguilar puffed out his chest. "We will arrive in Mexico soon, and Captain Cortés has tasked me with gathering information. Which of you girls can tell me about Mexico?" One slave averted her eyes when their gazes intersected, while the other faces kept the same blank expression. "You," he said, pointing to the slave who looked away. "Tell me about Mexico. Is there gold there?"

She shuffled her feet. "Yes."

She had played dumb—already she seemed the smartest to Aguilar. He realized the slave, more a woman than a girl, was the one who belonged to Puertocarrero. "What else do you know about the place?"

The slave girl lifted her chin and stared at him. "You do not want to go to Mexico." The confidence in her voice was as surprising as her candor. He suspected she had some kind of education when she was younger.

"Why not?"

"They kill there," said a different slave girl. He looked at the one who had just spoken. She cast her eyes downward once she realized she was being appraised, and Aguilar was able to study her features without distraction. Whereas Puertocarrero's slave was tall and lithe, the slave girl that had just spoken looked short and meek. He doubted, however, that either of them had been spared the switch. The Lord knew he had not been spared beatings when he had still been a slave.

"Who kills?" he asked, hoping the same girl would answer. She did not. Instead, she cast her eyes down and shuffled her feet.

"The Mexica kill."

Aguilar looked to see who had spoken and realized it had been Puertocarrero's slave. "Who are the Mexica?"

The slave girls looked at each other. Some appeared incredulous whereas others appeared scared. But without saying a word to each other, they must have agreed it was best to stay silent because not a single one of them made so much as a whisper.

"Talk!" Aguilar commanded.

"Forgive us, master," said Puertocarrero's slave. "We are all... confused. We know nothing about you pale people. Not all of us can answer your questions, but if you tell us about your land and your people, many would be more forthcoming."

The slave girls stopped their incessant shuffling and focused their undivided attention on him. Aguilar pursed his lips. He could not tell if Puertocarrero's slave was trying to help him or force his hand. He straightened his posture. It couldn't hurt to teach the girls about civilization.

"My people come from a land far away called Spain," Aguilar said. "Our Spain is a mighty country with a mighty military. Our king goes by the name Don Carlos and may be one of the most powerful men to ever live."

One of the slave girls asked what a king was. Aguilar had not realized he had used a Spanish word for king, and he searched his memory for a Yoko Ochoko word that would mean something like king.

"A king is a leader. The main leader."

A few nodded. "Of a village?" one girl asked.

"Of a..." he trailed off. He did not know a Yoko Ochoko word for kingdom either. "A group of large towns controlled by a very large town."

Vacant faces flickered with understanding. "Like Motecuhzoma?" Puertocarrero's slave asked.

"Who is Motecuhzoma?"

"He is the leader of the Triple Alliance. His people call him Great Speaker. You would call him king."

Aguilar rubbed his ear lobe and tried to remember if he had ever heard Motecuhzoma's name during his time as a captive.

"What is the Triple Alliance?"

"An alliance of the three most powerful *altepetl* in Mexico: Tetzcoco, Tlacopan, and Tenochtitlan. He rules everything from Tenochtitlan."

Aguilar mulled over the information. He had heard the term *altepetl* before, but he had never known it was a Nahuatl word. It translated to something like city-state. An alliance among prominent cities suggested a certain level of complexity and politicking that he had always felt beyond the Indians' capabilities.

"Who are his..." Aguilar trailed off again, his ears burning. He did not know a Yoko Ochoko word for vassal any more than he knew a Yoko Ochoko word for king or kingdom. Seeing no other option, he concluded the sentence by saying vassals in Spanish.

"We do not know this word."

His nostrils flared. "Who are his people? What people does he rule over?"

"Everyone."

Aguilar shook his head. "What are his people called?"

"The Mexica."

"And they're the ones to fear? The people who kill?" Aguilar asked.

"Yes," said Puertocarrero's slave.

"And they have gold?"

"All of it."

Aguilar smiled. Cortés would be very pleased by the news. It mattered little that some daft slave girls thought the Mexica were dangerous. They had probably thought the Potons were powerful before the Spaniards crushed them. He considered taking his leave, but curiosity got the better of him.

He focused his attention once more on Puertocarrero's slave. "Why do you know so much more about Mexico than the other girls?"

"I am from there."

Aguilar scratched his chin. "Are there other girls like you in the group?"

"No. They are Mayan. I am Nahua. I come from a small village at the edge of the Mexica lands, near the Maya lands, called Painalla."

"I am still learning your terms. How is Nahua any different than Mexica? Or Mayan?"

"Nahua refers to many peoples." She spoke slowly, the same way one would with a child. "Mexica refers to one group of Nahuas. There are Mexica people and there are Tlaxcala people and Totonacs, but they are all Nahua. Maya is not the same as Nahua. Maya are very different, a different group entirely. Do you understand?"

Aguilar nodded. Nahua referred to people of a certain region the same way European did and Mexica referred to a specific type of Nahua people. He found it troubling the girl would suggest that Mayan and Nahua were fundamentally different, but he did not care enough to correct her.

"So, you divide yourself along Nahua and Maya lines?"

"No. Few think of such things. We identify ourselves by our homes. I come from the village Painalla, so I am Painallan. Those from Potonchan are Poton. Those from Tenochtitlan are Tenocha."

"I think I understand," Aguilar said. Many in the Mediterranean still identified by city-state so it was not an altogether foreign concept.

"What's that dangling from your neck?" asked a slave girl.

Aguilar looked down. The only item dangling from his neck was his rosary. It dawned on him the girls had been inducted into Christianity but not educated on it.

"It is a symbol of the greatest religion on Earth. Long ago, a man named Jesus walked this Earth who endeavored to bring enlightenment to all good people. He performed miracles no mere human has ever been able to duplicate. He was put to death on this right here"—he held up his cross for all the girls to see—"because the sins of humanity were too great for him to be properly received. Yet his divine power let him conquer death, and He watches over us from the Heavens even now."

One asked him if Jesus watched over us alongside the god Huitzilopochtli, while another noted there was no dead man on his cross. One even asked what sin was. Dismayed, Aguilar turned away from the heathens.

"So, your God is great and loving?" Puertocarrero's slave asked.

"In ways we can barely understand," Aguilar said and turned around to face the girl again.

"Do people ever kill for your God?"

Aguilar did not know whether to feel slighted or embarrassed. "At times. Why?"

"The Mexica have very different beliefs, but they do the same. Maybe they already know your God," she said with a sly smile.

Aguilar scowled and stormed his mind for a clever rejoinder. An uncomfortable silence took root, and his color rose. He muttered a curse under his breath and left to report his findings to Cortés.

Chapter 11

The slave girl fastened her hands around the wooden railing and watched as a *pirogue* brimming with villagers drew nearer. The oarsmen were making steady progress against the gentle ocean swells, and she knew the villagers would soon reach the Spanish ships.

The *pirogue* could not have looked more different from the *carrack*. Slim and sleek like the shaft of an arrow, the *pirogue* glided through the water. The *carrack* was long and bulbous, like an egg stretched out on both ends, and rammed through waves with frightening brutality.

She closed her eyes and exhaled. She had no reason to be on deck; staying above could result in punishment, but she could not miss the chance to see people of Mexico once again. She squinted at the handful of indistinct figures crowded into the *pirogue*. Their features were obscured by the distance, but she was certain they were Nahua.

When the Spaniards first anchored at the place they called San Juan de Ulúa, she was skeptical they had actually reached Mexico. They had only left Potonchan three days ago, and it seemed impossible they could have traveled so fast, so far, so effortlessly. Earlier in their voyage they passed what looked like the Coatzacoalcos River, a place she once played with family and friends. Still, she clung to disbelief. However, her doubts disappeared like the morning mists once she laid eyes on the *pirogue*.

Many of the Spaniards were unsettled by the approaching boat. The Yoko Ochoko speaker even questioned her about it. He could not understand why they were being approached after only being in the bay for an hour. He claimed Indians were too docile to ever initiate dialogue with pale people. She asked him what an Indian was. He shot a wary glance her way and disappeared.

She thought of the dreadful things the future might hold, and her heart hammered. Just hearing the name Mexico was enough to send a shiver down her spine. The land had never been kind to her, and she had no reason to think it would be now. Then again, she had the Spaniards for travelling companions.

They made for interesting company. They had wild stories to tell, stories that seemed to be the work of pure imagination. She eventually learned the Yoko Ochoko speaker was named Gerónimo de Aguilar. He told her fantastic tales, of places called Europe and Africa and Asia and the West Indies, but he spoke largely of Spain. It was obvious he had great pride in his homeland, but the more she heard about where the pale people came from, the more frightened she became.

The Spaniards did not seem that different from the Mexica. Both did unspeakable things in the name of their beliefs, both prided themselves on mighty militaries, and both had only recently carved out a place for themselves in the world—yet neither had let this stop them from becoming a dominant power. A vast ocean had separated these kindred people for ages but they were finally reunited... and she suspected the union would be bloody.

Spaniards gathered at the railing to view the approaching *pirogue*. Some came too close for comfort, and she backed away. Any man could order her to leave, and she would have to obey.

The *pirogue* was much closer now, but the villagers still did not appear daunted by the gaggle of Spanish onlookers. Many of the villagers reciprocated the attention and engaged in some shameless staring, too. However, the villagers looked quite alarmed when the Spaniards stabbed a hooked shaft into the lip of their boat.

When they realized they were not under attack, that the Spaniards were only using the hook to pull the *pirogue* closer, they stopped rowing and let themselves be pulled forward. After much shouting and cursing, the Spaniards managed to turn the *pirogue* and dock it alongside their ship. The *pirogue*, so daunting when she was a child, looked pitiful next to the *carrack*.

The Spaniards threw down a rope ladder to the villagers. The material must have intrigued the villagers because they took turns pulling on it before they began climbing. A crowd of Spaniards milled around the ladder, and the slave girl spotted Cortés among them.

While she had long known him as the leader, she had not learned his name until recently. He said something in Spanish to his men. Some gathered around the ladder to help the villagers up while others retreated to form some sort of defensive half-circle. It was odd to watch free men follow orders, and she wondered what had happened in their lives that convinced them to sacrifice their individual will.

The first villager had climbed high enough to be given a helping hand and was hoisted onto the deck. He stood erect as a beam, projecting strength more befitting a young man than a wizened man with a lazy eye. His stoic expression revealed little, but his roving eyes betrayed curiosity. His gaze settled on her as he recognized a familiar skin tone. She wondered if he might have said something to her had she been something more than a slave girl. While the first villager succeeded in keeping a collected composure, the others were less successful. Some went slack-jawed, others went ashen-faced as they took in their new surroundings. The old man shot a stern look their way, and they recovered themselves.

Edward Rickford

The villagers formed a line. The Spaniards kept to their half-circle formation, and the two peoples stood across from each other. The villagers waited for their hosts to initiate the conversation, but the Spaniards did not oblige. They were either too spooked or too dense to know proper custom. Confused that the Spaniards had not greeted them, the villagers started to talk amongst each other.

Cortés, perhaps recognizing that something was amiss, gave Aguilar words to say.

"Greetings on behalf of Hernando Cortés, emissary of Spain," Aguilar announced in Yoko Ochoko.

The villagers looked at him quizzically. Yoko Ochoko was not their language.

"We do not speak that language here," said the old man in Nahuatl. The slave girl felt her heart flutter at the sound of his words. She had not heard the language in almost a decade, but her knowledge of it came rushing back, and she was startled by how much she remembered.

Having heard Nahuatl instead of Yoko Ochoko, it was now Aguilar's turn to look surprised. He tried saying the same phrase in Yoko Ochoko once again. He spoke slower this time, as though he was speaking to somebody hard of hearing.

"We speak Nahuatl here," the old man said.

Aguilar tried a different dialect of Yoko. None of the villagers bothered to answer. It was obvious that Aguilar could not speak Nahuatl. The slave girl could hardly believe it. The Spaniards had traveled all this way to Mexico without even knowing the language. They knew next to nothing of the land and must have assumed it was like the other lands they had visited. She wondered if they thought all the New World people were the same and struggled to fathom such appalling ignorance.

Perspiring due to the heat or his humiliation, Aguilar tried to explain the situation. Cortés erupted in rage, shouting at Aguilar with such force that spittle flew from

97

his mouth. Aguilar wilted and shriveled like a flower deprived of water.

He turned to the villagers and gestured to them with hand motions. They glanced confusedly at one another, but they did not respond otherwise. The entire affair was beginning to feel like a farce. They started making preparations to leave.

In her head, she saw what would happen next. The villagers would leave, and the pale people would try unsuccessfully to communicate with others in the land. They would eventually take her away from Mexico, and the place that had once been her home would, once again, disappear forever. The place of her family and friends—just thinking of them hurt. She realized that she had to learn their fate before the Spaniards took her away and stepped forward, drawing many eyes but thinking little of it.

"Does Motecuhzoma press his thumb down on Painalla?" she asked in fluent Nahuatl.

The villagers stared at her and muttered to each other in low tones. She remembered her condition more acutely as she took in their reactions. A slave had no business addressing free people without the permission of her master.

"I'm sorry," she muttered. "My family... my friends.... they are in Painalla. It's in Coatzacualco. I lived there once—I just want to know if...."

She trailed off. She felt horribly conspicuous. Ashamed even. She could only imagine the beating she would receive later. She looked up from her dirty feet and was surprised to see that the villagers had not already departed.

"The arm of Motecuhzoma grows longer and stronger with every moon," the old man said. "His influence can be felt in the farthest reaches of the One World, and his thumb hovers over Painalla like a dark cloud."

His eyes darted to the other villagers, as if to check their reaction. None objected aloud to his description, but some shuffled nervously. Motecuhzoma was so far away that it would take a week to reach his palace, and still he had the power to make these men hedge words. Her lip trembled as she thought about what would happen to the people she once loved if Motecuhzoma pressed his thumb down on Painalla. She stared at her feet and berated herself for showing weakness.

The old man asked, "Do the pale people also have a long reach?"

Jarring as it was to be addressed rather than commanded, she still had enough sense to nod yes.

"How long?"

She let her gaze drift up from her feet and beheld the villagers. It all felt like a dream yet she knew better than to question the turn of events.

"We left Potonchan three days ago," said the slave girl.

The villagers muttered among themselves. On foot, it could take up to a week to reach Potonchan from here. Despite the tremendous distance, she suspected that news of the battle had already reached the villagers. Word had an uncanny ability to outpace the fastest of feet.

"Are the pale people friendly?" asked the old man.

Before the slave girl could open her mouth, Aguilar interjected in Yoko Ochoko, demanding a translation from her.

She turned toward the people that had ravaged Potonchan and was surprised to see she had their rapt attention. She had only wanted to ask the villagers a question and now she seemed to be the focus of everyone.

The stares were mixed. Aguilar looked indignant, others looked confused, but Cortés looked pleased. By her. She smiled back at him, her head feeling light.

"Speak, slave!" Aguilar yelled.

Perhaps it was his tone or the word, but she felt a sharp pang in her chest.

"He wants to know if you are friendly," she murmured in Yoko Ochoko. Already she was expected to act as a bridge.

"Speak louder, dog!" Aguilar commanded.

She pursed her lips and cleared her throat. She felt something stirring in her, rebelling against her treatment. "He asks about your intentions. He wants to know if you are friendly."

Aguilar looked dumbfounded. Perhaps he had never asked himself the question. All the same, he recovered himself and passed on the question.

"Tell them we are friendly," Aguilar replied on behalf of Cortés.

The slave girl swallowed hard. Travel was going both ways on the bridge now. She should have been scared, yet she felt calm more than anything else. "They want you to consider them friendly."

The remark prompted heated discussion amongst the villagers. She felt her curiosity overcome her, and she asked if they were in Mexica lands.

"Motecuhzoma has done us a great honor by absorbing our poor village into Mexico," the old man said in a melancholy voice.

The slave girl nodded. The villagers were probably nothing more than tax subjects for the Great Speaker, but they could still send word to Tenochtitlan. And if they did that, the Great Speaker could send his wrath.

"Where do the pale people come from?" the old man asked.

She turned toward the expectant but worried Aguilar. A warm sensation washed over her as the full gravity of the moment dawned on her. She alone had the power to continue the conversation. She tried to remember a time in her life when she had ever felt so in control. Nothing came to mind.

"The villagers are part of the kingdom of Mexico," she said to the inept translator. "They would like to know where your people come from."

Aguilar spoke to Cortés, but the commander did not bother to look his way. Instead, Cortés kept his eyes riveted on her. She puffed out her chest, feeling proud, but she did not dare to meet his eyes again. Still, she noticed that he perked visibly at the mention of Mexico, like a snake that sensed prey. After a pause, he gave Aguilar words to say.

"We come from a land many leagues to the east and we are honored to"—Aguilar paused to collect himself—"speak with you."

He refused to look her in the eye and, for some reason, that made the slave girl feel more triumphant. The rest of the conversation was a blur. She knew there had been some convivial words, but the nebulous dream-like quality of everything blurred specifics. By the end of it all, the villagers and the Spaniards were exchanging gifts. The specific words that led them to this point were hard to recall, but it mattered little because she knew she was the conduit. The Spaniards would finally recognize she had greater value than a mere bedside comfort.

By the time the villagers left, she was weak with exhaustion. She stumbled into a seat and rested her head in her hands. Her face was slick with sweat, and her skin felt hot. She laughed, but she stopped when a hand lightly caressed her shoulder.

Irritated, she looked to see who was disturbing her rest and found that she was looking at Cortés. Aguilar stood at his side, but it was clear Cortés was the one who had something to say to her. Never taking his eyes off of her, he passed on his words to Aguilar.

His translator listened dutifully and gave a few perfunctory nods every now and then. But something shocking must have been said for Aguilar wheeled toward Cortés agape and pale. He let loose a string of objections, but Cortés silenced him with a wave.

Tears brimming in his eyes, Aguilar translated. "Cortés would like you to know he is very grateful for what you did today... and he would like to know if you could serve as translator. If you can, Cortés will gift you liberty and riches."

The final words seemed to kill him. But the life lost soon flowed into the slave girl. Her eyes widened, her heart quickened, her mind froze. She heard something snap close by. Intuitively, she knew the sound was probably just a natural one but in her heart, she felt it was something different. She was convinced it had to be the chains, the invisible bounds that had always restricted her movement. Already she felt she could move her hands and her feet with more freedom.

"No longer a slave," she mumbled under her breath in disbelief. All because she could do something as simple as speak her own language.

"Is this agreeable to you?" Aguilar asked nervously in Yoko Ochoko.

"Yes," she said. But when she spoke this time, she said it in the language the pale people used.

She was pleased she had remembered their word for yes and, looking up, she saw that Cortés also looked pleased. He gave new words to Aguilar.

"Cortés would like to know your name."

The slave girl stiffened. She had no real name. When she had been a child, she had been named Malinalli. But that was just the temporary birth name that so many other girls were given. Those who loved her were supposed to give her a new name once she became the proper age, but

102

they never did. They sold her into slavery long before that.

She thought about the kind of name she would like. She was important now. She deserved something nice.

"Malintze," she said.

"Malinche?" Aguilar asked.

She shot him a caustic glare. "Malintze."

Aguilar relayed the name to Cortés, and Malintze was dismayed to hear him pronounce her name as Malinche once again.

"Cortés says Malinche is not pretty enough a name for someone so beautiful. He says he will call you Doña Marina from now on. So will the rest of the Christians. Many of our high ladies from home are referred to with this honorific, and he knows you will enjoy the name."

Cortés took his leave after saying this, and Aguilar trailed behind like a sad dog desperate to reclaim the affection of his master. Malintze pushed herself to her feet and gripped the railing for support.

She gazed out on the land of Mexico and felt strength seep into her muscles again. She had a name now, and she had power. She would make sure the land knew both.

Chapter 12

Aguilar shifted his weight to his left foot. The sun had been beating down on him for hours now, and the proximity of camp to a marsh only made the heat more unbearable. He wanted nothing more than to find some shade, lie down, and drift off. He had no doubt the soldiers wished for the same. Like him, they had been standing at attention since mid-morning by order of Cortés. However, unlike him, they wore full armor while he wore nothing more than light chain mail.

It was almost noon, and Cortés had yet to give a stand-down order. Moreover, he was unlikely to give such an order since scouts claimed to have sighted a large Mexica party heading their way.

Aguilar cursed himself for telling Cortés about the Indian ambassador. Had he not told him, Aguilar could have gone about his day as usual without all the nonsense of standing in rank and file to impress some dignitary that might not visit camp. The slave bitch—some were calling her Doña Marina now, but he refused to address her as anything other than Malinche—was just as much to blame as him, but that knowledge did little to ease the pain in his back.

Ever since they'd gone ashore to encamp, a steady stream of Indian dignitaries had trekked through marsh and jungle to reach their camp. Some of the visiting parties came bearing lavish gifts—a beautiful feather garment adorned with rings of gold, a jet-black mirror made of stone, a magnificent shield that somehow changed color in the light—but all of them came bearing messages in need of translation. Their statements covered everything from Motecuhzoma's tyrannical ways, to Motecuhzoma's awesome might, to Motecuhzoma's intent to send the Speaker of Cuetlaxtlan to the Spanish camp. Once Cortés learned that he would be receiving an ambassador to Motecuhzoma, Cortés did more than expect a visit: he prepared for one.

Aguilar shook his head and kneaded the stiff muscles in his lower back. Doing so brought him precious little relief, and he motioned to a slave standing nearby with a water pail.

The slave hobbled toward him and, despite a slow pace, managed to spill water. The slave offered not a word of apology as he placed the pail at Aguilar's feet, though he did have the good sense to bring a full ladle to Aguilar's lips.

Aguilar tilted his head back to receive the water, but he did not take his eyes off the slave. The slave looked to be a Moor, a rather dark-skinned one at that, and had only one good eye. When he finished drinking, Aguilar ripped the ladle from the slave's hands and bashed it against his temple.

"Move faster, next time," Aguilar growled and threw the ladle to the ground. The slave nodded, scooped up the ladle, and shuffled off at the same slow speed.

Cortés glared at Aguilar. "Be petulant some other time. We ought to present the best image to our visitors today."

Aguilar pursed his lips and straightened his back. Were he a braver man, he might have reminded Cortés that the expected visitor, Motecuhzoma's supposed ambassador, had yet to arrive.

He glanced at Malinche. Like him, she was also situated to the right of Cortés. Unlike him, she was situated right next to Cortés. Were it not for her, he might have been standing next to Cortés. He wished he could use the ladle on her.

Pedro, positioned to the left of Cortés, shaded his eyes. "There's movement up ahead—I think it's the Indians we've been waiting on. They should reach us in a few minutes."

Aguilar heard a quiet shuffling as the soldiers behind him straightened their posture and adjusted their gear.

"Seems they didn't send any scouts ahead. Interesting, isn't it?" Pedro asked.

"Indeed. I suppose it means they aren't scared of us—or that they scouted us without our knowledge. Let us pray it is the former." Cortés shot a smug glance toward Pedro. "I believe we can easily correct the former."

Aguilar hoped that was the case and scanned the horizon. After just a few minutes, the first row of the Mexica delegation crested a nearby dune. Eight marched abreast, and he was sure he was looking at the entire party. Much to his surprise, another row came into view. And then another. And another.

Aguilar looked to Malinche for understanding. At first, she did not notice his staring and when she finally did, she made no attempt to clarify anything.

Aguilar stabbed an angry finger toward the approaching party. "Why are there so many? You said the Mexica were sending one ambassador."

"An ambassador for Motecuhzoma does not travel alone," she said. "He travels with guards and attendants. Many, many guards."

Aguilar turned back to the Mexica party. The entire delegation was now visible and he counted almost two hundred total. No other delegation had been even half that size. The Indians served a wealthy ruler, judging by the jade-studded litter at the center of the delegation.

Aguilar thought back on the fate of Potonchan. It didn't matter how powerful these Indians were. They didn't have firearms, they didn't have cavalry, they didn't have Cortés.

The Mexica laid the litter down, and a cadre of attendants stepped forward to open the curtain. A tall figure, the ambassador, emerged from the litter, bearing smoldering incense and crimson-stained reeds. A thick blanket of bright colored feathers had been draped over his shoulder, and it looked as if he could take flight just by flapping his arms. Most Spaniards would blush at the thought of wearing something so colorful, but the ambassador appeared unmistakably proud of his appearance, haughty even.

The ambassador stopped after a few steps, joined two fingers together, and pointed them toward the heavens. All members of the delegation mimicked his motions down to the smallest details, joining and elevating the same two fingers. When he knelt, the others did the same. When he rubbed his fingers in the dirt, the others did the same. When he pressed those fingers against his wet lips, the others did the same.

Once the Indians finished with their ceremony, Cortés called forward Father Olmedo to conduct mass for their guests. Aguilar translated for Malinche, but he was disappointed to see that most of the Indians maintained a dejected appearance as they received Christian blessing. Father Olmedo might as well have given sailors a speech on farming techniques.

Father Olmedo retreated, and the Indian ambassador advanced toward Cortés, stopping only when he was a pike's length away from Cortés. Unlike his Mexica counterpart, attendants flanked Cortés on both sides. To his left, trusted swordhands like Pedro. To his right, Aguilar and Malinche. If the ambassador felt intimidated, he did not show it. He extended his hand toward Cortés, offering him incense and reed with a poise and dignity befitting a Spanish courtier.

The dignitary announced something in Nahuatl, and Malinche translated to Yoko Ochoko for Aguilar.

"The dignitary wishes for us to know that he is the Speaker of the *altepetl* Cuetlaxtlan and servant to the great Motecuhzoma who rules far away from his great palace beyond the mountains," she said. "He goes by the name Tentlil—"

Aguilar raised his hand to stop her. She looked affronted, which elicited a triumphant smile from him, but she remained silent while he translated for Cortés. If the dark expression on Cortés' face was any indication, the captain did not share his joy. Aguilar let his hand down and motioned for Malinche to continue.

"And he humbly begs us to accept gifts from Motecuhzoma, who cannot be here for he has much to attend to in Tenochtitlan, the capital of the mighty Mexica kingdom," she said, her voice a tad less prideful. "He requests permission to bring some gifts forward."

Aguilar did his best to translate, but he stumbled over words like Tenochtitlan and Motecuhzoma. Cortés replied in a level voice that he would be honored to accept the gifts. Much as Aguilar resented his diminished status, he was impressed Cortés' inscrutable expression never slipped. Sometimes it felt as if Cortés was playing a perpetual card game, one with no end and only one objective.

Tentlil motioned for his attendants to step forward. The attendants carried ornate chests of dark, marbled wood, so heavy that each required multiple porters. Once they were close enough, they laid the chests down in the sand and opened them for the Spaniards to marvel at the treasures.

The soldiers gaped over the magnificent feather work, the shimmering gold items, and the splendid jewelry. If any of the men had doubted the riches of the Mexica, none did now. This one delegation had brought finer presents than any party before them. Aguilar's mouth went dry.

Now more than ever he believed they'd find the gold Cortés had promised so long ago. He looked back to the man responsible. He was surprised to see Cortés betray his feelings in the form of a restrained smile, but not even the Pope could have stopped himself from smiling in the face of so much gold.

Cortés cleared his throat and hid away his smile. "We are pleased to accept your gifts and would like to present our own."

While Aguilar translated to Malinche, Cortés motioned to his soldiers to bring forth gifts. One present was just a simple cap. The cap was adorned with gold and featured a picture of Saint George battling a dragon, but artful decorations could not belie its plain nature. Two soldiers came forward bearing an armchair and set it down in front of Tentlil. Well-crafted and inlaid with intricate carvings, the armchair was more pleasing to the eye than the cap, but neither item was impressive in terms of aesthetics. Tentlil seemed to recognize as much and studied the chair with a critical eye.

"Perhaps I can sit upon it when I have the good fortune to meet Motecuhzoma," Cortés said.

Tentlil reeled back and gave Malinche a response within seconds.

"Tentlil finds it curious you have only now just arrived and already ask to speak with his king," Aguilar told Cortés. "He warns against similar suggestions in the future."

Silence settled over the Spaniards near enough to hear the translation.

"Do forgive me," Cortés said after a pause. "I too serve a most powerful king, far across the ocean to the east, and I am here on his behalf. As it happens, I have been instructed by my great monarch to personally meet with Motecuhzoma, and he expects me to succeed in my endeavor. Motecuhzoma's greatness is so well known

109

that word of his glory has crossed the whole Atlantic to reach my people. I did not mean to offend. I have traveled thousands of leagues to be here, and I am simply doing as commanded."

Tentlil kept his eyes trained on Cortés as the translators passed on his words. Aguilar did the same and prayed that Tentlil would not see through Cortés' facade. Spaniards in Cuba did not know of Motecuhzoma, let alone Spaniards in Spain.

Tentlil said something new and Malinche translated once again. "What is a league?" she asked on behalf of the dignitary. Aguilar released his breath. It was better that Tentlil questioned Spanish units of length rather than Spanish lies.

Even after receiving an explanation, Tentlil did not look any more enlightened. Cortés asked, "Do you know what a pace is?"

Aguilar answered no for Tentlil. Cortés took a pronounced and deliberate step forward. "That's a pace."

Having seen a pace for himself, Tentlil informed them he knew what a pace was, but simply had a different word for it in his language.

"Good," Cortés said. "One league has more than 3,000 paces. Do you follow?"

Once again, word had to trickle not just through Aguilar, but also through Malinche.

"Tentlil says they have a similar unit of length. It is a little less than 3,000 of our paces. They call it a long-run," Aguilar said.

"How many long-runs to get to Tenochtitlan from here?" Cortés asked.

Tentlil clenched his teeth and glared at them. It took a few moments before he could pry his jowls apart and give words to Malinche. "Too many for weary travelers such as yourselves," she answered for Tentlil.

Aguilar translated for Cortés and suppressed a laugh. Tentlil must not have understood Cortés' nature if he thought that difficult circumstances would deter him from accomplishing a goal.

"We are capable of many great things," said Cortés. "Allow me to show you."

He turned his back to Tentlil and made his way toward the soldiers standing nearby. Tentlil followed, and Aguilar hoped Cortés' military demonstration would be enough to convince the Indians to submit to Spanish authority. Shamefully, doubt had found a place in his heart.

The lavish gifts and the impressive delegation made it clear the Indians here commanded considerable power. Nonetheless, Tentlil's compliance did give him some comfort. It indicated a passiveness on the part of the Indians that would make conquest easier. At least that's what he hoped. Having once been a slave, Aguilar knew that a man assured of his own power had little reason to fear the weak.

~ ~ ~

The roar of the cannons snapped Vitale out of his heat-induced stupor. Hundreds of startled birds took to the air, cawing and shrieking with such volume that Vitale had to grit his teeth to bear it. Looking around, Vitale could see the birds were not the only ones shaken by the cannon demonstration. Many in the Indian delegation ducked their heads, and the Indian ambassador, so composed when he first greeted Cortés, staggered back in shock.

Cortés' eyes sparkled with mirth as he took in their reactions. Vitale was given to pity more than anything else. If the Indians knew anything about their mighty weapons—the scarce ammunition, the cumbersome firing process—they would not have been half as terrified. Nonetheless, he understood the value of fear as a weapon and hoped with all his heart that the Indians would never learn those shortcomings.

As the Indians prepared to make their departure, Vitale's eyes settled on the ambassador. His pursed lips, his tight-knit brow, his distrustful eyes were plain to see and Vitale's feelings of pity returned. He realized with alarm that Tentlil noticed his staring and was now pointing at him. The ambassador shouted something in some foreign language.

Vitale's knees stiffened. He pointed to himself in confusion and was dismayed to see the ambassador nod in his direction.

Vitale wondered if the Indian was offended by his staring. He worried the Indian would insist he be punished. Vitale looked to Cortés for assurance and was surprised to see that Cortés was approaching him. Fear gripped his gut even tighter, but he somehow managed to stand straighter as Cortés took a place by him.

"This one?" Cortés asked and beckoned to Vitale.

Tentlil nodded.

"The Indian likes your helmet. Hand it over, son," Cortés commanded.

Vitale furrowed his brow at the quizzical command. He realized his hands had wrapped themselves around the hilt and sheath of his sword, but he pried them off so he could remove his helmet. Why the Indian wanted it was beyond him, but he knew better than to disobey a direct order from Cortés.

He tugged the helmet off and felt a wave of relief as he pulled his head out from its muggy confines. Heart thumping, he handed the helmet to Cortés.

Cortés took the helmet without even looking at him and offered it to the Indian. Just as he extended his arm to receive the helmet, Cortés pulled the helmet back, much to the chagrin of the Indian.

"I will give you this helmet," Cortés said, "on one condition: you must return this helmet full of gold. Can you agree to this?"

Vitale looked on as Aguilar and Doña Marina translated.

"Tentlil wants to know why you would like gold," Aguilar said in Spanish.

"Tell him... tell him we Spaniards suffer from a disease of the heart that can only be cured by gold."

Cortés' smile was mischievous enough to make a thief seem virtuous. Some of the soldiers who heard the audacious claim could not help but smirk. Much to Vitale's surprise, Tentlil appeared to consent to the bold demand because Cortés proceeded to hand over his helmet. Tentlil spared only a small glance toward the helmet before gesturing to his attendants. As one, they proceeded to leave.

The last of the knots in his stomach came loose as the last member of the delegation departed. Vitale relaxed his shoulders and shook his head in disbelief. He had the strangest sensation he had played a part in something far larger than himself.

Chapter 13

Cortés waited outside of Aguilar's tent as two of his guards summoned the inept translator. The day had gone well, and the night would still be young by the time he finished talking to Aguilar. Today being Easter Sunday, his family had probably hosted a small celebration at their estate in Medellin. Here in the New World, Cortés spent the day entertaining Tentlil, the uppity dignitary that had seen fit to gift him with treasures worth thousands of *escudos.*

He smiled. The encounter was a reminder of everything he loved about the New World. The possibilities in this place were truly endless.

Still, it bothered him that he could only guess why Motecuhzoma had given him so much. If Motecuhzoma was just trying to communicate his prestige, he had succeeded. But that explanation was too simple; there needed to be an ulterior rationale. Cortés closed his eyes and took a deep breath. He had been tasked with solving a riddle posed in a foreign tongue, but he swore, with God as his witness, to not give in to frustration.

He thanked God not everything the Indians did was puzzling. Tentlil had sent him nearly a hundred porters, and Cortés found them easy to understand. They were here to help with labor—and report back useful information to Tentlil. Unfortunately, Aguilar had been little help when it came to identifying the spies. Chances were Cortés would have to turn to Pedro or Doña Marina, as he was so wont to do these days.

Aguilar stepped out of the tent and performed a hasty salute.

Cortés smiled. "Walk with me."

Aguilar took a place by his side, and the guardsmen followed behind. Aguilar's eyes widened, and he looked to Cortés for assurance. Cortés waved away the guardsmen, but he did not bother with any comforting words.

"Have you summoned me just to walk?" Aguilar asked as they strode out of camp and into the dark.

"Aguilar, you worry so much. We are friends, aren't we? Brothers in arms?"

Aguilar nodded with a touch too much enthusiasm. "Of course."

"You understand we are waging war against the Indians, right?"

Aguilar hesitated. "Cortés, I don't—"

"Answer the question."

"Yes, I know we are waging war."

"Good. So, you would agree that a campaign of conquest cannot succeed without effective communication?"

"Yes. But I don't see what can be done about that," Aguilar said, his voice plaintive and his expression pleading.

"Leave the thinking to me."

Aguilar stopped. "Well, what do you think would be best?"

Cortés paused, wiped the sweat from his brow, and turned toward Aguilar. "I think we need to simplify the translation process. Two translators really is too much."

"I couldn't agree more! Let's send the bitch away and sail down south again where we have no need of her. Surely, there is more gold there."

Cortés closed the distance between him and Aguilar with a single step. They stood so close that their chests almost touched. "And just who are you so kindly referring to?"

Aguilar cast his eyes downward like a sullen dog. "Nobody, m'lord."

"Good. A Christian ought to speak kindly of respectable women. We know there is gold here, so we will be staying here. But let me cut to the point to avoid confusion: I want only one translator. I can no longer have the duties divided between you and Doña Marina."

"What do you propose?"

"You will teach her our language. That way communication will only have to flow through one translator."

"Cortés, please don't do this to me," Aguilar whimpered. "Being translator means everything to me."

"We have no other choice, brother. You do want this campaign to be successful, don't you?"

"Of course. But there are other ways. I can learn Nahuatl—"

"Aguilar, my friend, you place too large a burden on yourself. You have only recently been released from captivity. It is too much to ask of you. After all the hardship you have endured, you have earned the right of leisure. All I ask is that you teach Doña Marina so she can serve as translator, while you rest your bones and regain your strength."

Aguilar sniffled and wiped his eyes. "Regain my strength? You think I'm weak, don't you?"

"Aguilar, calm yourself—"

"I will not!" Aguilar spat on the ground.

Cortés' hand shot forward with viper-like speed to slap Aguilar full in the face. Aguilar staggered back, his eyes wide and his jaw slack.

Cortés sighed. "I apologize for my rudeness. I have little tolerance for low manners." The meek translator nodded. "I appreciate your understanding nature," Cortés continued. "So, when can you begin teaching our new translator?"

"Never," Aguilar whispered under his breath. For a moment, he was brave enough to hold Cortés' stare.

"Listen here, you low-born degenerate," Cortés said. "You will teach Doña Marina, and you will commit your every morning to the task until your services are no longer needed. Then, you will retreat to whatever wretched remove I consign you to, and pray that I forgive your impudence. Should she struggle to learn our language, should her progress be slow, I will attribute the failure directly to your poor teaching skills. You will be made an example of in front of all the men. Do we have an understanding?"

Tears came to Aguilar's eyes. "Of course. I a-apo-apologize."

Cortés laid a reassuring hand on Aguilar's shoulder. "Know your place from now on." He brushed past the translator who once seemed such a boon to the mission. Now, he was nothing more than a sad wretch passing on the torch to someone far worthier.

Cortés strode back to camp, his mind abuzz and his step light. He hated to treat a fellow Christian so poorly, but Aguilar had given him no choice. Aguilar lacked Doña Marina's gift for language, and he could not risk the expedition by entrusting translation duties to some rattled fool. She had committed herself to learning Spanish only a few days ago, and already she had learned enough to answer questions, so long as they were simple and direct. With a teacher, Cortés had little doubt that she could become fluent. Her talent was apparent to all. As was her beauty.

Even Cortés was taken by her looks, although he wasn't supposed to think anything untoward about Doña Marina. Not so long ago she belonged to Puertocarrero, and fancying her could estrange him from the lieutenant best positioned to help Cortés curry favor with the nobles. Without the support of prominent nobles, all the gold

117

Cortés had acquired would disappear into the coffers of some well-heeled bureaucrat.

He took a deep breath and focused his mind on the hurdles he had yet to overcome. Yet when he lay on his pallet that night, he found himself thinking not of the gold or the power that awaited him, but the pleasure he'd have if the Indian woman were beside him. Thoughts of his wife never came.

~ ~ ~

"So, the leader of the pale people insists upon meeting in person?" Motecuhzoma spoke to Tentlil in a calm voice that belied his agitation.

"Yes, Great Speaker, most insistent." Tentlil had arrived less than an hour ago, but once he was seen crossing the causeway to Tenochtitlan, Motecuhzoma had him directed to the Serpent Keep.

"Where are they now?" Motecuhzoma fixed his eyes on a nearby snake enclosure. One of the snakes had recently shed, and its scales had taken on a pale hue that reminded him of milk. The snake was dormant at the moment, but he knew it could not remain so. A snake did not wait; it lay in wait.

Motecuhzoma had long been fascinated by snakes, by their nature as much as their appearance, and kept dozens in the serpent keep. Here they were mere pets that could never do him harm. So long as they were caged.

"The pale people are near Cuetlaxtlan, as they were when the relay runners first brought news of them," Tentlil said. "They cannot be more than seventy long-runs from Tenochtitlan."

Motecuhzoma frowned. "Not so far for the eagle, but quite the distance for the serpent."

He stroked the wooden slats that separated him from his reptilian pets and wondered why the pale one took such an interest in his person. Not that it mattered. So long

118

as the snake was unable to overcome its surroundings, they would remain separated.

"Tell me, what do you think of the pale people?" Motecuhzoma asked.

"They are abominable. They stink worse than a tapir, and they know nothing of manners. But they are powerful. I have seen their weapons myself. They have weapons as loud as thunder and as powerful as lightning."

Motecuhzoma tugged at his thin beard. The pale people that came last year could also summon the ear-splitting eruptions that scattered the deadly volley. "The pale people, did they mention anything of gold?"

"They spoke of little else. They claim to suffer from some heart malady that can be cured only by gold. A child could not fall for such foolishness."

"Do not be so quick to pass judgment. Unfulfilled desires can sicken pure hearts too."

Motecuhzoma wondered if his own heart had fallen victim to the same disease. He thought on the wars, the sacrifices, the terrible choices made in pursuit of his ambitions. "Were they pleased with the golden sculptures?"

"Of course. Our artistic works are without equal."

Motecuhzoma turned his gaze toward Tentlil. "Did you give them a great deal of our precious art?"

"Only a fraction of what you have entrusted to me." Tentlil paused. "You would like me to meet with them again, wouldn't you?"

"Observant as ever. Yes, I will have you meet with them again."

Tentlil nodded. "Are we to cure their hearts with more golden sculptures?"

Motecuhzoma laughed, and a smile cracked the weary corners of his face. "They seem to have a preference for gold, so perhaps there is no need to send them fine feather work or green jade."

Tentlil made a quiet hissing sound.

"I see that you consider yourself the possessor, rather than the custodian, of the fine tribute I have placed under your protection," Motecuhzoma added. "Should more pale people arrive in our lands, I may have you send them fine gifts. This time, however, the pale people shall receive treasures from my own keep."

Tentlil's eyes widened. "You would put me in charge of transporting your treasure?"

"Of course. I trust you as I trust my own family. Such a treasure cannot be transported without guard, however. I am sending my own kin and my guardsmen to accompany you. The journey will not be without difficulties, but I promise you shall make it there and back safely."

"Only a fool would doubt the Great Speaker," Tentlil said.

Motecuhzoma huffed. "I am the Great Speaker, and I assure you I am not immune to doubt. Sometimes giving gold to the pale people seems the sensible thing to do, and sometimes it seems a terrible mistake. Am I a fool for doubting myself?"

A flush crept up Tentlil's face. "Great Speaker, I did not mean to—"

"Think nothing of it. I know you do not mean to give offense."

Tentlil ground his sandal against the floor and stared down. "When will the gifts be ready?"

"Tomorrow morning." Motecuhzoma lifted Tentlil's chin with a single finger. "Rest. You will journey back to the coast soon."

Tentlil swallowed. "More pale people may come in the future. Will you call on me to send treasure again?"

"You worry I would make a pauper of you?"

Tentlil did not answer, but his grim expression said enough.

"Should more pale people come, I might call upon you to send fine gifts their way. I ask the same of all governors in the outer provinces."

Tentlil gritted his teeth, and Motecuhzoma wondered if Tentlil had fallen victim to the gold disease as well. Or perhaps it was the jade that had sickened his heart. That was more likely. Jade was far more valuable.

"Great Speaker, why do you have us collect fine tribute only to parcel it out to these strange people?"

Motecuhzoma touched his diadem rather than answering. So long as it rested upon his head, Tentlil and many more would look to him for guidance. At least the pale people had not shown an interest in it. A man could only part with so much. Willingly, at least.

"When the pale people last came, they spoke of another world filled with many pale people," Motecuhzoma said. "They could be lying, but I am inclined to believe them. Unfortunately, we know little of the pale people in these faraway lands. The ones who visit us are just as mysterious. Giving them fine gifts communicates to them our love for the gods and inclines them to be friendly to us."

Tentlil took in a deep breath. "Great Speaker, may I speak my mind?"

"Please do. You are one of my highest-ranking officials to meet with the pale people, so it is imperative you do."

Tentlil squared his shoulders. "I am not so naïve as to think purchased friendships lack value. The might of the Triple Alliance is a testament to the strength of strategic partnerships. But I do not see the sense in cultivating a friendship with the pale people. They are not worthy of our friendship. Or our gold."

Motecuhzoma fingered the slats of a nearby enclosure, tutting all the while. "Surely the excrement of the gods is not so precious that we cannot give some away. The gold we have given the pale people cannot represent more than half a moon's worth of tribute, and Tenochtitlan does not lack for vassals that could replenish depleted stores. Besides, we still have our riches. We are not giving away our cocoa beans after all."

Tentlil pursed his lips and exhaled through his nose. "I am grateful you have not asked me to send them cocoa beans for that would truly pain me. I do not see why we send gifts their way though. They do not seem worthy of our friendly gestures."

"Perhaps they are not," Motecuhzoma admitted. "But it is usually better to be kind than hostile to a stranger, especially if that stranger commands a great deal of power. Gold does little when it sits in a hold, but it can do a great deal for us when we send it to these people. It will convey our piety, it will convey our power, and it will help us keep their monstrous weapons out of our home. Your journey could not be any more important; otherwise, I would not give you my own treasure. You must let the pale people know they are not welcome in Tenochtitlan, and that I cannot meet with them under any circumstances. They must understand this."

Tentlil straightened. "I will not fail you."

"Then you must do exactly as I command. Give them my gold and make them understand they will gain little by staying in our lands. By now they have heard of our great gold stores, but you must convince them that we have given them all that we possess. They need to understand there is nothing to be gained by traveling to Tenochtitlan, and that we can take by force what we have given by choice should circumstances call for it."

Tentlil gave a perfunctory nod, but his mind seemed elsewhere. Perhaps he was thinking of the destruction the pale people could wreak with their terrible weapons. Motecuhzoma hoped the memory of it would not sap his strength.

"Rest," said Motecuhzoma. "You will need your strength and your wits."

With that, Motecuhzoma waved him away as he would a pest. He wished he could do the same with the pale people. He looked again at Tentlil and was surprised to see he had not left the room.

Tentlil cleared his throat. "Great Speaker, there is more you should know." He paused. "Some of the villagers are no longer calling them pale people. They are calling them *teteo*."

Motecuhzoma shook his head. *Teteo* was a term for powerful sorcerers. In a matter of days, they had convinced his subjects they commanded power so great it could not be understood within traditional norms. With enough time, it seemed possible that all the Triple Alliance would fear these *teteo*.

Chapter 14

Aguilar stared at Malinche's sleeping figure. A few weeks ago, she was a lowly slave that belonged to Puertocarrero. Now she had her own pallet and private tent. Thinking on it was enough to get his blood boiling, but his anger faded as he studied her soft features.

Aguilar still remembered the day when the Potons had given her away. Her beauty had been the talk of camp for days. He once thought the bawdy whispering crude. Now he entertained some depraved fantasies of his own.

She stirred on her pallet, and Aguilar's reverie was broken. He reached forward and shook her awake. Her body tensed, and her eyes flew open. However, once she recognized him, weariness replaced the fear.

Aguilar's heart pounded with a power and force that made him clench his teeth. He wondered how he'd come to be so weak, so meek that he could not inspire fear in a former slave, a woman no less. To be disrespected by Cortés was one matter, but to be disrespected by Malinche was too much.

"Wake up, slut," he commanded in Spanish.

She brushed aside her blankets, and Aguilar was amazed to see how sparse her nightdress was. His anger was no match for the desire that overcame him.

"What does this word slut mean?" she asked in Yoko Ochoko as she came to her senses.

Aguilar colored. "It's not important," he muttered in Yoko Ochoko as he fetched the water pail in the corner of the room.

She stood up from her sleeping place and stretched her arms. "I suppose I shall ask Cortés then."

Aguilar grimaced. The bitch really knew how to get under his skin. "He will not take kindly to having his time wasted. Stop bothering about trivialities. We have important business to attend to."

He dropped the pail, and the water splashed on her feet. She shot a withering glare his way. "Always such a temper, Aguilar. What have I done to you?"

She knelt and cupped the water in her hands so she could rub it along the length of her shapely arms. He expected Malinche to avert her accusing eyes, but she kept them fixed on him the whole time.

"We have important work to do and you are wasting time," he said.

Malinche gave a half-hearted nod and turned her attention back to the pail. She splashed the water on her face and rubbed her wet hands through her hair.

"Why do you always do that?" he asked.

"Do what?"

"Splash the water all over yourself. Is it some ritual of your people?"

She smiled as if he had said something ignorant. "I suppose you can say so. It is what we do to keep clean. We try to wash at least twice a day. Do your people not do this?"

"Washing regularly is bad for the health. All the doctors of Europe would tell you the same."

Malinche looked at him askance and muttered something under her breath before standing. She made her way to the corner of the room where her day dress hung from a knobby stand.

She slipped out of her night dress. "What is the important business? Tentlil will not be back for many days and there are no expected visits today."

Malinche kept her back to him, and he was powerless to look away from her bare figure. His greedy eyes roved over her tight thighs, the gentle curve of her hips... and the scars that lined her back. The abuse he suffered as a slave came rushing back to him, and he averted his eyes.

Aguilar swallowed the lump in his throat and focused his gaze on Malinche's luscious hair, admiring the way it glistened in the light. "I am going to teach you our language. Cortés says it will make translation easier."

Malinche finished slipping into her day dress and wheeled around. Her eyes twinkled, and she looked as radiant as the sun. Her face darkened, however, as she looked Aguilar over.

"Were you staring at me while I changed?" she asked.

Aguilar blinked. The tips of his ears burned like Greek fire.

"Do you *teteo* spend all your time staring at bare figures?"

"You have to understand," he stammered. "We dress much more conservatively in our countries. It's unusual to see a woman wearing so little. Christian women aren't supposed to…"

"I've heard the stories. It's probably easier to tell people to hide everything under heavy clothing when the temperature is…"

"Agreeable?"

"Mild," she corrected. "So, where shall we have the lessons?"

He dragged over a stool for himself. "Here." She looked hurt by his tone, but it didn't stop her from taking a seat across from him.

"How much of our tongue do you know?" He wondered how much longer he would have to speak Yoko Ochoko with her. It could be taxing at times, switching so often between Spanish and Yoko Ochoko. He was tempted to speak only Spanish to her, if only to remind her he still had that power over her, but he knew Cortés would not approve.

She tried to answer in Spanish, but gave up and switched over to Yoko Ochoko. "I don't know that much."

"We will start with basic words then, basic words you have heard, but cannot put a meaning to. Say any Spanish word, and I will tell you the meaning."

A sly smile spread across her face. "Slut."

Aguilar rolled his eyes. Her giddy enthusiasm made her ignorance all the more galling.

"Pick another word."

She looked slighted. She repeated the word again, with more force.

His hand clenched into a fist. "No."

"Did Cortés send you here to teach me?"

"Yes."

"Then teach me."

He let out a weary sigh. "Do you know of Adam and Eve?" Her blank face said enough. "Adam and Eve were the first people on all the Earth." A quizzical look flashed across Malinche's face. She looked as if she were tempted to interrupt, as if she had a different story of the first people. Fortunately, she stopped before mentioning any blasphemy.

He cleared his throat and continued. "They lived in a beautiful garden and knew nothing of sin. It was paradise on Earth. The garden gave them all they would ever need. However, it was not enough to give them all they would ever want. The evil snake lurking in paradise knew this well and soon came to Eve. The snake offered her sustenance that had always been denied to her, and the weak-willed woman accepted the snake's offer."

"What made her weak-willed?"

"Being a woman."

Malinche pressed her lips into a line so thin and tight it seemed impossible for any words to escape.

"Eve then offered the forbidden fruit to Adam," Aguilar said. "Adam loved God too much to seek out the sustenance, but the woman was very beautiful. She tempted him, and he forgot his love of God."

"Perhaps man is just as weak-willed as woman then," Malinche noted.

Aguilar stared at her incredulously. A child could be more sensible than these Indians.

"They enjoyed the fruit together, but nothing was the same afterward. Having seen Adam and Eve's transgression, God knew they could not live in paradise anymore. They knew too much of sin. Paradise was now forbidden to them, so they made a new home for themselves and brought forth new people into the world. That is the story of how people came to be on Earth."

Malinche bobbed her head up and down as if she understood. "How does this relate to slut?"

"Slut is what we call women who remind us of Eve. Had Eve never tempted Adam with her body, Adam would not have partaken of the forbidden fruit, and he would still be pure. Women are supposed to hide away their bodies so men do not fall prey to the same temptation that Adam did. If they do not hide themselves from covetous eyes, if they welcome the affections of all, then men cannot be faulted for indulging in the flesh."

"Why are women to blame? Can't men be taught to control their temptation?"

"Men cannot."

Malinche huffed. "It seems men are the weak ones then."

Aguilar closed his eyes and pinched the bridge of his nose in frustration.

"If men have such problems resisting the flesh, does that mean women have power over men?" Malinche asked.

Aguilar shifted in his seat. "You will only cause yourself trouble if you think like this. There are certain things women are not supposed to exercise power over. The body of a woman is never really a sovereign thing. It belongs to us—it's our right."

"And who says this?"

"The only holy book that matters."

"Your holy book does not sound like a woman's book."

"It is everybody's book. Everyone who cares about following the true path, that is."

Her eyes narrowed. "What else should I know about following the true path?"

"That a servant ought to obey in all matters," he grumbled.

She regarded him with a mixture of curiosity and contempt.

"Why does power matter to you all of a sudden?" he asked.

A sullen look crossed her face. "You were never a slave like I was."

Her voice broke as she said the word slave. Aguilar cleared his throat and considered enlightening her. Perhaps it would bring her some comfort.

"Malinche—"

"Do not call me that! Call me Doña Marina or Malintze, but whichever you choose, at least pronounce it properly. I deserve that much. I am not a child who can be sold to traders anymore."

She stared down, indignant. Her nostrils flared every time she exhaled, and she dug her fingernails into her thighs with enough force to draw blood. It had been some time since he had seen a woman so angry.

"I will fetch us some food. We can continue with the lesson later," he said and left the slave girl. Perhaps some other time he would let her know she was not as alone as she thought.

Chapter 15

Tezoc looked on anxiously as a detachment of guards and attendants marched down the street. The palace ledge provided him an excellent vantage point, but seeing the royal procession in its entirety only made the sight more painful.

Owing to his position as a high-command general, he had seen many royal processions pass through Tenochtitlan, but he had never seen one leave with so much gold. Fine tribute always flowed into Tenochtitlan, never out. He felt like he was looking at a river that had somehow reversed direction.

As he watched the procession grow smaller, he wondered if sending the pale people precious art would be enough to dislodge them from Mexica territory. Reports from the villagers indicated that the pale people hailed from an *altepetl* more than a thousand long-runs away. The Mexica had always held gold in high esteem, but they could never be compelled to travel that far for gold alone. Sure, it could be crafted into stunning works of art, but it was nowhere near as precious as green jade.

Tezoc was convinced the pale people had come for something else. Part of him even hoped so. If they wanted gold only, they would inevitably take an interest in Tenochtitlan. And since they had already braved the waves, he doubted the trials of an inland journey would deter the pale people from marching on Tenochtitlan.

"Troubling, is it not?"

Tezoc did not need to turn his head to identify the voice. It could only be Milintica. *Impossible to be alone in Motecuhzoma's palace.* He sighed. "I haven't the slightest idea what you are talking about."

"Do you enjoy watching our gold leave Tenochtitlan, then?" Milintica took a place by Tezoc's side.

Tezoc sneered. "I did not know you cared so much for gold. Have you become a patron of the arts since last I saw you?"

"I have always appreciated the finer things in life. Just another reason I value your company so highly."

Milintica reached out to squeeze his shoulder, but Tezoc caught his hand. He bent Milintica's hand backward, thinking about how easy it would be to break his thin little wrist. No harder than snapping a twig. "Have I ever given you cause to doubt that I feel the same about you?"

"Of course not." Milintica tugged his hand back in small jerks until Tezoc finally let go. He massaged his palm, smirking all the while. "I would advise against feigning any great affection, however. I assure you I would easily sort out the truth."

Tezoc shrugged. "I've never been much good at lying." He cast a sidelong glance toward Milintica. "Some of us lack practice."

"Such resentment, so little reason. Careful who you insult, Tezoc. I can whisper foul words in many ears."

"You should have the ear of Motecuhzoma only. And I know no reason why honest advice would need to be whispered." Tezoc withdrew from the ledge into the chilly corridor.

"You are naive indeed if you think that advisors have never whispered a foul word to a Great Speaker. How is it you think that Tlacaelel gained so much power?" Milintica asked.

Tezoc stopped. He wanted to remind Milintica that he'd never have the same power as the legendary advisor

Tlacaelel. He closed his eyes and inhaled. "Why are you here? Have you sought me out deliberately?"

"Indeed, I have."

"For what reason?" He turned and was surprised to see Milintica had not moved from the ledge. He shook his head and made his way back.

"Tell me what you see, Tezoc, when you look out at that royal procession leaving our city."

Tezoc trained his eyes on the vast crowd of attendants and guards assigned to the procession. Had the gold been rendered into compact units, it would have been far easier to transport, but only an uncultured fool would do such a thing. A metal so soft begged to be crafted into the most intricate of shapes, the most unwieldy of objects. Looking over the fine golden sculptures—some crafted in the image of the gods, some in the image of sacred animals— that winked and shimmered when touched by the light, he knew the Mexica artisans had done right by their trade. "I see a gold-laden procession heading out of Tenochtitlan for Teotitlan, in order to firm up our new alliance."

"You flatter me, Tezoc. Do not let me think Motecuhzoma trusts me so much that only I was made privy to the true destination of the caravan."

Tezoc tucked his tongue into his cheek. "I see a procession filled with gold heading out of Tenochtitlan for the *teteo* camp. I see a procession so valuable to Motecuhzoma that he sent his own family to guard it. I see a procession filled with gold that belongs—"

"Here, in Tenochtitlan," Milintica finished. "We are looking at history, my friend. The pale people have yet to send any fine presents our way, but we honor them with mountains of golden sculptures, as if they are faithful allies. I fear we are bringing great shame on our ancestors."

"Careful now. You forget our history. We have much to be proud of, but there was once a time, not so long ago, when we groveled before the Culhuacans and the Tepanecs."

Milintica laughed. "Itzcoatl should have never stopped at burning the history codices. If he really wanted the past to stay dead, he should have cut out every tongue that did not belong to a *pilli* and broken the hands of every scribe. The past would've stayed buried much better that way."

Tezoc snorted. "He would have been the most beloved Great Speaker that ever lived."

"A Great Speaker cannot only be loved and respected; he must also be feared." Milintica paused, as if expecting Tezoc to interject. When Tezoc said nothing, he sighed and continued. "You know our history, then? You know the gods urged us to settle here because this is where we found the eagle and the cactus. The gods knew that no other people could turn fetid swamps into a bustling metropolis that brings glory to all the One World. Where there was no habitable land, we made the most beautiful of gardens from mud and baskets. Tens of thousands now live in our city on the water, and hundreds of thousands wish they could live here. You know the resilience of our people. You know how strong we are."

"I am responsible for leading our forces into battle. I assure you I understand the strength of our people."

Milintica's eyes flared with passion. "Then you know that no nation can match the Mexica, that we could crush the pale people under our heel if we chose to! Instead, we choose to honor them with fine gifts and receive nothing in return."

"Why do you tell me this? Your job is to advise the Great Speaker, not me."

"Our wise Great Speaker recognizes that in times like these, he cannot rely on the counsel of just one. If he thought he could, he would not have ordained a meeting of the Great Council within half a moon."

Tezoc frowned. He had not known Motecuhzoma would be convening a Great Council. Tezoc knew that he would receive a summons soon, the Great Council was a collection of all the prominent *pilli*, but learning of it from Milintica rankled him. *How did he learn of it before me?* He cracked his knuckles and studied Milintica with a critical eye. "What are you proposing?"

"Nothing. I am simply here to point out that you and I have long provided counsel to the Great Speaker. Our opinions carry far more weight than any of the *pilli* who will be at the Great Council. Now imagine if our opinions were one and the same, if we had a—"

"Consensus," Tezoc finished.

"Exactly."

The smile on Milintica's face was so gleeful Tezoc felt himself fall under its sway, much as it irked him. "Consensus on what?" Tezoc asked. "That the Mexica are strong?"

"Certain platitudes are so obvious they do not need to be spoken aloud."

"Do tell what sentiments ought to be spoken at the Great Council."

Milintica squared his shoulders. "The *teteo* put on quite the show when they were entertaining Tentlil. Seems they wanted us to know they command a great deal of power. We ought to show them the same is true of us."

"So, you do not believe our first delegation convinced them?"

"I believe a military delegation could serve our ends better. After all, the pale people have yet to depart our lands."

Tezoc rubbed the calluses on his hand. Never a day passed when he did not train with a weapon, though it had been years since he took up arms against an enemy. "It seems as if you suggest we send the army."

"Better than sending them precious works of art, wouldn't you say?"

"Tell me, how will we gather the resources and finances for such a campaign? Will we march on the pale people with a portion of our army and risk sending too small a force? Or do we spend months mobilizing the entire army, knowing full well the rains will have returned by the time we start marching and that the pale people could learn of our intentions weeks in advance?" Tezoc leaned toward Milintica. "But most important of all, what happens if battle breaks out between our forces and theirs? Our army is our nation's most precious asset—more valuable than our gold, our riches, our accomplishments. Without the army, there wouldn't be a Tenochtitlan. And you suggest we risk it to preserve some golden sculptures?"

Milintica sneered. "I suggest we use that army to protect our hard-fought victories. I do not think that is a terribly radical idea. If battle breaks out between our forces and their forces, then we crush them."

"Some foes can be quite resilient."

A sour look flashed across Milintica's face. "Tlaxcala will bend the knee soon enough."

"I am a warrior of the Shorn Order, and I am a general on the Council of Four. Remind me why I should defer to your military opinion?"

"Let's not forget, we've both fought on the battlefield."

"Let's not forget, I have spent far more time on the battlefield than you," replied Tezoc. "And I'm all too aware of your combat experience. I heard that you took your kills on the battlefield. Is it true? Did you deny the Givers captives for sacrifice just so you could wet your knife?"

"You deflect," hissed Milintica. "Is the Cutter of Men scared? I come here seeking your help in protecting our *altepetl,* and all you can do is quibble about the past. We do not even know if these people are worthy of fear and here you are, quivering in your sandals, because I suggested we send our warriors their way."

Tezoc smiled and shook his head. Milintica arched his brow.

"A great man once told me that the ignorant ought to be the most cautious," said Tezoc. "You may know him. I believe you have whispered in his ear on some occasions."

Milintica pursed his lips. "Think on what I have said. The united voice rises above the clamor."

With that, Milintica took his leave. Moments later, a courier came running toward Tezoc with a summons. He did not need to open the summons to know that it would inform him of the Great Council convening. He looked out at the horizon and shook his head. Power was an unfaithful lover.

Chapter 16

Cortés sat up in his makeshift bed. It had never been a comfortable thing, nothing more than a pallet strewn across some wooden crates, yet sleep found him most nights. But not tonight. Like the angel of Passover, the specter of sleep passed him over in search of others.

A few days before, Tentlil had returned for a second meeting and gifted the expedition with generous helpings of gold. Cortés had been quite pleased to accept it, despite being less than pleased to hear Tentlil claim Motecuhzoma could send no more. Cortés explained he could leave for Spain if he had more gold, perhaps forgoing a personal meeting with Motecuhzoma, but Tentlil did not appear swayed. Still, it seemed a promising sign that Tentlil would journey back to the capital, and Cortés prayed he would return with more fine presents.

Just the thought of it was enough to buoy Cortés' spirits. At first. But Tentlil had been gone less than a week, and the high that once lifted his spirits had faded. These days, all his men did was grumble. They complained the midday sun was intolerable, so he had more hovels built, and then they griped that was not enough since the sand was scorching hot all hours of the day.

The men did not stop there. Many seemed to have forgotten that prior to making camp, a loud contingent had insisted upon a location close to the shore but removed from all Indian settlements, even if it meant camping next to a marsh.

The marsh drew an ungodly number of mosquitoes, and he had been assaulted with a barrage of unending complaints ever since the first day of encampment. Just earlier, he heard men grumbling the heat was spoiling the preserved food, that the fresh water stored onboard the ships was being poisoned with salt. The only men who did not grumble were those who had fallen sick with some unknown fever. When they regained their energy, he knew they would join the chorus.

He ran a hand through his sweat-slicked hair. Just thinking about all their complaints made his blood run hot. Some of the more brazen men suggested they leave the cursed marsh and return to Cuba with the gold they already had. They did not seem to realize that their enormous winnings were far less impressive once the proper cuts—the Royal Fifth owed to the king, the fifth owed to Cortés—were allocated. An elephant could feed many, but not all.

Hoping to placate the crew, Cortés sent scouts in search of friendlier locales. Pedro, who had proven himself loyal on multiple occasions, would head one expedition and Montejo, who had proven himself less than loyal on multiple occasions, would lead the other.

A lazy smile spread across Cortés' face as he considered the indignities that may have befallen Montejo's scouting party. Most of Montejo's company consisted of men who were either weak-hearted or, even worse, sympathetic to Governor Velázquez.

However, that was not enough to purge the camp of the undesirable elements, so he had sent away the rest with Juan Velázquez de León, cousin to the esteemed governor of Cuba, to conduct a scouting mission deep in the jungle. The vast expanse of untamed wilderness haunted the dreams of many, and he saw few cheerful faces in León's company when they departed. The weak-kneed naysayers could simmer in their own cauldron, but they'd deprive him of sleep no more. As for the Indian woman…

139

Cortés stood and advanced toward the wine keg. He took a hearty swig, perhaps too hearty. He had hoped the drink would dull his senses, but it focused them instead. Cortés was unable to think of anything other than Doña Marina, the enchantress that visited his dreams so often. He made his way back to his pallet. Just looking at it reminded him of the beautiful woman he was not supposed to have.

He distracted himself by thinking on the soldiers again. Nearly thirty had died. It made him feel powerless, and every death was a mark against his leadership. He shook his head. Hostile Indians could be put to the sword, but there was nothing he could do to stop the men from succumbing to war wounds and fever.

A sudden need to feel powerful gripped him, and he returned to the wine. He placed his cup under the tap and let the sweet contents pour inside. Cortés stared into the dark pool of crimson and wondered why men so welcomed the sight. Revulsion seemed so much more appropriate. He put the cup down. There was only one way he could feel powerful tonight.

He strode out of his tent and told the guards stationed outside what he needed. He saw a glimmer of envy in their eyes, but he knew he could trust them to be discreet. Cortés stepped back in and surveyed his tent interior. His lodging was no royal palace, but it would suffice. He sat in his chair, surprised by his own anxiety. Cortés considered returning to the wine, if only to calm his nerves. But he did not want to be calm. He needed to be sharp.

He mulled over what he would say. Perhaps with more time, something would have come to mind, but he could already hear the guards returning. His hand shook, and he closed it to hide the tremors.

The enchantress entered calmly. Doña Marina deserved ballads and sonnets every time she stepped into a room. Instead, his steely stare and cold countenance greeted her. Her eyes found him and matched his stare with frightening strength. In the past, she would have never been so brazen, but those days were gone. She was no longer a slave.

Or perhaps she was.

Cortés had summoned her the same way he would a lowly servant. He reminded himself that she could have refused to come when she had been informed that Cortés needed her presence. He reminded himself that he had sent armed guards.

Silence reigned. He could not tell if the atmosphere in the tent was one of heightened tension or gradual deflation. She opened her mouth to speak. Before she could say a word, he commanded that she take off her dress.

Her brow furrowed. He could not tell if she was surprised by his brazenness or his command. But she uttered not a word of protest. Cortés liked to think it was because she also saw something pleasing in him, but he knew it was possible that she had learned long ago not to object. The half-smile playing on her lips confused him the most.

She pulled her dress off and stood before him. He ordered her to lie on the pallet. Once again, she looked surprised, but she obeyed. Cortés took a deep breath and closed the distance between them. Still fully clothed, he looked over the beautiful woman lying on his pallet.

The darkness of her skin blended in with the coverings so perfectly it seemed dreamlike. He wanted to reach out to her, stroke her skin, confirm she was flesh and blood. His pallet was strewn across waist-high crates and he would not even need to bend over to touch her.

The shaking once confined to his hand spread to his whole body. His thoughts flew to his wife, but the thoughts disappeared as fast as they came once he felt Doña Marina's hand settle against his chest.

That small touch was enough to know. He understood why she was here and what she wanted. It all made sense. Whereas others had made a slave of her, he had freed her, if only to do his bidding. Whereas others had looked upon her as a bedside comfort, he had shown everyone her greater talent, if only to use her as she had been used before.

His hand drifted to the drawstring that secured his britches. All he would have to do was tug on it, and they would fall to the ground. He would finally be able to give himself to Doña Marina. He hesitated, thinking of all the reasons he shouldn't.

He might have gone on like that, standing over her, admiring her fine body, but something pulled him, and he was suddenly on top of her. He knew no more, could think of nothing besides the great gift God had given him. Yet for some strange reason, when it was all over, he found himself wondering not about the pleasures of the flesh, but if the snake and the garden were meant for each other.

Chapter 17

Tezoc looked over the members of the Great Council. Most were dressed in fine robes, covered with fine feathers and jade, but some of the poorer ones had only gold jewels. Nearly every *pilli* of importance was in attendance and for good reason; today, the council would discuss the prudence of sending a third envoy to the pale people.

Seeing so many *pilli* in one space unnerved Tezoc more than he cared to admit. A simple roof collapse would leave every prominent member of the Republic dead. He shuddered to think of the paralysis that would grip Tenochtitlan.

A light tap on the shoulder caused Tezoc to turn. Chimalli, his vice general, leaned in close to whisper in Tezoc's ear. "The historic nature of the council session makes me think I should give a speech."

Tezoc chuckled and shook his head. The thought of Chimalli rousing a crowd with his mellow voice and stolid persona was quite the entertaining prospect. "What would you say to our esteemed *pilli*?"

"I don't know. Perhaps some nice poetry." Chimalli scratched his chin and lowered his voice. "I do know, however, Milintica believes I ought to advocate for a march against the pale people."

Tezoc swallowed down the anger building in his chest. He had given Milintica no affirmation that he would support the march against the *teteo*, and Milintica's decision to reach out to his second in command for support was a serious breach of decorum. "Do you know who else he approached?"

"An exact count would be difficult." Chimalli sighed. "But I predict he will have many mouthpieces in this room."

Tezoc nodded and turned toward Milintica, who stood at the front of the room. All the other *pilli* rested upon soft reed cushions and could choose to stay seated even when delivering a speech. Nonetheless, Tezoc knew every single one of them would have traded places with Milintica. Only he had the privilege of standing near Motecuhzoma. Milintica was so close he could rest a hand on Motecuhzoma's shoulder. Or whisper in his ear.

If Milintica noticed Tezoc's glare, he did not show it. Instead, he blew into a death whistle. The eerie screeching could not be ignored and all members of the Great Council turned toward the front of the room to behold the Great Speaker.

The room quickly quieted as they took in his fierce visage, his jade-studded diadem, and his imposing figure. Motecuhzoma's arresting stare reminded Tezoc of an eagle ready to swoop down on unsuspecting prey and he suppressed a shudder.

Milintica cleared his throat and puffed out his chest a fraction. "The Great Speaker now calls forward Tentlil for an account of his talks with the pale people."

Tentlil stood up from his seat in the front row and turned to face the *pilli*. He studied the crowd the way a warrior would study a hostile army. He then bowed his head to Motecuhzoma and waited for permission to speak. The Great Speaker signaled his assent with a small hand gesture.

"I have met with the pale people on two separate occasions now," said Tentlil. "When I first visited their camp, I gave them the finest feather work, jewelry that would impress even the Toltecs, and golden sculptures crafted by our most skilled artisans. The pale people were interested only in the gold. Once they finished examining it, they proceeded to show me their weaponry. The weapons they possess have no equal in the One World." Tentlil took a deep breath and shook his head. "One weapon, long as a reed but many times thicker and stronger, can sling a bead no bigger than my thumbnail with deadly speed. Another weapon, a great cauldron with a tapering end, can sling a projectile with a force that shakes the skies. The sun has risen and fallen many times since I first beheld their weapons, but even now my ears still ring with the sound of those terrible weapons."

Muttering spread throughout the room like fire during the dry season.

"Can you present any of the items you speak of?" a balding councilor asked.

Tezoc turned around to see which councilor had spoken, but over a hundred served on the Great Council. Trying to pick out one was like trying to distinguish one chilli seed from another.

"I cannot. They were reluctant to part with their weapons," Tentlil said.

"You must know we can't just take the word of a villager on something so important," a different councilor said. "Do you have even a single *teteo* weapon you can show us?"

This time, Tentlil was able to identify his questioner and treated him to a testy glare. "During my parley with the pale people," Tentlil said through gritted teeth, "I brought with me many artists to put in picture what I put in words. Look over the reed paintings and decide for yourself if you think I intend to frighten for theatre. I will be the first to admit my words do not do justice. The issue is not that my words are too frightening—the issue is they are not frightening enough."

Tentlil motioned to the porters scattered throughout the room who then started distributing the reed scrolls. A porter came directly toward Tezoc and handed him one.

He accepted the scroll with a touch of trepidation, undid the binding string, and hurried to unroll it.

His heart skipped as he took in the picture. Smoke and fire spewed from the snout of the ugly cauldron weapon, as well as two startlingly round projectiles connected by some sort of tether. The snout was directed toward a fallen tree. He hoped that he was somehow misinterpreting the picture, but the implication was inescapable.

The parchment quivered in his hand, and he decided he had looked at it for long enough. Chimalli sat behind him, so he turned and passed the parchment to him. His vice general was so surprised by what he saw that his breath caught.

"In my second parley with the pale people, there was no weapons demonstration," Tentlil said. "Nonetheless, we exchanged gifts like the first time. During this second parley, I gave them more gold and they were very pleased. With the permission of our Great Speaker, I'd like to bring out the gifts they have given us."

The room pivoted to Motecuhzoma once more. He nodded his approval.

"Bring out the gifts!" Tentlil bellowed. The porters returned within moments bearing a number of strange objects. Once again, items were distributed throughout the crowd except for one item that was placed at the front of the room. Tezoc wondered if his eyes were playing a trick on him. The item at the front of the room looked to be nothing more than an armchair, but that seemed too simple, too plain.

Tezoc pored over the chair to see if he could discern some fine craftsmanship that may have escaped his first glance. The more he looked, the more he was disappointed. The chair was well crafted and inlaid with various carvings, but that was not enough to make it beautiful. He did not have to peer hard to see the fine streaks of salt and grime. Cushioning ran along the armrests, the seat, and the back, but it did little to accentuate any fine features. More than anything, the cushioning contributed to the sorry appearance. What may have once looked beautiful was now torn. White fluff sprouted out of the chair like mushrooms from a rotting log.

Tezoc had seen plain chairs before, but never had he ever seen one given to the Great Speaker. For that matter, he could not recall a time anybody had given Motecuhzoma such a plain gift. It was hard to know whether he should be angry with the pale people or whether he should pity them for being so poor.

Tezoc looked at one of the *teteo* shirts being passed around. The sleeves were exceptionally long, extending all the way to the wrists, and the material had an odd, waxy sheen. Yet for all its mystery, the shirt did not seem any finer than the chair. The fluffy cap and the goblet being passed around did not seem very fine either.

A swarthy councilor stood to his feet. "Did the pale people bring these items from their home?"

"It is difficult to know," said Tentlil. "The pale people speak of many homes, but speak most of a far-away land called Spain. I do not know if these gifts come from Spain. They call the clothing a Dutch shirt and the glass a Florentine goblet."

The murmuring returned with a vengeance. *Pilli* throughout the room asked what a Dutch was, asked about the location of Florentine, asked whether Florentine and Dutch were villages in Spain, and a host of other questions in such rapid succession it was impossible for Tentlil to answer all of them.

Motecuhzoma raised his hand high for all to see and slowly lowered it. The noise and his hand dropped in unison.

147

"Many thanks, Great Speaker," Tentlil said. "I cannot answer questions on their home and where they come from because I understand little of it myself. However, I do know their home is very far from here."

"Are they like the pale people that came with Grijalva?" Once again, it was the swarthy councilor who asked.

"This new group is far more numerous and voracious," Tentlil said. "They hanker after gold like madmen. I gave them ample amounts in our first parley and more in our second parley. They are still unsatisfied. They want more. They know of our gold stores and wish to see Tenochtitlan. I have told them they are not welcome, but my words fall on deaf ears. We have much to fear should they prove hostile, and I fear that they may have designs on Tenochtitlan."

Silence thundered through the room.

"How many are there?" asked a *pilli* near the front.

"Reports vary. Many of the pale people stay aboard their water-houses. Some say fewer than a thousand, some say a thousand, and some say thousands."

The fear, so palpable earlier, was replaced with scorn. The *pilli* shouted about their inability to make a decision without all the facts, Tentlil's various failures as an emissary, the might of the Mexica army, and the ability of Tenochtitlan to withstand any attack.

Just when it seemed the din of shouting would grow so loud that no one voice could be distinguished, a councilor leapt to his feet and yelled, "If we know they are to march on Tenochtitlan, then let us save ourselves the waiting and march on them!"

The clamor that had invaded the room vanished. The remark was bold, resonant, and far too intuitive to ignore. Something about it also felt contrived, and the smile spreading across Milintica's face only made Tezoc more suspicious.

"Great Speaker, how soon can the army be mobilized?" asked a councilor.

"The bulk of the fighting force can be mobilized in less than three months," said Motecuhzoma. "To march to the shore with such a large force would be a considerable undertaking, though. There are logistics of food and supply to consider."

The Great Council absorbed the news in silence. Moments earlier, it seemed the room would catch fire. Now it felt like the room had been doused in cold water. But looking around, Tezoc saw that some embers still had life.

"The rainy season will be upon us in less than forty days," a councilor said, his voice almost as solemn as his demeanor. "If we are to make battle against these people, we must do it before the rains start. We cannot mobilize the bulk of our forces in forty days, but we need not mobilize the entire army to chase these people from our lands. We can crush them with a fraction of our army."

Heads nodded in agreement. Tezoc swallowed down his dread. The members of the Great Council represented the elite of Mexica society, but so many had grown accustomed to posturing, to exploiting their office for graft, that he had to wonder if any of them could grasp all the complexities of the debate.

"Why march on them if we're not sure they're enemies?" asked a councilor. "All we know is that they are powerful. Perhaps we can entice them to use that power against our enemies."

The chamber reverted to silence as the war movement came to a grinding halt. Tezoc felt like he was watching a boulder teeter on the edge of a precipice. He would throw himself against the boulder to prevent it from going over the edge if need be. He was not opposed to battle with the pale people, but he was opposed to rushing into battle, especially if there were better alternatives.

"Can they be trusted, Tentlil?" Tezoc asked. "Should we set them on our enemies?"

Tentlil shifted his weight. "I cannot answer with certainty. They have been very pleased in the past when I have given them gold."

"Will they vanquish our enemies if we give them gold?" a councilor, sitting far in the back of the chamber, asked.

"Perhaps. If the stories from Potonchan are true, they are quite skilled in battle. But sending them more gold may not be enough to deter them from marching on Tenochtitlan. I am told they have orders to personally confer with Motecuhzoma."

"Orders from whom?" asked the swarthy councilor.

"Their own Speaker. They seem most keen to earn his favor, and they will travel all the way to Tenochtitlan just to have their meeting with Motecuhzoma. My spies among the porters tell me the *teteo* have lost many to sickness. They must long for home, but every time we confer, they insist upon a personal meeting with our Great Speaker."

An uneasy tension settled over the chamber. Motecuhzoma had already made it clear he was opposed to such a meeting. Any councilor who advocated such a meeting risked execution. Even the most powerful of them would be fortunate just to be given a Flowery Death.

"If they are determined to march on us and cannot be deterred with any of our intrigues or riches, we have only one option." All the *pilli* waited with bated breath for the trembling councilor to say more. "We must have war. There is no other way."

Tezoc allowed himself a rueful smile. He did not think less of the man for omitting mention of the other alternative.

"We are safe here in Tenochtitlan," countered a different councilor. "Our city has never been taken, though our enemies have tried many times. If they travel from the coast to the valley of Tenochtitlan, we ought to attack. They will be weakened by their journey, and we will be strengthened by our proximity to our great capital. We have never been bested when we have fought on our own lands—there may be no better place to make war."

Tezoc's chest tightened.

"We Mexica have the bravest and best warriors in all the One World," replied a solemn councilor, "yet even they would struggle to stand tall before these *teteo* weapons. Just imagine what these weapons can do to our homes, our temples. Battle with the *teteo* would not be a Flowery War, and we should not court hostility with such powerful foes. If they want to start a war, they can send the war shields and the arrows. We need not do it for them."

There were a few somber nods, but nothing universal.

A councilor with a massive nose plug stood. "My fellow councilor, you touch upon some important truths. Putting our army in harm's way is no simple decision. We ought not forget there are *pilli* in the army. If we were to throw our whole army at them, we could lose noble blood. But even more noble blood will be spilled if battle happens near our precious Tenochtitlan. Battle never stays confined to one place and will spill into our homes if we wait to march until they are in sight of Tenochtitlan. Far less good blood will be shed if we march on them now and do battle with them on the shore. Better to have battle spill into far off villages than our dear valley."

Pilli signaled their agreement with nodding and cheering.

"Let's spare the *pilli* and march on the *teteo* with an army of commoners. We'll get rid of two problems that way!"

There were chortles of laughter as well as murmurs of approval. Both were disconcerting to Tezoc.

"Don't be ridiculous," one councilor chided. "An army of commoners could never succeed. They'd all scatter into the jungle at the first sight of deer."

The laughter was even more uproarious. Tezoc pinched the bridge of his nose in exasperation and saw that was Milintica stifling laughter. Tezoc waited for his blood to cool and forced himself to his feet.

"Have we argued enough over which Mexica deserve to die most?" Tezoc asked.

The eyes and ears of the room snapped toward him. He noticed a number of unfriendly faces in the crowd and his indignation grew.

"We have important issues to discuss," he continued. "While we debase ourselves, a foreign people take root in our land who pay no heed to the gods and spit upon everything proper. The scope of their power and the size of their ambitions are almost completely unknown to us. They may not even send the shield and the arrow before battle. What we do know is piecemeal: we know there was a battle at Potonchan and we know the Potons were routed. We do not know who initiated hostilities, but we do know the Potons greatly outnumbered the pale people on the battlefield."

"Perhaps you would be kind enough to tell us something we don't already know then?"

It was the same councilor that had suggested a pre-emptive march, the one who was probably a mouthpiece for Milintica. Tezoc laughed and continued.

"As my dear friend has already pointed out, we need more information. So serious is this predicament that we seem to have forgotten that we are not the only ones short on information. The pale people also lack critical information. Perhaps they are holding meetings of their own, discussing the best course of action. They should be." Nervous laughter trickled through the crowd. "We are familiar with these lands—they are not. We are

152

familiar with the peoples here—they are not. We are familiar with our weaknesses—they are not."

"What do you propose?" asked a councilor.

"Let's keep them unfamiliar. That ignorance will be their downfall. Our spies among the porters have obtained valuable information for us, but they have exhausted their utility by now. We must meet with the pale people again, and we can use it as an opportunity to recall the porters. I think we can all agree that we ought to check the ambitions of the pale people, and I hope we can also agree there are ways to do that other than a military march. The porters have made life easy for the pale people, and so has their ability to trade with the neighboring villages; we must deny them these comforts from now on. If they flounder, we will know they are weak. If they are resourceful, we will know they are strong. Either way, we gain information that would be useful for a march."

An uneasy chatter took hold of the room. Tezoc turned toward Milintica and saw the smile was gone from his face. If Milintica's scowl was any indication, the *pilli* would not be lending their support to a brash all-out assault on the pale people. At least not yet.

Tezoc focused his gaze on Motecuhzoma. It was too soon to know what specific recommendation the Great Council would offer. But no matter their recommendation, the burden of the final decision rested with the Great Speaker.

Chapter 18

Malintze's fingers tingled as she stared at Tentlil's fine gifts. Nearly ten days had gone by since they had last spoken, but he had finally returned to the *teteo* camp for a third meeting. He brought less gold this time, and the gold he did bring was less shiny, less polished.

When the gifts were first unveiled, Cortés muttered something about Tentlil standing by his bluff. Ordinarily she would have tried to decipher the phrase, if only to surprise Aguilar by using a Spanish turn of phrase, but she was far too enraptured by Tentlil's gifts to give it much thought.

While Tentlil had brought little in the way of gold, he brought much in the way of fine feather work, sweet incense, and jade so beautiful it could have only come from the Great Speaker. Never in all her life had she expected to stand in front of such treasure, but judging by the disappointed expressions of the nearby *teteo*, they were not impressed.

Mouth still agape, Malintze looked back to Tentlil. The triumphant smile plastered to his face turned her stomach, but she returned his smile. His jovial expression faltered just a fraction, and she suspected they were not supposed to be pleased by the latest batch of presents. Or maybe he just did not like seeing a former slave girl regard him as if they were equals.

"We are pleased you find such joy in the treasure we have brought you," Tentlil said, a smirk pulling at his lips.

"We are pleased," Malintze said, "you honor us with such fine presents and hope we have honored you with our presents." She savored the look of disgust that flashed across Tentlil's face.

Tentlil pursed his lips and cleared his throat. "While the Great Speaker wishes he could send the *teteo* more, he cannot. He is most pleased he could aid your sick friends, but the Great Speaker can help no more as he has honored them with all the gold in his possession. He hopes the *teteo* understand they will have better luck finding gold once they leave Mexico, as Motecuhzoma's domain is a poor one." Tentlil tutted and shook his head. "The Great Speaker understands your *teteo* may be disappointed that he cannot send any more gold, but he sends fine jade and knows this will assuage any misgivings."

Malintze stared at Tentlil. It was not the rash presumptions that startled her the most, nor the implicit demands, but the blatant lying. The *teteo* had received generous helpings of gold, but it was impossible to believe Tenochtitlan had no more, that Motecuhzoma had somehow exhausted all his gold stores. Mexico was the most bountiful land in all the One World and no city had even half as much gold as Tenochtitlan.

She furrowed her brow, struggling to understand why he would lie, and it dawned on her that Motecuhzoma did not want the *teteo* in his home. The Great Speaker, frightened? For years, his traders had sold little girls into slavery, but he did not fear reprisal. His warriors subjugated villages far and wide so he could reap greater tribute, but he did not fear reprisal then. And now he feared these Spaniards all because they had strange skin and loud weapons.

She looked to her travelling companions. They seemed right not to trust Tentlil. Cortés was so distrustful he had his men stand at attention in full battle gear. If Tentlil made a single misstep, if Cortés got the slightest impression the exchange was little more than a pretext for

155

ambush, the *teteo* would fall upon Tentlil and his attendants without mercy. Her translation could hasten bloodshed or prevent it. Regardless of the outcome, she had no interest in translating Tentlil's lies.

"The Great Speaker—" she stopped. The *teteo* were still unfamiliar with Mexica terminology. "The Mexica King presents this great treasure in the hopes it will help with your sickness. He is sorry that he cannot give you more, but…" Malintze trailed off. She could not say anymore without lying, without helping the Tenocha. The same people that forged an empire from blood and misery, the same people that often bought little slave girls.

Aguilar looked at Malintze and his face brightened as she struggled to translate Tentlil's statement. Hope glimmered in his eyes, and her heart pounded.

"But his gold is very precious," Malintze continued, "and he must keep it in Tenochtitlan for the sake of his people. He passes on good wishes in your search for more gold. He hopes you enjoy the jade."

She knew her translation lacked her usual polish, but judging by Aguilar's crestfallen expression, she had banished his dream of reclaiming his position as main translator.

Aguilar conferred with the captain in Spanish and then said to her, "Cortés is pleased to learn that the rumors of Motecuhzoma's generosity are true, but is sad to hear that Motecuhzoma can part with no more gold. He asks the great king where more gold can be found. Jade will do little to help our hearts, but gold will do much."

Malintze passed on the words to Tentlil verbatim. She wondered if she should have changed the words of the *teteo* to make it clear they did not need the gold. A good translator facilitated dialogue and rote translation often inhibited communication. Euphemisms had to be explained, turns of phrase had to be contextualized to have an honest exchange. But she was cautious about changing the words of the *teteo* as she did not always know enough about their beliefs and their practices to sort out the truth. Sometimes she wondered whether they could sort out their own truths and falsehoods.

"Travel to the land of the Totopecs, and you will find plenty of gold," Tentlil said. His expression was too fixed, his response too prepared; she needed no special skills to know he was lying.

She considered changing what he said again to make his deception obvious. But she had manipulated enough today and had lost her taste for making truth clear. She passed on the words to Aguilar who in turned passed them on to Cortés. They asked how close they were to the Totopec lands. She let them know that it was even further away than Potonchan and on the opposite coast. Cortés grimaced when he heard.

"My esteemed friend, we are unfamiliar with these lands," Aguilar said on behalf of Cortés. "Perhaps your king could guide us to the Totopec lands. We could not fail if we had such a great king for a personal guide."

Malintze passed on the words to Tentlil, never once breaking eye contact with him.

Tentlil shook his head. "A pleasing thought indeed, but it can never come to fruition. There are simply too many affairs to attend to in Tenochtitlan. It would be most unwise for our Great Speaker to traverse the many mountains and jungles and deserts that separate him from you—it would be even less wise if your *teteo* were to make the same journey. They are, after all, quite unfamiliar with these lands, are they not?"

When Cortés' heard the translation, his eyes twinkled as if he was holding back a smile. He set his face in a deep frown and placed a hand over his heart. He told Aguilar that being unable to meet with the Great Speaker saddened him like the loss of a brother, that it would be impossible to present himself before his own sovereign without having accomplished the chief objective of his expedition.

"I am sad the sun must go away each night, but certain things cannot be changed." Tentlil gave a dramatic sigh. "You are free to stay on the coast as long as you need to. The Great Speaker has every expectation you will enjoy your stay."

Cortés trained his eyes on two large discs gifted to him by the Mexica. One was stark gold, the other bright silver, and each one was so heavy no single man could move it. Malintze doubted that Cortés knew the gold disc represented the sun and that the silver disc represented the moon. She knew, however, that Cortés could not be contented with what he already had.

Cortés muttered something to Aguilar and turned his back on Motecuhzoma's delegation. Malintze barely had the chance to pass on Cortés' gratitude and warm wishes before he disappeared from sight.

~ ~ ~

Vitale leaned forward on the rock to keep the fishing net submerged beneath the placid waves. The ocean seemed even darker than the heavens above. It wasn't that late, but he could feel himself drifting off. He had been in a state of hypervigilance ever since Tentlil had left camp yesterday, and that constant alertness was taking a toll.

Vitale stayed awake most of last night expecting the Indians to attack under cover of dark. Tentlil had come too many times with words of peace and welcome not to be suspicious. Much to everyone's surprise, no attack occurred after Tentlil left. Many gave thanks to the Lord when the sun rose on a peaceful horizon, but the relief that came with dawn soon turned to dismay once the sleep deprived men finished stumbling around the camp perimeter. The Mexica porters always slept on the outskirts of camp, but none could be found the morning after the third parley with Tentlil.

Men of all stations were seized by despair once news of their absence spread. Many claimed that camping next to the marsh was not much different than camping in hell. If that was true, then the porters had been their angels. They had only been with them for a few short weeks, but they had managed to become an essential fixture. But now they were gone, along with all the Indian traders that once frequented the camp. Overnight, it seemed as if every Indian in the area had vanished.

Vitale lifted his hands from the water. They were stiff from the cold, and he doubted he could keep a firm grip on the net. He missed the porters already. If they were still around, he would not have to worry about catching fish as he could trade for it instead. If he was hungry, he would eat it himself. If he was feeling generous, he could bury some near the beach so that Solomon could find it.

He considered going to one of the slaves for help. If he wanted to eat the fish himself, that might have been a good idea. However, since he was trying to get fish for Solomon this time, it was best not to draw attention to himself. He could only imagine the jeers and abuse should others discover he was willingly helping a Moor.

Vitale rubbed a hand through his hair. He would have to cut it again soon. He wondered how much time had gone by since he last cut it. Summer was in full swing and it was hard to keep track of time anymore. When the weather was agreeable, the men practiced drills and exercises. Since the weather was rarely agreeable, most of the men frittered away their time playing cards and fantasizing about their future riches. Days felt like weeks, but life in the camp was still preferable to life outside the camp. He would not have traded places with any of the scouts. The raw power of the untamed landscape filled him with a dread so great he preferred the mosquito-infested marsh to the jungle.

He cast his gaze toward the sea, hoping he could make out just one bright spot on the horizon. No matter how hard he looked, he could not, and a profound sadness overtook him. He stood up, stretched, and trudged back to dry land. He tossed the net over his shoulder, keenly aware of its emptiness.

The camp lights came into view. Considering the time, he was surprised the camp was so well-lit. The sun had already set, and most of the men should have been preparing for sleep. Instead, he saw a number of men milling about as if it were still light out. He picked up his pace. A crowd was gathering inside camp. Without thinking, he joined it. He did his best to fight his way to the front, but the throng had grown too thick.

"Calm yourself, men," Cortés commanded.

The crowd did as instructed, but not without some jostling and infighting. Vitale caught a sharp elbow in his ribs. He turned, looking for the culprit and noticed a familiar face. Try as he might, however, he could not remember the man's name.

"You part of Puertocarrero's company?" Vitale asked.

"No. I serve under Pedro de Alvarado. But we all serve Cortés, don't we?" The soldier flashed him a radiant smile.

Vitale nodded. "What name you go by?"

"Bernal Díaz del Castillo." The name sounded familiar to Vitale, but he could not remember why.

"Know what's happenin'?"

"Only that Cortés wishes to speak with us."

"About what?"

Díaz shrugged.

"Perhaps we'll soon be leaving?" Vitale asked.

Díaz reeled back. "Did you not see the gold plates they brought us yesterday? They were as big as carriage

160

wheels! There is too much treasure in these lands to be leaving anytime soon."

Díaz's words cut like a dagger, and Vitale turned away from him. He peered anxiously past the shifting bodies in front of him to catch a glimpse of Cortés.

"Men!" Cortés cried. The crowd responded with an enthusiastic, but not overwhelming, hurrah. "We have been away from Cuba for almost half a year. In that time, we have won every battle and extracted more treasure from these lands than any explorers before us. The glory we have won will always be remembered with affection and love. I know not an army in all of history that has fought so bravely and gained so much, all while hardly lifting a finger! Our might is such that a single campaign has yielded more success than all the Crusades."

Cortés waited for the cheers to die down.

"But I understand that some care more for the comforts of home than for glory and riches. Tonight, I ask that you share your thoughts, your reservations. We are at a critical juncture in our search. We can turn back now, return to the familiar embrace of our loved ones with the little we have, or we can see just how much more this land has to give. Are we to carry on the search to its end, or should we leave while there are still winnings on the table? I could not in good conscience decide the entire future of our campaign myself, so I ask you, my dear countrymen, to voice your sentiments and tell the proper course. I hereby offer the floor to anyone kind enough to offer their advice."

An uncomfortable silence settled over the group. Vitale heard some murmuring, but nothing intelligible. He was struck with a powerful desire to speak his mind, to tell everyone how much he hated this land and how desperate he was to leave. He would let everyone know that it was no insult against Cortés' leadership, that his exemplary command was the only reason he had not objected before, but he simply could not abide the mosquitoes or the heat or the Indian hostility or the jungle anymore.

Yet even more powerful than Vitale's desire to speak was the pain in his gut when he thought about speaking before his countrymen. He would only draw unwanted attention to himself. He was an anonymous soldier with no claim to great heritage. He had never distinguished himself in battle, never endeared himself to the officers. Perhaps Cortés truly did wish to hear every opinion, and Vitale could let everyone know he wished to return to Cuba without fear of punishment—or perhaps Cortés would reward his candor by sending him on a scouting expedition deep into the jungle. Vitale looked to his fellow soldiers for help, hoping one of them might have the courage to do what he could not.

"I have something to say," a man announced.

"Well, by all means!" Cortés shouted.

The man cleared his throat much more than needed. It was comforting to know that others struggled to find their voice in front of a crowd. "Cortés, these mosquitoes are… untolerable. At least an Indian can be cut down with a sword. But these mosquitoes—they come in hordes even greater than the Indians."

The murmurs of approval were universal.

"Fear not, my countryman," said Cortés. "Soon we will be gone from this wretched marsh and making camp in more favorable lands. The last of the scouts will be returning by week's end, and I am sure they will bring favorable news."

The approval was obvious, but Vitale sensed shallowness to it. There was a small commotion as a different man stepped forward. Once again, Vitale could not see him.

"These mosquitoes are a curse from hell, but it has been an honor to fight for you, Captain. I have just one request—" the voice broke and succumbed to sobs. "My friend Carlos died—damned fever! If we are to be legend, make it said that he died fighting Indians rather than fever. There is more glory that way."

Other voices took up similar pleas. Vitale scoffed. He was surprised by his callousness but unashamed of it. Even he knew battle lacked for glory, and he was still wet behind the ears.

"Of course, I only urge we stay the course. This land has not been drained of all its treasure yet."

There was a tremendous roar of approval. A man yelled that the king in the mountains hoarded all the gold, another yelled about not fearing a king of savages, and then all the men started yelling about what it would take to defeat such a wealthy king.

"We have beaten strong Indians before and we can do it again!" Cortés yelled, much to the crowd's approval.

A gaunt-faced soldier stepped forward. His pinched countenance spoke to a lifetime of deprivation, of living hand to mouth with little expectation of more. "Cortés," he said in a strong voice, "will we return to Cuba soon?"

A disquieting stillness settled over the crowd.

"The decision should not be mine alone," Cortés said. "Men, tell me what would you have."

The statement lingered in the air. Vitale felt the urge grow stronger, but his gut was no less pained and his knees no stronger.

"Leave here," Vitale whispered. He said it again and prepared to say it aloud for all to hear when a voice beside him screamed: "Onwards to more gold!"

The crowd erupted in cheering and for a terrifying moment, Vitale thought he had uttered the terrible words. Confused, he looked to his side and saw that it had been none other than Díaz. He finally remembered that Díaz was the one who had savaged Solomon.

Cortés, perhaps sensing the crowd momentum, returned to his former self. "I will lead you past Scylla and Charybdis, but we cannot triumph if some lack the heart for battle. I must know now: will we flee from the Indians?"

A resounding no.

"Will we return home before we have enough gold to make King Midas seem a pauper?"

The same answer again with even more enthusiasm.

"And you will follow me to victory and gold, no matter the hazards?"

The answer was an emphatic yes like Vitale had never heard. Cortés bellowed the search would continue, and the men went wild. The taste of bile flooded Vitale's mouth, and he rushed out of the crowd. He barely had time to find somewhere private before the retching began, but that was time enough for the self-loathing and pity to sink in.

Chapter 19

Pedro stared into the fire, contemplating Cortés' latest bid to defy Governor Velázquez. The flames licked at the wood without any true energy and seemed as exhausted as him. He rubbed a whetstone along his sword, and the rasp of steel against stone filled the air. Normally, the sound would send shivers of excitement down his spine, but he was too tired for that tonight.

"Explain it again, please," Pedro said, irritation coloring his voice.

Cortés tutted and squeezed Pedro's shoulder. "You heard the men tonight. They do not want to return when there is still so much gold to win. To return to Cuba with the little we have would be unconscionable."

"Returning would be dangerous for some," Pedro countered. "Not for me."

Cortés flashed him one of his winning smiles. Pedro surprised himself by returning it, albeit less enthusiastically.

"We are friends, are we not?" Cortés leaned forward to tend the fire. The flames responded eagerly to his attention. "Surely you do not wish to see your friend run afoul of Governor Velázquez."

"So, I should run afoul of him because you have?"

"Follow my instructions to the letter, and we will never have to worry about the fat *hidalgo* again. We will have enough gold to make ourselves kings."

Pedro grunted and focused again on the flames, straining his ears for the soft cackle the logs made when protesting the incessant heat. "I am not one who gives in to fear easily. A man like Velázquez will never frighten me, nor will his gallows. But I do not understand why I should cross the man when I gain so little. Where is the gold I defy him for?" He stabbed the tip of his foot into the ground and sent a spray of dirt flying into the fire. The fire hissed, and the flames dimmed. "You want me to risk my life for a cut of gold that I could fit in my hand. It's madness."

Cortés squared his shoulders. "You know there is more gold here."

"The Indians don't seem to think so," Pedro grumbled.

"And how many Moors claimed destitution when Christian soldiers knocked at their doors? These Indians are no better, my friend."

"The Indians lie because they want us gone," Pedro said. "They are hardening to us, and you know it. Or did you forget that all of Tentlil's porters disappeared overnight? That villagers no longer frequent our camp? We can't even trade with the damned savages anymore. They've cut our legs out from under us, and you don't even want to retaliate!" Pedro shook his head and said under his breath, "You just want to crawl away to some new hiding spot."

"We must bide our time to build our strength," Cortés replied. "I suspect that king in Tenochtitlan played a role in our current predicament. If he is growing suspicious of us, now would be a terrible time to launch a march. We must make allies of the locals before we commit to battle."

Pedro gritted his teeth. "Well, how in the hell are we supposed to get more gold from that king in Tenochtitlan? I doubt that Indian ambassador will soon be returning with gold, and the king won't be travelling to our camp while he still has his senses. Let's leave this hellish marsh and march on his city if you're so convinced he's gilded."

"Not yet, Pedro. These are foreign lands. Navigating them will not be easy. We have neither maps nor guides.

166

And the king will not sit idly by as we march toward his city. He could even raise that army we keep hearing so much of."

"I pray he does. We'll annihilate his army with the cavalry like we did at Potonchan, eh?" Pedro gave Cortés a friendly nudge in the ribs.

"Your levity is ill-suited," Cortés warned. "Even if we won, it would be a Pyrrhic victory. And I'm not sure we could win right now."

"There you go again with those phrases nobody understands. Craven talk is still craven when you use fancy words. We Spaniards are not ones to be bested by savages."

Pedro took a swig from his canteen but kept his gaze on Cortés.

"We have cavalry, but they have arithmetic," Cortés responded in an even voice. "Fear not, Pedro. We will march on them—when we are stronger. In the meantime, we have other priorities. We must wed the men more firmly to the mission, or they will demand we sail back to Cuba. Tonight's speech will not appease them long."

"It would help if we move out of this Godforsaken marsh since the Indians won't be helping us anymore," Pedro growled.

"This I already know. The maritime scouts found a new site for our camp, and we will soon relocate. But leaving the marsh will not be enough. If we are to find the gold, we must set down roots. We have to establish a colony."

A lizard darted across the ground, and Pedro skewered it on the end of his sword. He brought the lizard closer to admire his work. It kicked and wriggled on the tip of his blade, determined to deny the inevitable.

He frowned. If the lizard gained anything from its protestations, Pedro was none the wiser as the creature remained just as skewered. After one last twitch, the creature finally stilled.

Pedro flicked the lizard into the fire. The smell of the singed flesh wafted upward and made his stomach rumble. He was tired of cassava bread and pork, tired of waking up with rashes and mosquito bites. Most of all, he was tired of waiting. He wanted to march on Tenochtitlan and seize the gold already, if only to put an end to all the interminable waiting.

"Is your mind elsewhere, Pedro?"

Pedro strained his eyes to find the lizard in the fire. "Of course not."

"Good. Will you support me in founding a new colony then?"

Pedro thought of his poor prospects in Cuba, the past reprisals he had suffered for defying Cortés. If he refused to help, his subordinates could suffer the price. Worse yet, his family might. Three of his brothers served the expedition in junior roles. Pedro shook his head. He never should have let them join. Pedro let out his breath and turned to his captain-general. "As long as it helps us find more gold. What will the name of our colony be?"

"Villa Rica de la Veracruz," Cortés said with a grand flourish. "We arrived in these lands on Good Friday after all."

"And how will this colony be different than a camp?"

"That is the beauty—it won't be."

"I don't understand," Pedro grumbled.

"It will be a colony on paper, but a camp in practice."

"And you are doing this so you will not have to answer to Velázquez anymore?"

"Precisely. By founding a colony, we absolve ourselves of all legal obligations to Velázquez. And his orders."

"How so?"

"Because the colony will be founded for the good of the king."

Pedro frowned. "And that is reason enough?"

"My friend, we have reason and law on our side. The *Siete Partidas* stipulates that the king and his subjects are obliged to promote the common good. Even strict orders can be set aside for the common good. If a town lord ordered the townspeople to attack all ecclesiastical passers-by, not a single townsman would have to follow that order because it would violate the common good. Now we must be like the town people and sever our binds to Velázquez so we can collect more gold for our king."

"And after establishing the illegal colony, we give ourselves the right to make it legal."

"Beautiful, isn't it?"

Pedro sheathed his sword. "Your studies as a notary have done you some good yet."

"All of us, Pedro. All of us."

Pedro went back to staring at the logs. The heat had broken most of them. "What do you need me to do?"

"Bring the royal notary and the other officers to my tent tonight. We must convene to decide on the proper leadership roles in our new colony. Once the Velázquez sympathizers return from their scouting missions, we will not be able to."

Pedro nodded and stood up. He flapped the hem of his shirt as he walked away, his clothing damp with perspiration. The heat of the fire could be overwhelming at times, but he knew he could not do without it.

~ ~ ~

Solomon peered out from behind the edge of the tent at the two men confronting Cortés. Both had ceased their shouting to let Cortés speak, but neither seemed moved by his words. The bull-necked one, Montejo, looked as if he was ready to strike Cortés whereas León, nephew to

Governor Velázquez, just seemed interested in getting his words out intact.

Solomon crept forward to hear Cortés better. So far, he had heard only snatches of conversation, but he understood why León and Montejo were so furious. Not only had Cortés relocated camp while they were scouting the interior, he had also declared the camp a colony.

"No longer answer to Governor Velázquez?" Montejo shouted. "That's mad talk—he's the one who commissioned this search mission!"

"We held elections and the men made it clear they wish to found a colony," Cortés responded in a calm voice. "We are calling it Villa Rica de la Veracruz, and I pray you will lend a hand to construction efforts. Veracruz could make good use of men with your talent."

"You seriously intend to found a c-colony in these godforsaken lands?" León asked. His deep, baritone voice almost made him seem a man, but only a child would have trusted Cortés to honor his commitments.

"Of course. I fully intend to bring God to these lands."

"Why on Earth would you want to found a c-colony here?" León asked. He took a moment to compose himself, praying perhaps that his occasional stutter would leave him in peace. "None of our c-cartographers have mapped this part of the New World. Once we leave, you'll never be able to find your way back h-here."

"Fear not, I know exactly where we are. I am told we are quite near a village called Quiahuiztlan."

Montejo squared his shoulders. "That means nothing to me."

Solomon was willing to wager most of the men shared the same sentiments. He was also willing to wager that the vast majority of the men were grateful to vacate the marsh to encamp near Quiahuiztlan. There was much to be said for camping near a remote Indian village as opposed to a mosquito-infested marsh.

"Veracruz's surroundings will come to mean quite a lot to both of you," Cortés said. "Your fellow settlers are very satisfied with the new arrangement, and I urge you to take consideration of them."

"Settlers—what is this fiction?" Montejo shouted so loudly it seemed as if he would burst the veins in his neck.

Cortés shook his head. "You should not denigrate what you do not understand. Veracruz is just as much a legal entity as Cuba. Ask the royal notary yourself. He has been party to all the important developments."

León's face darkened. "Governor Velázquez did not give you p-permission to found a colony. He will not be pleased when he hears about this."

"A shame you think your uncle so unreasonable, León. Alas, I will lose little sleep over your uncle's happiness. Sadly, I find Velázquez is moved more by cupidity than any other passion. This colony serves the king, and I am far more concerned with pleasing his Highness."

León gritted his teeth. "Governor Velázquez commissioned this s-search. We serve him."

Cortés looked at him askance. "Are you suggesting we should serve somebody else before the king?"

Some men nearby laughed. León opened his mouth to object, but stopped himself. Montejo looked astounded that León had not already answered, and his veins bulged out with newfound rage.

Solomon suppressed a snigger. He found the infighting among Spaniards amusing long before he was forced into slavery, and his new station in life made him appreciate it even more.

"Where is your damned authority for all this hogwash?!" Montejo bellowed.

"The sacred laws of Spain, the *Siete Partidas* of course."

Montejo fumed. If the flush creeping up Montejo's neck was any indication, he had little knowledge of the *Siete Partidas*.

"What of Velázquez's charter?" León asked. "I'd imagine his charter would take priority h-here since we are in new lands, not Spain."

"Not Spain?" Cortés arched his brow. "In our every victory, I have claimed the land for the Crown. If you thought it so objectionable, you should have raised your concerns earlier. You cannot claim these lands do not fall under the auspices of the king, and his laws, only when it is convenient."

"So," León said, "Velázquez's charter does not g-give you any authority for what you have done?"

For a moment, it looked as if León had caught Cortés off-guard. Solomon felt a brief touch of admiration for him. A struggle for power was always more interesting between worthy foes.

"A compelling argument can be made for Article Twenty seven," Cortés said. "But don't just take my word on it."

Cortés motioned to the royal notary who went off to fetch the charter. Solomon marveled at the compliance of the men who served Cortés. He had been elected to the position captain-general and chief justice only two nights ago, but the men waited on him as if they had served him for years. Within moments, the royal notary had returned with the charter and handed it to Cortés after performing a quick salute.

Cortés dismissed him with a wave and handed an upside-down charter to Montejo. Montejo stared at the charter, unable to make heads or tails of it.

"Read it for us, Montejo. Please elucidate my authority for all my men to hear. Surely no illiterate man would claim a great knowledge of legal code."

The crowd laughed, and Montejo clenched his jaws shut. León ended the charade of literacy by snatching the charter away from Montejo.

"Will you be doing us the honors of reading Article 27 then?" Cortés asked. "If your stammer will allow."

León colored and shot a quick glance at the crowd. He lowered his voice a fraction and said, "Should c-crisis befall your mission, you are hereby authorized to undertake the m-measures that best p-provide service to God and their Highnesses..."

"I hear nothing in there that gives you the right to betray our Governor!" Montejo shouted.

"Crisis has befallen our mission—just look at how many have died from the fever. We must establish a colony if we are going to survive. In the interest of serving God and king, we ought to do so sooner rather than later."

"Is it just a coincidence that this c-c-colony also serves your interest?" León asked.

"You mustn't think of it that way," Cortés said. "Surely you would not dispute we are expanding Christendom with our mission? We have already converted twenty slave girls to His Holy Faith, and we can convert even more Indians by founding a colony."

"That remains to be seen," León hissed.

"When we make it back to His Highness' court, we can settle the issue there. I wonder if I can make twenty-one new converts before then," Cortés said.

León snorted and went back to poring over the charter. Cortés pulled it from his grip with a kind smile. León's grip tightened for a moment, but a resigned look passed over his face, and he let go.

Cortés rolled up the charter and returned it to the notary who wasted no time making himself absent again. Solomon suspected the charter contained provisions Cortés wished to keep secret, but one did not need to be an Al-Azhar scholar to know that it was dangerous for slaves to volunteer an unprompted opinion.

Cortés opened his arms for a hug. "Let's put this disagreement behind us. We are fellow citizens of Villa Rica de la Veracruz, and we should not argue."

Solomon tensed as León stepped forward. Montejo, however, did not move. León directed an expectant glance toward his recalcitrant friend, but still Montejo did not move. Onlookers that pretended to be busy dropped all pretense and stared unabashedly.

"I will not be part of this mutiny," Montejo growled.

The murmuring of the crowd came to an abrupt halt. Even Cortés was taken aback by the accusation. "Perhaps you should save the theatrics for when you next see Velázquez. But then again, he may not much care what the joint chief magistrate of Veracruz has to say."

Montejo reared back. "You made me joint chief magistrate?"

"Of course, I did. You and I will help administer justice in Veracruz—"

"I will not serve with a mutiner," Montejo shot back. He spat on Cortés' boot.

Cortés nodded. He shot a quick glance toward the soldiers who took positions near and behind León and Montejo. They did so with so much tact and stealth that neither of the two officers noticed. Solomon's insides coiled like a compressed spring as he thought about what would happen if Montejo and León had time to draw their weapons. Word had it that León was one of the best swordhands in the entire expedition.

"Would you care to make your friend recant his statement, León?" Cortés asked.

"Montejo, shut up. This is not the t-t-time," León warned.

"Conduct your shadow campaign against Cortés without me," Montejo said. "I will not be silenced, and I will let everyone know where I stand!" He huffed for breath and leveled a finger at Cortés. "I will not take any more orders from this mutiner."

Cortés sighed. "Very well. Arrest them both!"

The soldiers seized Montejo before he could even grab the hilt of his sword. León did little better and was wrestled to the ground before his sword was half out. Montejo shouted and bellowed but quieted after a soldier smashed a mail-plated fist into his face.

Solomon rubbed his jaw. If high-ranking officers were not safe from violent reprisal, he wondered if anyone was safe from the captain-general. The scars on his back tingled, and he retreated backward with downcast eyes.

"For all of you who need to know in the future, mutiner is not a word." Cortés' icy tone brought Solomon to a halt. "The proper word is mutineer."

There were some hearty peals of laughter, but they were too scattered and nervous to seem genuine. Cortés took his leave, and Solomon went back to unloading provisions as if nothing had happened.

Chapter 20

The horse nickered loudly and Malintze tightened her grip on the saddle. Everything about the animal—its size, its noises—was foreign and she had yet to conquer her fear of the slobbering beast. She doubted sometimes she ever could.

It dealt nothing at all with personal animosity. She found horses quite beautiful. A rider who knew his way around a horse could look very elegant, regal even. But Malintze did not know her way around a horse, and climbing atop one was enough to quicken her pulse. Had it not been for Cortés' urging, she would be walking on her own two feet with the rest of the company.

She tried to loosen her grip on the reins, but her body refused to obey. The inability made her feel powerless, reminded her too much of her former station in life. Malintze tried to remember how many years had passed since she was first taken from Painalla. Impossible to ever really know.

Malintze was certain, however, that she had been young when she had been taken. In some ways, she wished she had been younger. Then, perhaps, she would not have understood what was happening when the traders took her from her family. And she would not have had a happy childhood to remember, a source of constant torment during her years of bondage.

She tensed, remembering her time as a slave. Those days were over, but she often needed convincing. Just looking at Cortés was enough to give her doubts sometimes. She was not surprised he pretended as if nothing had happened between them, but she was very surprised he had not summoned her to his tent again. Perhaps shame stopped him, perhaps disgust; she did not dwell on the reason long. Even if she lived to a hundred, she wasn't sure she'd understand the way men thought about intimacy.

Despite the confusion Cortés inspired, Malintze felt she was coming to understand the Christians better. She certainly knew their tongue better. Soon there would be no use at all for Aguilar. He seemed to realize it too, and he spent most days pouting or sulking or both. She had a child for a teacher, but he was not the only child in her midst. In a way, all the *teteo* reminded her of children.

Everywhere the *teteo* went, they gaped over the wild fauna and the vibrant flora. Seeing a parrot was cause enough for celebration, and the men would marvel at the yellow beaks, the blue eyes, the raucous cawing hours after a sighting. The simple cluck of a turkey could make them giddy with joy. Many of the men had insisted upon stroking the verdant foliage and only stopped once the rashes started breaking out. Nonetheless, they were dangerous children. The sighting of an exotic bird elicited crossbow arrows, as well as oohs and ahhs.

While their destructive impulses were foreign to her, she could understand their sense of wonder. She understood they were currently travelling in a domain controlled by the Totonacs, but she knew nothing about the lay of the land. Nevertheless, just knowing about the Totonacs made her vastly more knowledgeable than the *teteo* who insisted upon calling them Indians for some strange reason.

Malintze was glad the *teteo* could at least see the Totonacs were different from the other peoples they had encountered, even if she was less glad to hear them remark upon those differences for hours on end. The first Totonac envoys visited Veracruz yesterday, and the Christians had still not stopped talking about their

177

outlandish facial piercings and blackened teeth. Many of the men wagered that the Totonacs had ear plugs thicker than a crossbow shaft. None of the men made any wagers about their mutilated lips, though. They were far too horrified to do anything besides guffaw and gape.

Perturbed as the *teteo* were by the appearance of the envoys, they still agreed to meet with the Totonacs in their capital Cempoala. The march to Cempoala had begun only a short time ago, but she predicted the march would not end for many hours. While the distance between Cempoala and Veracruz was relatively short, the *teteo* were not inclined to rush. Some of this dealt with the grueling June heat and a difficult landscape, but most of it dealt with Cortés, who insisted upon sending scouts ahead and marching at a cautious pace.

Much to her surprise, the prospect of a long, slow march fraught with danger had done little to dampen the spirits of the men. She wondered how many more would have to die for them to stop feeling immortal.

She looked up. One of the scouts was riding back. No, galloping back. *He must have seen something shocking.* A chill passed through her. She felt vulnerable sitting atop the horse, but she did not trust the animal or herself nearly enough to attempt a dismount. Her hands tightened around the saddle horn so much it hurt.

Commands rang out from every corner of the formation, and the marchers came to a standstill. To Malintze's surprise, her horse stopped as well.

The scout continued to gallop toward them. Many of the men nearby grabbed at their hilts. It was a welcome sight as she had great confidence the *teteo* could protect her from any hostile force. She looked back to the scout who had all but closed the distance. He was in such a hurry he brought the horse to a stop just a few paces from Cortés.

"Captain Cortés, you must see this!" the scout shouted between haggard breaths.

"See what?" Cortés asked.

"There's a city of silver up ahead!"

Cortés' eyes grew wide as dinner plates. All at once, every man began shouting and hurrahing for attention. Within a few moments, it seemed everyone around her had gone mad.

"Where?" Cortés asked.

"Straight up ahead," the scout said, his voice full of glee and certainty.

"Was it whole city or pyramid?" Malintze asked in halting Spanish.

The scout's face went red. "Only a pyramid, I suppose," he mumbled. "But it's the biggest pyramid of silver I've ever seen!"

Malintze let out a small laugh at the scout's naiveté. The men around her went quiet, and the rest of the formation followed suit.

"Is something amiss?" Cortés asked.

Malintze looked around at the *teteo,* and she noticed many faces were just a touch indignant. She could not help but laugh more.

"There no city of silver!" She laughed and wiped her cheek. "Your scout see a pyramid coated in lime!"

The scout's face fell. "But it looked so silver...."

"Then it freshly painted," Malintze said. The men looked at her as if she had robbed them of a miracle.

Cortés shaded his eyes to peer into the distance, probably wishing he could see the pyramid himself. Malintze turned back to the scout. Her smile fell when she noticed the angry gleam in his eyes.

The scout scowled at her and dropped a hand to his sword hilt. "You trust an Indian woman over an honest-bred Christian, Cortés?"

Her heart skipped a beat. The men were not ready to have their silver city taken away. It looked as if some would resort to violence just to keep it.

She shot an anxious glance at her only protection. Cortés did not seem to notice. He instead kept his gaze leveled on the scout. "She is a native here—of course I place great stock in her word."

Malintze sighed. Looking around her, she could see that many of the Christians had been calmed by the words of Cortés, their Lord on Earth.

The scout flared his nostrils. "But—"

"If the city of silver is up ahead, we shall encounter it very soon," Cortés said. "You can gallop ahead to the pyramid if you want. You won't get there much sooner than us. But if you find a pyramid coated in lime, we will all remember you as the fool who clung to his ignorance in the midst of truth. Do you wish to be remembered that way?"

The scout hesitated. "Guess the pyramid won't be moving anywhere, so no need to rush," he murmured.

Cortés nodded and gave orders to resume marching. Not one person objected, and the march continued as before.

Her horse plodded forward again, but she hardly noticed the swaying and the plodding anymore. Her mind was elsewhere. The tools of the *teteo* indicated they were very intelligent. Thinking a whole city could be made of silver indicated just the opposite. The contradiction was baffling, but it helped her understand them better. Some *teteo* had to be smart; otherwise, none of them would possess such powerful weapons. But she now saw the true genius of the *teteo* wasn't their ability to manufacture cannons and muskets. Their true genius was their ability to make great tools so simple even common fools could use them.

~ ~ ~

180

"The Cempoalteca would like to know if the horses are always so wet," Aguilar announced. Cortés pinched the bridge of his nose in exasperation. They had spent hours marching to Cempoala, capital of the Totonac confederacy, and when they finally arrived, he assumed the most trying part of the day was over. Then the translations began. Or tried to begin.

None of the Cempoalteca that first greeted them spoke Nahuatl. They did not speak Yoko Ochoko either. They spoke something and none of them knew the language, let alone the name of it. Even Doña Marina, fluent in so many Indian languages, did not know it.

Thankfully, Cempoalteca soon arrived that did speak Nahuatl, but they had only a basic understanding of the language so conversing had proved frustrating as well as tiresome. Anytime Cortés spoke, his word had to travel through Aguilar, then Doña Marina, and then the Cempoalteca translators to reach the crowd of locals who had joined them in the central plaza.

Not only were the Indians determined to ask questions about every single tiny detail, but Aguilar also saw fit to translate each and every single question, important or unimportant.

Cortés sighed and turned toward Aguilar. "Aguilar, are our horses always wet?"

His brow furrowed. "No."

"Then tell them that. You can answer a simple question just as well as I can."

"Should I let them know the horses are wet because we had to travel through rivers during our march?"

"Yes, Aguilar. Be sure to let them know the rivers were very big and very wet."

Aguilar's face turned to curdled milk, and he returned to his translating work. Cortés focused his attention on Pedro. Even now, in the midst of the fawning crowd, Pedro looked prepared for violence. His hand had been attached to his sword hilt ever since they entered Cempoala.

Cortés would not have had it any other way. He needed men like Pedro. Men like him were always on edge, always tense, always ready for violence. It made things easier knowing he could delegate the worrying to others.

Despite some horrifying reports—Cortés had sent scouts throughout Cempoala and they returned with stomach churning stories of human sacrifice—it was easy to feel safe in the city. The gruesome piercings, outlandish tattoos, and blackened teeth gave the locals a rather striking appearance, but they seemed friendly enough. For the first time in all their expedition, it seemed they had finally found Indians they could be peaceable with.

At least, he hoped so. The city was quite beautiful and it would be a shame to sack it. Everywhere he looked he saw beautiful buildings made of stone and stucco polished with stunning shades of yellow, blue, red, and green. He was a touch disappointed the pyramids were coated in lime rather than silver but did not dwell on it. Neither did his eyes dwell on the pyramids long. The lime coating gave them a sheen so brilliant it hurt to stare. He averted his gaze toward the manicured landscape, marveling at the neat, orderly rows of palm trees that ran parallel to the major streets.

He could spend all day admiring the city, but he could not indulge the pleasure yet. The town chief, called upon so long ago, and his retinue had been spotted on the horizon and would arrive in a few minutes.

Cortés straightened in his saddle, much to the protest of his back. He had been sitting in the saddle for hours now, but he would not dismount before speaking with the chief. He was far more imposing atop his horse, and he needed to look every bit daunting.

He considered riding out to the entourage, but decided against it. It was better to leave the hurrying to the Indians. He bid his translators and guards closer. The Totonac entourage, fifty strong, ground to a halt as they came within a few paces of the Spaniards. Some person of importance, the chief he assumed, was carried forward by means of a massive sedan chair that hid the occupant from view with a thick curtain.

Cortés suppressed a chuckle. He had his horse, and the chief had the sedan chair; perhaps men on every side of the ocean needed conceits. The curtain of the sedan chair was brushed aside to reveal the chief, and Cortés' laugh caught in his throat. The chief was so obese his stomach rolls spilled over his armrests, and Cortés seriously doubted he could stand without assistance.

The chief cast only a brief glance toward Cortés' entourage. Once he locked eyes with Cortés, he started bellowing and gesturing toward the horizon. Cortés had not the slightest clue what the chief was saying and turned to the translators. They were struggling to keep up, and seemed to capture only a fraction of what he was saying.

"What's Fat Chief so excited about?" Pedro asked.

"If he ever slows down, we might one day find out," Cortés said.

Fat Chief ended his tirade with a final huff. Cortés waited patiently for word to percolate through the translators. It was a sad sight. Rivers were not meant to pass through spigots.

"Malinche says the Cempoalteca speak very broken Nahuatl," Aguilar said. "She can only translate pieces."

"Tell her to translate what she can," Cortés snapped. Aguilar passed the command on to Doña Marina and was no kinder in tone.

"The chief says his name is Xicomecoatl. He has heard we are very powerful, and he hopes you will think of him as a friend," Aguilar announced. "He also wants to know if we are friends to the powerful people who live in the valley, the Mexica people."

Cortés nodded. "Tell him we have not yet decided if the Mexica are worthy of our friendship. Are the Cempoalteca friends to the Mexica?"

"No," Aguilar said. He paused as he waited for Doña Marina to translate more. "They are mortal enemies, but the Cempoalteca have been forced to submit to the Mexica because they have been bested in battle. Now they are forced to pay tribute to them. He wishes fervently he had the power to improve his situation. The Cempoalteca have no wish to continue paying tribute to their Mexica overlords."

"Ask him if he is willing to go to war to end the tribute payments."

Some of Cortés' guards stiffened at the mention of war. The importance of the moment seemed lost on Aguilar, however, and he translated for Doña Marina in the same droll tone. Doña Marina widened her eyes when she heard and passed the statement on to the Cempoalteca with only some hesitation. Cortés almost rolled his eyes when he realized he would have to endure another cumbersome translation. Once again, Fat Chief launched into a lengthy tirade as rapid and as animated as the first.

"The Cempoalteca have gone to war for the sake of tribute and will do it again, as will many others, but only if they know they can win independence. He doubts he can triumph against the Mexica on his own because he does not have your power."

"Remind him that war with the Mexica would be a difficult undertaking," Cortés said. "Let him know that any who make war against the Mexica could use Totonac help."

Cortés inhaled deeply after releasing the words. There was a chance the Cempoalteca were lying about their enmity toward the Mexica. This entire meeting may have been nothing more than a ruse on the part of Motecuhzoma to trick Cortés into revealing his true intentions. They could be in the middle of a trap. If so, they were doomed. Motecuhzoma would have no choice but to treat him as an enemy if he discovered their plans for an offensive march.

"He says there are over thirty towns in the Totonac confederacy and thousands upon thousands live within its borders. He says every single town would contribute to the war effort so long as we spearhead the offensive."

Cortés' heart pounded in his chest. He felt faint for a second. To command an army of thousands… truly, there was no higher calling.

"He also says there are many more who would fight alongside us who are not Totonac," added Aguilar. "He talks of Tlaxcala. He says they are in active revolt against the Mexica. They would gladly aid our cause. They would also contribute many warriors. The chief says he is willing to act as intermediary with Tlaxcala. He says…" Aguilar stopped mid-sentence. He gulped and asked Doña Marina to clarify something. Satisfied, he resumed the translation. "The chief says we could command an army with hundreds of thousands should we go to war with the Mexica."

Cortés' calm demeanor finally cracked, and a smile split his face. His heart soared, his breathing deepened, his being calmed; he felt as if the heavens had opened and he had received manna from the Lord Himself.

"Let him know we can agree to those terms," Cortés said. "Tell him that if his word is good, we will be marching on Tenochtitlan by the end of the year."

Chapter 21

Tezoc breathed in the scent of *octli*, savoring the fruity smell. He didn't have the stomach for alcohol he once did, but he could still put away many younger men. Looking across the table at Milintica, he wondered how well Motecuhzoma's top political advisor could handle his *octli*. Milintica was younger than him, but had spent far more time navigating the corridors of power. By the end of the day, Tezoc hoped to know who had the stronger stomach.

However, Milintica had yet to express interest in drinking or even conversing, giving his full attention only to Tezoc's collection of Toltec pottery. Tezoc suppressed a smile. The brilliant wax finish and the dazzling color range seldom failed to catch the eye of guests. Tezoc was not one for ostentatious displays, but he was proud of his collection.

"An impressive lineup of Toltec pottery, isn't it?" Tezoc asked.

Milintica guffawed, but he kept his gaze fixed on the Toltec pottery.

"I would be happy to send a vase to one of your litter-bearers, should you wish to take one home with you," Tezoc said.

"A fool's gambit, to carry a Toltec vase and a litter." Milintica chuckled and uncrossed his arms. "Besides, none of your vases, pretty as they are, would match any of mine."

Tezoc resisted the urge to roll his eyes.

Milintica strummed his thumb up and down on the table's lip. "You have such fine tastes in art, Tezoc. It's a shame we have so little else in common."

Tezoc tutted and shook his head. "Milintica, don't be so dramatic. We both wish to protect our people, don't we?"

Milintica's face darkened. "I did not know you cared for my wishes. I wish to expel the pale people from our land, but I fear I am alone in that regard."

"You are not. I also want the pale people gone from our land. I objected to your march because there are better ways of achieving their removal."

Milintica narrowed his eyes. "Removing them will be far more difficult now that they have taken refuge in the Totonac lands. The pale people have grown quite comfortable here in the One World, haven't they? I wonder how much longer until they start referring to our lands as their home."

Tezoc smiled thinly. "You sound like Cuitlahuac and Itztli."

"They make a lot of sense these days. If only they had attended the Great Council. They could have calmed some of the more dramatic *pilli*."

"They were firming up our military alliances. We generals do not have the luxury of spending all our time in Tenochtitlan," Tezoc said. "But let's put aside our misgivings. We have important issues to discuss."

Milintica furrowed his brow. "Is that so?"

Tezoc nodded politely, but Milintica did not seem moved. He probably wanted Tezoc to grovel, but Tezoc was not willing to do that—yet.

"Hard to imagine you would have anything important to discuss with me," Milintica hissed. "Unless, of course, you intend to admit that your genius ploy of withdrawing the porters has failed to dislodge the pale people from our lands."

Tezoc pursed his lips. "We dislodged them from Cuetlaxtlan area, and we better understand their nature now that they have aligned themselves with the Totonacs."

Milintica flared his nostrils. "Your ploy failed. You are a failure. Admit it."

"Do not forget you are a guest in my house," Tezoc said.

"And quite a nice house it is. Really. Almost as big as mine."

Tezoc waved over a nearby servant who set two glasses of *octli* on the table.

"Are we celebrating now?" Milintica asked.

"I suppose." Tezoc picked up his glass and motioned for Milintica to do the same. "Alcohol precipitates so many great friendships, does it not?"

"Often precipitates much more than that," Milintica said. "Tezoc, do you think you can ply me with alcohol? That I will simply forget how you wronged me?"

Tezoc shrugged. "If you feel it prudent to abstain, I understand. It's easy for men like me to manipulate men like you. And when alcohol is involved, then it's almost too easy."

"Oh please, surely you can goad me better than that."

"I'm not goading at all." Tezoc brought the cup to his mouth. A mischievous smile spread across his face. "But I will have you know this *octli* is very expensive."

"Very expensive you say?" Milintica asked in a piqued voice.

"Worth more than an entire garden of cocoa beans. I have never had the same taste for decadence as you, but even I must admit that this *octli* is well worth the expense. I have been saving it for a special occasion—it just might be the best *octli* I have ever had."

"So, it's your favorite?"

"Without question."

"Better for it to be in my belly than yours, then." Milintica picked up his glass and took a healthy swig. "Hmm, that is… different."

"Perhaps to the uncultured tongue," Tezoc teased.

"Still casting barbs, are we?"

"Forgive me. Old habit."

Tezoc waved the servant over to bring new drinks.

"Why did you invite me here, Tezoc? Surely your pride must have protested."

"You know me well." Tezoc took a drink from his new glass. Milintica followed in his example, albeit more cautiously. "But," Tezoc said, "my pride is not nearly as important to me as the good of our *altepetl*. As you noted, the pale people have grown quite comfortable here in the One World. I feared they would be resourceful, but I didn't think they would be so resourceful as to deliberately seek out our enemies and make a pact with them."

"Aye, your little test has shown them to be very smart. All the more reason we should have crushed them while we had the chance."

Tezoc shook his head. Milintica still didn't understand that engaging an enemy of unknown strength was foolish at best and suicidal at worst. "We may still have an opportunity to crush them."

Milintica stared at Tezoc in disbelief. He scoffed, downed his new drink, and stared at the bottom of the empty glass with an uneasy expression. "I may never understand you. Not so long ago, I sought you out and advised that we both advocate for military action against the pale people. I urged we present a united front against the pale people. You not only refused to join ranks with me, but you took a giant *macuahuitl* to my plans and sliced them to little bits right in front of the Great Council.

"I did not think—"

189

"You humiliated me!" Milintica snarled. "In front of the entire Great Council. Prestige and influence that I have been building for years—gone in an instant. And now that we know the pale people are resourceful as well as powerful you want to march on them? It was already an uphill battle to win support for a march before the rainy season began, before the pale people started receiving Totonac succor. Winning *pilli* to our side will be almost impossible."

"We should focus our efforts on the Great Speaker, not the *pilli*. And I am not advising a military march just yet."

"Then what are you advising?"

Tezoc waved the servant over to bring new drinks. "I advise subterfuge. Four years ago, we marched on the capital of Tlaxcala. We were supposed to rout the Tlaxcalteca forces. Instead, our forces were defeated. Why do you think our march failed?"

Milintica shrugged. "Perhaps it was poor leadership. The military is full of fools these days."

Tezoc huffed and raised his cup to take another drink. He motioned for Milintica to join him. Milintica flicked his eyes toward his own cup, but made no attempt to reach for it.

"Don't be such a sour guest," Tezoc said in a plaintive voice. "My house is your house. Please, you really must share this drink with me."

Still hesitant, Milintica lifted his cup, but did not take a drink until he saw Tezoc finish. When Milintica finally finished his glass, he grimaced and muttered something about strong *octli*.

"I suppose, in some respects, it is fair to blame military leadership," Tezoc admitted. "Our campaign against Tlaxcala failed because we relied on strength alone. Tlaxcala knew months in advance that we would be marching on their capital with a massive force. They were able to form alliances, prepare defenses, hoard supplies—everything we didn't want them to do."

Milintica looked at him askance. "Of course, Tlaxcala knew we would be attacking. We were raising an army to invade their home. No amount of subterfuge could make them forget that."

"But it could have enticed some of their allies to join us, or at least not sabotage our plans. Wouldn't you agree that underhanded tactics can achieve a great deal?" Tezoc asked.

Milintica snorted and turned away from Tezoc, focusing once more on the priceless Toltec art perched atop the nearby cupboard. Tezoc motioned to his servant for a new round of drinks. Before he could lay the glasses down, Milintica protested that he had already drunk too much. The servant laid the glasses on the table anyway.

Milintica stared incredulously. "Is your servant deaf?"

"In some ways. He comes from the Huastec lands, and he is still learning Nahuatl. His family sold him when he was not quite young and not quite old."

Milintica leaned back in his chair. "What good is a servant who can't understand you?"

"I speak more than just Nahuatl. As you may know, our enemies often speak languages other than Nahuatl."

Milintica said nothing. He narrowed his eyes and took a small sip of his *octli*. He rested his fingers on the cup's lip and then pushed the cup away. Tezoc arched his brow, but did not press Milintica to drink anymore. Instead, he finished his own cup, knowing that Milintica was studying his features for any sign of weakness or pain.

"What is it," Milintica stopped to suppress a burp, "you propose we do? How should we employ subterfuge against the pale people?"

"I propose we lift the stay on tribute collection in the Totonac lands and send collectors to the town nearest the pale people."

191

Milintica's hand drifted to his midsection. "Elaborate."

"If the pale people do not interfere when we send our tribute collectors into the Totonac confederacy, we know that we do not need to fear their presence. We can carry on the affairs of our nation as before and ignore the pale people. I doubt the Totonacs will have much interest in preserving a pact with a do-nothing ally."

"And what happens if the pale people attack our collectors?"

"Then we have the perfect justification for war. Raising an army can take months under ordinary circumstances, but if our tribute collectors were attacked, we could raise an entire army in mere weeks. Tetzcoco and Tlacopan also rely on tribute and could supply thousands of fighters."

"It all sounds very interesting. But did you forget that Motecuhzoma is opposed to sending tribute collectors to the Totonac lands while the pale people are encamped there?"

Tezoc narrowed his eyes. "I haven't. Otherwise, I would not have invited you here. You know as well as I that it is dangerous to go against Motecuhzoma when he has his mind set. But he respects us. If we could both agree that we should send collectors to the Totonac lands, he may reconsider."

Milintica rubbed his throat and coughed. "It's not a bad idea. I prefer marching on them, yet I could settle for your proposal. But remind me why I should help you when you have done so little to help me? Need I remind you of a certain Great Council session?"

"You need not remind me. My apologies for not paying you greater heed—"

"Remind me why I should do you such a great favor."

Tezoc leaned back in his seat. "This conflict is bigger than us. You are not doing me a favor. You are serving your *altepetl*."

"Well I would be happy to help my *altepetl*—once you help me," Milintica replied.

Tezoc pushed down his anger. If Tezoc wasn't so desperate for Milintica's help, he would have excoriated him for his selfishness. "Will you help me only if I do you a favor?"

"Correct."

Tezoc snorted. "I have never known you so honest."

"You have never known me so drunk." Milintica shook his head and rubbed his temple. "You have always thought me selfish. It's why you despise me."

Tezoc clenched his hand in a fist beneath the table. "There is only love between us."

Milintica laughed. "What favor will you do for me? You did ruin my plans for a march, after all."

"I owe you no favor. You have your opinion, to which you are entitled, and I have my own, to which I am entitled. The purpose of the Great Council is to speak our own sentiments, not the sentiments of others. I owe you no debt."

"So, you will do me no favor?"

"If reason cannot convince you to publicly support a plan you favor, then no amount of groveling would help."

Milintica did not try to hide his smirk. "You may be right, but what a pretty sight it would have been, to see you grovel like some beggar." Milintica took a sip from his drink, and his face curdled like he had consumed something rotten. "Could almost make up for this awful drink you call *octli*."

Tezoc nodded toward his servant who positioned himself behind Milintica, looming over him like an oak would a sapling. It would be such an easy thing to snuff out Milintica's life. All of Milintica's servants were outside, he was unarmed, he was drunk... and because of that, Tezoc had to be sure no harm came to him. While he was inside the house.

Tezoc rubbed the lip of the glass and spoke to his servant in Huastec. "Please escort our guest out."

Milintica arched his brow. Despite being unfamiliar with Huastec language, he seemed to intuit he was being dismissed. "You're not even going to try to convince me that I am making a terrible mistake?"

Tezoc shook his head. "I see no reason to waste my breath. Besides, I suspect you will come around to my way of thinking sooner than you think. But I should tell you: if you cannot agree to my proposal regarding the tribute collectors, you will not be stepping foot inside my home again."

Milintica let out a raucous laugh. "Consider your proposal rejected. I wouldn't want to sully myself by stepping inside this place again anyway."

Tezoc nodded and motioned to the Huastec to help Milintica stand. Milintica let the servant help him to his feet, but pushed him away with a brusque shove once he was standing on his own two feet. Despite his initial objections to physical assistance, he let the Huastec lead him toward the exit, swaying all the while. At no point did he seem to realize he was being led to the back exit rather than the front exit.

The conversation with Milintica had left a bitter taste in Tezoc's mouth and he downed more *octli* to dull the guilt welling in his stomach. Alcohol often precipitated great friendships, but it could also precipitate scandal. Members of the upper class could be put to death for being drunk in public. Milintica would be learning that lesson very soon. Unless Tezoc told his Huastec servant to escort Milintica out the front exit, where his litter-bearers awaited him. They could escort him home, and the authorities would be none the wiser as to Milintica's inebriation.

Tezoc stared into his cup and wondered what Milintica would do if their roles were reversed. He shook his head and cast aside the dark thoughts. It did not bear thinking about. All that mattered now was making sure the authorities learned of Milintica's poor state. So long as no one outside the household realized that Tezoc had laced Milintica's drink, Tezoc would gain much needed leverage with Milintica.

The back door closed and Tezoc rose to his feet, glass in hand. He advanced toward the door and pressed his ear up against it. All he could hear were muffled voices. He fixed the glass to the door, placed his ear against the base of the glass and strained his senses to hear better.

"Where are my litter-bearers?" Milintica asked.

The Huastec servant replied, "They are at the front entrance. You must walk around to the other side of the house to reach them."

"Speak Nahuatl, not Huastec, you stupid beast! Where are my litter-bearers?"

"You must go around the block to reach them," the Huastec said. "It is not a long walk. You wil only have to pass a few houses."

"I cannot understand you when you speak Huastec," Milintica growled. "Let me back in to the house and take me to the other exit."

"I am not allowed to let you back in," the Huastec said. "You must walk around the block to reach your attendants."

Tezoc tried to imagine Milintica's reaction. He was probably glowering, fuming like some child that realizes a toy is out of reach. Tezoc was surprised that Milintica hadn't started shouting for his attendants. It would be better if he was shouting. Then the neighbors would hear him and others could corroborate testimony regarding Milintica's poor public state.

"Fetch my litter-bearers," Milintica said, a hint of desperation in his voice.

"I must stay here. You can walk to them."

"I will not stand outside this house like some vagabond in need of charity. You will take me to my litter-bearers, or you will bring them to me."

An excruciating silence took hold. Tezoc's pulse quickened. He had enlisted the Huastec's help specifically because he had such poor knowledge of Nahuatl. Any servant that understood Nahuatl would have long since agreed to help Milintica. But even if the Huastec could not understand Milintica's words, he could understand gestures and emotion. He knew the dangers of crossing someone powerful. He had to know that all he had to do was obey Milintica to spare himself a terrible wrath. Tezoc closed his eyes and prayed that his servant would stay loyal.

"It is not a long walk," the Huastec repeated. "You can walk around the block to them."

"I will remember this," Milintica spat. "I will make you suffer for the rest of your days, and you will rue the day you entered Tezoc's service."

Tezoc breathed a sigh of relief as he heard Milintica's footsteps fade from hearing. He returned to the table and took a small sip of the *octli* Milintica had been drinking. His stomach roiled like Lake Tetzcoco during a tempest. He knew little of herbs or potions, but he was certain Milintica would struggle to make it halfway down the block after consuming such a potent concoction.

One of the neighbors would surely notice Milintica's poor state, and Tezoc had every confidence he would be arrested before day's end. He also had every confidence he could convince the authorities to release Milintica before dawn and was more than willing to—so long as

Milintica agreed to support his plan regarding the tribute collectors.

But if Milintica still refused to lend support, Tezoc would not lift a finger to save him from royal punishment. He wondered if he would miss Milintica. He knew with a startling certainty he would not. The capital did not lack selfish *pilli* that would put their own interests before their own *altepetl*.

Chapter 22

Vitale's leaden feet begged for relief, and he wondered why he thought it would be a good idea to embark on a late night walk after spending so much of the day practicing drills and digging post-holes. The world around him teemed with energy—jungle animals proclaimed their existence with abandon and the full moon bathed the landscape in an eerie glow—but it did little to enliven him.

He took a deep breath and stared at the road ahead. Vitale had never seen anything like it in Spain or the West Indies. The Totonac road was smooth and level like a beam of wood and would take him all the way to Cempoala, a distance of almost seven leagues, if he travelled the length of it. He wondered if it could perhaps carry him as far as Tenochtitlan. "Solomon, do you think this can last?"

"I'm afraid I don't know what you mean."

Vitale laughed. Nobody understood what he meant these days, and gloom hung over him like the sword above Damocles. He was so desperate to find just one person who could understand how he felt that he sought out Solomon and freed him. Temporarily, at least.

Freeing him had been easier than he expected. All he had to do was tell the guards stationed by the slave quarters that he needed to borrow a slave. Before they could pick one for him, Vitale chose Solomon. Vitale worried the guards would ask why he needed Solomon in particular, but they handed him over without question and resumed their card game after reminding Vitale to return the slave by daybreak.

"I don't know the word for it," said Vitale, his voice as weary as his feet. "I think Cortés used the word expedition."

Solomon narrowed his eyes and tried to hide a smirk. "Expedition is a choice way of putting it. I think plundering is a more apt description."

"I don't mean the plundering," Vitale spat. Solomon was so taken aback by the outburst he stopped walking. Vitale exhaled and sat on a fallen log. Vitale knew his sword arm had become stronger during the course of the expedition, but he forgot sometimes that his temper had gotten shorter. "I mean this. Just being here, in the middle of all this… newness. Not the warring, just…"

"The exploring?" Solomon asked.

"Yeah, that. How much longer do you think it can last?"

"There is more world to be seen," Solomon said. "I suspect the game of exploration will continue long after we die."

Vitale drew in a slow, deep breath. "The Cempoalteca treat us like royalty. They even got that special word for us, *teotl*. Lost track of all the times I've been called that."

Solomon chuckled. "Chances are, they never called us *teotl*." Vitale stared at him confusedly. "They use *teteo* to refer to a group, *teotl* when they are talking about only one man," Solomon said.

Vitale shrugged. Nothing of their language made sense to him. "I thought slaves were only supposed to have an ear for whips and chains."

"I wasn't always a slave," Solomon said. "I used to have quite the ear for language. Had to, since the vernacular changed so much from port to port. Maybe if I learn enough Nahuatl, I can set up trade here also."

"So, you used to trade? Before the Emirate of Granada fell?"

"Aye. I was a merchant. Went everywhere in the Mediterranean. Went outside a few times, but never any farther than the Red Sea. I was a different man then. An ignorant man. Did some terrible things. But that was another life." Solomon shook his head. "What does it matter to you how the Indians see you?"

Vitale ran a hand through his hair. He had cut it so short he had nothing more than stubble atop his head. So long as he had Old Christians for company, he would always have to. His natural curls raised too many troubling questions about his heritage.

"I've always had to worry about what others see," Vitale said. "That's what it means to be a New Christian. But the way the Cempoalteca look at us—I'm not used to it. It's like they think we're salvation, like they think I'm salvation. Never thought anybody would ever look at me like that."

Solomon huffed. "They do think of you as salvation. The world looks different with a yoke around the neck. Becomes possible to mistake swords for shears."

Vitale nodded. "We been in Totonac lands for almost two months now. Least that's what I hear; the drills and the training make all the days blur together. Been here so long we've almost finished building the defenses for Fort Veracruz. And the Cempoalteca have been nothing but helpful the whole time. Washing our feet, lending us porters, givin' us food and drink—all because they think we will fight for them. I don't understand it."

Solomon gave Vitale's shoulder a light squeeze. "Friends with swords are almost as good as friends with keys."

Vitale sighed. "That's not what confuses me. I'm confused why I still hate it here." His eyes went misty. "I'm so pathetic—crying about my problems to a slave. Must sound like a madman. Probably am." He sniffled and wiped away tears. "Thought I could enjoy this place, even make something of myself here. And I figured I wouldn't have to worry about Don Carlos issuing any Expulsion Edicts while I'm an ocean away in lands he's never even seen. Thought I could be safe out here. I'm a bigger fool than my parents ever were."

He wondered what his parents would think of him now, fighting alongside Old Christians, drinking and breaking bread with them like they were kin.

"Some of the men talk about how if they get hands on the Mexica Indians, they're gonna give 'em the Judaizer treatment," Vitale continued. "Cut 'em up and flay 'em, just to see if all idolaters scream the same way. Worst part is I don't know if they said that because they know my heritage or because they don't. And if these Mexica get their hands on me, they'll tear my heart out for their sun god. Then they'll cut me into little pieces and eat me. I came here for something better. Now I'm stuck, doing everything possible to not get noticed by all the monsters surrounding me."

A wave of misery washed over him, and Vitale buried his face in his hands.

Solomon took a seat next to him. "If it weren't for the people, would you still hate this place?"

Vitale wiped his face. "Can't say. Too together for me to separate 'em like that. I can't just put things aside like that. This New World is hot, that's for sure. And humid. Not sure I like that." He paused and studied his surroundings. "Like the nature here, though. How colorful the plants are, how the animals so different."

"Probably won't last."

"What won't?"

Solomon cast a longing glance toward the horizon. "The nature."

"Why not?"

"The nature of men. Perhaps one day He will intervene and fix us. But He designed us this way, so maybe not."

201

Vitale furrowed his brow. "Designed us what way?"

"With eyes and hands. I can't see the sense in it. He knew we would use our eyes to behold his beautiful creations, but He must have known we would use our hands to destroy them. I can understand giving us one, and not the other, but both? Has all the makings of a tragedy."

Vitale pursed his lips. "Maybe things can change."

"Well, I suppose things can always get worse." Solomon flashed him a toothy grin, and his good eye twinkled. The bad eye, however, looked as dead as the moon. "Don't you grimace at my ugly face." Solomon laughed. "I'm not the only disfigured one."

Vitale stroked his maimed cheek. It was still sensitive to the touch. "I was wondering if you would notice."

"I was hoping you would just tell me, and spare me the asking."

Vitale stared at the moon. He thought about the cuts on his face, and his smile faded. "Got them back when we was still camping in the marsh. My gut started giving me trouble after we voted to stay and fool that I was, I left camp to go retch. Vomited so much, I had to lie down just to regain my energy. Woke up next morning covered with itches and sores. Them mosquitoes ate me alive."

"Mosquitoes did that to your face?"

"In part. Once I got back to camp, all I could do was itch. Some of the men saw, and they told me the trick to getting rid of the bites was heating up a knife to scrape it all off. Did most of my right cheek before they burst out laughing. Turns out they were just upset with me for beating 'em in cards the day before. Fool I was, I lunged for the four of them after I put my knife away. Really only got two punches in before the four of them pinned me to the ground." Vitale's eyes went misty as he remembered the humiliation.

Solomon shook his head. "Tucking your knife away was the smartest thing you could have done. Cortés would have made an example out of you had you seriously harmed any of them. Imagine what would have happened if one of those men was related to an officer. Attacking them because they goaded you into cutting yourself—"

"They didn't just goad me into slicing my cheek open. One tried to steal my necklace once they had me pinned down. The one thing I got to remember my mother by and the damn fool broke the clasp tearing it off my neck." Vitale rubbed the place his necklace used to be. "Bastard only dropped it because I bit him so hard."

Vitale pulled the necklace from his pocket. He hated keeping it there. He had lost count of all the times his hands had flown to his pockets in a panic, all because he couldn't feel the necklace through the fabric of his pants.

"I see why you have no fondness for the men," Solomon said.

"If you run off, I won't yell," Vitale whispered.

Solomon's eyes widened so much it seemed they would pop out of his head. He turned away from Vitale and looked at the dark jungle where it was so easy to disappear. "Running away into the unknown and finding my freedom. I'd like that."

Vitale waited, but Solomon remained seated on the log. "What are you waitin' for?"

"I can't run. I'm an old man with a ruined body and can't do much better than hobble these days. The best I could do is climb a tree and wait for the hounds and a pack of Spaniards to find me."

Vitale snorted. He hadn't thought that far ahead.

"Besides," Solomon added, "what would happen to the poor boy who helped me escape?"

"Torture, I suppose."

"They'd strappado you until you sang and strappado you more."

"León and Montejo seem to have gotten off fine."

"They weren't so upbeat in the brig."

"They were only there for a few days." Vitale shrank inward and fidgeted. "Besides, Cortés let them keep their rank afterward."

"I assure you it was more out of smart politicking than mercy. Many in your crew would sell the virtue of their own womenfolk for a quick profit, and Cortés is no different. But enough grim talk. We can reach Quiahuiztlan in less than an hour if we stay on the road. This time of the week, the locals like to celebrate and we can watch them do the flying pole dance."

The flying pole dance was not a dance in any traditional sense of the word, at least not to Vitale. To do their dance, four men would climb to the top of a very large pole and then lean so far back they would fall. When he first saw it, he thought he was bearing witness to some sort of mass suicide. Fortunately, he was quickly proven wrong. The dancers had fastened ropes around their feet and rather than plummeting to the ground, they swung round in a circle as the square whorl holding the rope gradually spiraled downwards. The most daring ones included acrobatic tricks in their routine, and just watching was frightening. Vitale had crossed the Atlantic and charged into battle, but he doubted he had the nerve for that dance.

"I don't even understand their dance," Vitale said. "How am I gonna enjoy something like that?"

"You don't need to understand something to know it's beautiful. Be Moses some other time. Let's enjoy a night here."

Vitale mulled the offer. "Go on ahead without me. I'll catch up in a bit."

Solomon shrugged and drew himself to full height. He looked back one last time and, seeing that Vitale would not be following him, tottered down the dim path alone.

Chapter 23

Tezoc dipped his fingers in the water bowl and rubbed away the food particles. The water clouded and he looked away, fixing his eyes on the clear blue sky above. Now that the rainy season had come, clear blue skies would be rare. He sighed. Sitting in the courtyard of his house, basking in the warmth of the sun, gave him unrivaled serenity.

He looked at Chimalli who seemed content to sit on the stone bench and ruminate in silence. It was hard to know with any certainty, though. Tezoc sometimes felt he barely knew what displeased Chimalli. Only in recent years had Tezoc begun to learn what pleased him, and he still had much to learn. For that matter, Tezoc had much to learn about his own tastes. He had always known something was missing from his marriage with Nemilitztli, the beautiful *pilli* woman who gave Tezoc his son, but he had never known he could find that fulfillment elsewhere. Chimalli had introduced him to a great deal that he would not have discovered otherwise.

A servant, the Huastec one that had helped him spike Milintica's drink, took away Tezoc's bowl. He looked unsuited to the task, or any simple household task. His shoulders were broad as a doorway, and his hands were the size of dinner plates. If he had been Mexica, rather than Huastec, he could have fought alongside Tezoc's warriors. Nonetheless, Tezoc trusted him more than he trusted many of his closest warriors, and he had every confidence that the Huastec would never report him, or Chimalli, to the authorities for their illicit relations.

"What made you release your servants?" Tezoc asked Chimalli.

"I had no need of them," Chimalli said after a long pause. There wasn't a trace of judgment in his voice. Nonetheless, Tezoc could not help but feel a twinge of guilt, or something like it, when he thought of his many servants.

"I often wonder if I ought to just release mine. Feels wrong, sometimes. We are military men and should not need them."

Chimalli laughed. "I doubt anyone needs them. How many years of service do yours have left?"

"None of my servants will be with me two years from now. I will be replacing the Huastec by the end of the year. If he lets me."

Chimalli arched his brow.

"He does not want to leave my service," Tezoc said. "Seems he has become quite accustomed to the trappings of fine life. And he can never return home. Tenochtitlan is all he knows."

Chimalli nodded. "He certainly wouldn't be the first to become attached to Tenochtitlan. Sometimes, it feels as if this *altepetl* is the whole world."

Tezoc did not answer. He thought of his late wife. He wondered if the Huastec would have been so eager to stay in his service if she were still alive. She had never been kind to the servants. She could be downright cruel at times. He often wondered if he was responsible for her mean-spirited ways. Perhaps she would have been kinder if he had feigned affection better.

"Would you have stayed in Tenochtitlan your whole life, if you could have?" Tezoc asked.

Chimalli shrugged. "I've never considered the possibility." His voice took on a more serious shade. "What has you so pensive?"

"I don't know." Tezoc stared at the small weeds that had made a home within the stone foundation of his courtyard. The weeds weren't supposed to be there, but somehow they had found a way. He ground them down underfoot. "The pale people, I suppose. Ever since they started coming to these lands, I've had a lot of questions. Their presence is very disconcerting."

"Are you worried perhaps for the tribute collectors?"

"I am." Tezoc exhaled. "Won't be long until they arrive in Quiahuiztlan. Strange they should face the pale people before us, no?"

"You need not fear for the tribute collectors. Do remember, most of them are warriors."

"They were warriors," Tezoc corrected.

"A warrior is always a warrior," Chimalli countered.

Tezoc was less sure. These days, the mere prospect of battle could make his joints ache with fierce intensity. "When did you last hear from Milintica?"

"Just before the Great Council meeting. Why?"

"No reason," Tezoc said, his voice as hollow as the lie in his words. "It's just, he's always planning something. And I haven't heard a word from him. It makes me wonder why I am being excluded from his plan, why we are being excluded." Tezoc thought more on his scheme with the *octli*. Just like he had hoped, Milintica had been arrested for public inebriation, and the threat of exposure had made him very willing to support Tezoc's plan. Almost too willing.

"It is not so hard to send a courier," Chimalli said.

"I think I will send one." Tezoc paused. "Not that Milintica has much reason to answer. He probably does not have much affection for me these days."

He thought more on his scheme with the *octli*. Guilt took him every time he thought about it. There was supposed to be a certain level of decorum among Motecuhzoma's inner circle. They often disagreed, but to resort to such heavy-handed tactics was almost unspeakable. But as great as his guilt was, it was not nearly as great as his certainty that he had no better choice.

"Are you worried he has not forgiven you for speaking out against him during the Great Council meeting?" Chimalli asked.

Tezoc laughed. "Perhaps I am worried that my successor general does not have a woman to call his own." Tezoc shot Chimalli a mischievous glance. "Some of the men under our command must wonder if you have never married because you have no interest in carnal matters."

Chimalli huffed, and his eyes crinkled around the edges, like they always did when he was holding back a grin. "I care only for your thoughts on this matter." Chimalli stared at him pointedly. "Would you have it any other way?"

Tezoc shook his head and stared at the ground. He wished he could say more, but there was too great a risk of being overheard by others. Not all his servants were as trustworthy as the Huastec.

"Are you aware your son is spying on us?" asked Chimalli.

Tezoc snapped his head up. He did not see his son anywhere, and he wondered if Chimalli was playing a trick on him. Before he could ask, Chimalli tapped him on the shoulder and pointed to a nearby pillar. Tezoc shook his head and made his way toward the pillar. Sure enough, Tlalli was hiding behind the stone column. Fear clouded Tlalli's eyes, but he held Tezoc's gaze.

Tezoc studied his son like a fresh recruit. He was already fourteen years old, so it would not be long before he entered the military school for *pilli*. Tlalli was slim as well as lithe, but carried himself like someone much larger. Tezoc hoped it was Tlalli's youth that made him

208

do so. Boys were often encouraged to think they were more than they really were. He had seen it far too often on the battlefield.

"I'm sorry," Tlalli said.

Tezoc pursed his lips. "It's all right. We were not discussing matters of state this time. But you must never spy on us again."

His son nodded a bit too eagerly, and Tezoc knew Tlalli would spy on his private conservations in the future. He smiled and tousled his hair. Together, they walked back to the bench.

"How is your niece, Chimalli?" Tezoc asked.

"Quite good. She has yet to outgrow her mischievous ways, too."

"I'm not mischievous," Tlalli demurred. "Just curious."

Chimalli laughed. "They're really not much different."

Tezoc sat on the bench. His son stood in front of him, awaiting permission to sit. "Tlalli, why do you spy on us?"

Tlalli hung his head in shame. "I want to be a good warrior. Like you," he whispered.

Chimalli's face softened when he heard his answer, but Tezoc maintained his stoic expression. "Spying on us will do you no good. Even if you did overhear us talking strategy, it would not help you become a great warrior."

His son stiffened.

"It is not because of your age." Tezoc lifted the boy's chin. "You do not have any experience on the battlefield. Nothing we talk about could ever make sense until you have endured the furor of battle." A chill ran through Tezoc as memories of his first battle came rushing back to him. "Tlalli, why do you deserve to be a great warrior?"

His son's brow wrinkled in confusion.

"Every boy in Tenochtitlan wants to be a great warrior," Tezoc continued. "Why do you deserve to be great when so many covet the same?"

"We can all be great," Tlalli countered.

Chimalli and Tezoc shared a knowing smile. A long time ago their teachers had told them those exact words.

"My son, there can be no mountains without valleys. What will you do to be great that the other boys will not do?"

His son pursed his lips. "I will train."

"So will the other boys. It will not be long until you and many other boys will go to school just to train."

Tlalli puffed out his chest. "I will train more."

Tezoc nudged Chimalli and put his arm out. Chimalli nodded his understanding and handed Tezoc an obsidian dagger. Tezoc weighed it in his palm before passing it to Tlalli.

"Show me what you have learned so far," he commanded.

A hard mask descended over his son's features. Tlalli took a few steps back and lunged to the right with surprising speed. He jabbed and stabbed the air as if it had soft spots. Perhaps because he did not know what to do with his free hand, he pushed and prodded the air with it. At one point, he almost stabbed his own hand.

"He fights like you," Chimalli said teasingly.

Tezoc smiled and bid his son over. Tlalli placed the weapon in his hand, but seemed reluctant to part with it.

"Tlalli, this is one of the most dangerous weapons you will ever wield. With a weapon like this, you can do great harm to your enemy as well as yourself. The club is but a plaything by comparison. When you handle a knife, you must always be aware of its danger. You must never be careless."

He handed it back to his son and motioned for him to try again. His son took a deep breath. For a moment, it looked as if Tlalli would launch another wild attack on the air. But then he surprised Tezoc by moving only one foot forward and thrusting only his knife hand into the air while using the other hand to sweep the air. He moved forward in quick, choppy bursts that combined deadly poise and impressive form and finished with a sweeping slash that could have disemboweled a grown man.

"Much better. You will make a very fine warrior when the time comes," Tezoc said. He put out his hand again and was pleased to see his son was much less reluctant to part with the knife this time. When Tlalli fully understood the import of the weapon, Tezoc doubted he would want to hold onto the knife any longer than he had to. Just holding a blade in his hand could make Tezoc's hand burn. He handed the knife back to Chimalli. A few moments later, he heard the commotion.

It sounded as if an entire tray of tableware had been dropped, but the most disconcerting sound was the scream. He barely had time to stand before the courtyard was flooded with members of the Royal Guard.

Tezoc took a defensive position in front of his son and scanned the plaza in search of an exit. None—unless he was willing to fight his way through seven Royal Guardsmen.

The guardsmen leader stepped forward. "General Tezoc, you are under arrest."

Tezoc narrowed his eyes. "What crime have I committed?"

"Poisoning an advisor to the Great Speaker."

Tezoc's stomach dropped. It felt as if his knees would give out. For such a crime, a man could be put to death. Or worse.

He cast a desperate glance toward Chimalli as the guardsmen advanced toward him. He expected to see righteous indignation, or at least confusion, and was surprised to see neither. Instead, the look on Chimalli's face promised violence for any that would harm Tezoc.

Tezoc thought of everything that would go wrong if Chimalli attacked the guardsmen. Chimalli was hopelessly outnumbered and even if he somehow managed to triumph against them, it would change nothing. More men would come and they would come much too soon to make an escape. Fighting them off would barely even give him enough time to say his farewells. Just thinking about the wrath that would follow such a brazen attack made his heartbeat quicken. He thought of his son, his family, Chimalli trapped in the middle of all that carnage… and he shook his head no.

That was all Chimalli needed as a signal. He tucked away his knife, and the murderous gleam in his eyes faded. The guardsmen did not seem to notice they had been spared the wrath of the man second in command to the Cutter of Men. Tezoc's stomach tightened as he realized that Chimalli might not be second in command anymore.

Two of the guardsmen grabbed Tezoc's arms and he did not resist as they dragged him forward. Guardsmen closed in on his Huastec servant. Even if he could understand their commands, he did not seem inclined to listen.

They wrenched the Huastec forward, and he instinctively pulled back. The defiance was short-lived. One of the guardsmen smashed a club into his face, and he went limp. He fell into their arms and they quickly dragged him forward, his feet trailing along the hard pavement.

Tezoc winced and cast one last look backward as he was dragged out of the courtyard. The horror etched across Tlalli's face was so palpable that Tezoc almost went limp himself. In that moment, he knew he had failed, not just as a statesman, but also as a father.

Chapter 24

Cortés watched as Pedro leaned over his saddle to clear his nose. It wouldn't be long until the Mexica tribute collectors arrived in Quiahuiztlan, the town nearest Fort Veracruz, and Pedro did not seem the slightest bit interested in presenting a dignified image. If they were meeting with Spanish officials, Cortés would have chastised him for his uncouth ways. But with the Mexica, it was more important to be intimidating than dignified.

Pedro straightened and wiped his mouth with the back of his hand. "You know, I was beginning to think we had civilized the Indians. Figured the Indian King wouldn't collect any sacrifice victims so long as we were around, and it took me by surprise when the Indians came running to Fort Veracruz hollering about tribute collectors." He tutted and shook his head. "Suppose there's a reason, after all, not to cast pearls before swine."

"You were right to think the Indian King had changed his ways," Cortés said. "The Totonacs tell me the Mexica are very punctual about collecting tribute payments. If the Mexica had kept to their past schedule, they should have come to this town weeks ago."

"You think there's a reason they're showing up now?"

Cortés had asked himself the same question, as did all the townspeople in Quiahuiztlan, but they were far less calm about it. Once news broke out that tribute collectors were coming, families took refuge in their homes and their temples. It bothered him none that the locals had gone into hiding. In many ways, it was beneficial since both his force and the Cempoalteca force would be more conspicuous.

Reports indicated that the tribute collectors were few in number. So long as the scouts were right, surrounding the tribute collectors would be easy once they entered town. The conditions were perfect for an ambush, and many of his officers hoped he would approve one. Cortés hadn't ruled it out, but he had to gather more information first. Once he knew why the Mexica were here, he would know the proper course.

"The tribute collectors could be here as part of a test," Cortés said. "See how we react to their presence. Force us to go all in or fold to test the strength of our hand."

Pedro shrugged. "They could be scouts."

"Perhaps. Maybe they will report back to a hidden army once they have assessed our forces. Are Puertocarrero and Montejo in place to alert us if they see anything suspicious?"

"Yes. The men will alert them, and then they'll light a smoke signal for us. We have nothing to worry about."

"We have much to worry about," Cortés corrected. He bid his horse forward. These days, he never met with delegates unless he was mounted, but Cortés was not the only one on horseback this time. Every single officer was mounted. Even Doña Marina had clambered onto a horse.

Cortés glanced back to make sure she was still behind them. She had fallen farther behind. No surprise considering her slow pace. Sometimes he feared she would never be comfortable on a horse. He prayed that wasn't the case. He had dreamed of riding with her many times. After the campaign was concluded, of course.

"Will we always be on horseback when we meet new Indians?" Pedro asked.

"As long as it's advantageous."

"Some of the officers have private objections. They prefer to be on their feet in situations that could break out in…"

"Hostilities?"

"Exactly."

Cortés stroked Arriero's mane. "Which officers?"

"They would like to stay anonymous," Pedro said. "Otherwise they would have gone straight to you."

"Your loyalties become more intricate with each day, Pedro. I will not press the issue. For now."

"Many thanks."

Cortés shooed away a large fly. "Pedro, do you remember what the Indians call our horses?"

"Not at the moment, but—"

"They call them stags without horns. Do you know why they do that?"

"Because they're mindless savages."

"Because they have no horses. They've never seen a horse, and they've never heard any stories of them, either. Before we came, not a single horse could be found in these lands. Perhaps if they had oxen or steer here, they would describe our horses as skinny oxen or tall steer. But they have neither, so they liken our horses to deer. My friend, we are strangers in a strange land and the more we remind them we are foreigners, the better."

Pedro's face scrunched in confusion. "Why?"

"The devil you don't know frightens far more than the devil you do know."

Before Pedro could respond, a scout called out that a group of Mexica had been spotted on the trail leading up to Quiahuiztlan. The call echoed throughout the town until every Spaniard had heard. Cortés waited for the scouts to specify the number spotted, but the shout never came. Months of drilling and training, but still he lacked a professional army.

Cortés turned Arriero eastward. The mare could not gallop as fast as his horse in Spain, but Arriero was stronger and, best of all, obeyed him unreservedly. He bid her toward a sloping trail and brought the horse to a standstill in the middle of it. Quiahuiztlan was a small town built into the side of a large hill and could only be accessed by one road, so it would just be a matter of time before the Mexica tribute collectors crossed his path. He took a moment to study his surroundings. No large Indian settlements in the immediate vicinity, but the occasional smoke column let him know others had also made a home in the area. Considering the lack of large settlements, Cortés was both surprised and impressed by Motecuhzoma's interest in Quiahuiztlan. Brave warriors could help conquer vast swathes of territory, but it took smart bureaucrats to administer a far-flung kingdom.

"I think I see them," Pedro said.

Cortés shaded his eyes and could just barely make out some indistinct figures slowly ascending the trail. A small animal rustled through the underbrush, an armadillo from the sounds of it, but Cortés kept his gaze fixed on the approaching figures. The collectors carried themselves well and projected an imperial air that reminded him of nobles from home. If one ignored the embroidered loincloths and focused on the extravagant robes instead, the pomp and flair of their attire had a noble aspect too.

They certainly did not lack useless trinkets, something the Spanish upper class seemed incapable of surviving without. Tucked into the arm of every tribute collector was a crooked walking stick that seemed to function solely as an aesthetic. For reasons he could not understand, each man also carried a rose. If wealth was measured by possession of items lacking practical purpose, the tribute collectors had wealth aplenty. Even their servants, who did nothing but fan the air for the collectors, looked well-dressed.

Cortés was transfixed by their appearance, but the Mexica delegation did not even glance their way. He expected them to at least stop in front of the horses, but instead they flowed past them like water around a stone. Besides bringing some roses closer to their noses as they walked past, the Mexica did nothing to acknowledge Cortés and Pedro.

"Apparently, we smell," Cortés muttered.

"Speak for yourself," Pedro said. "I washed just last month."

"More recent than half the men," Cortés grunted. "Let's tie up the horses to that tree."

As they made their way to the makeshift tethering post, Pedro summoned another fat glob of phlegm and sent it flying toward the ground. "Disgusting. Whole lot of them. Just look at the way those tribute collectors style their hair. Slicked back and knotted—like a woman. Makes me sick."

"They are backwards to us, and we are backwards to them," Cortés replied. "Such a vicious cycle, no?"

"You affront holiness with such talk."

"I will pray for forgiveness then. I have so, so much I must ask forgiveness for. Or so I have been told by many cuckolds."

"I will pray for both of us then," Pedro grunted as he dismounted from his horse.

Cortés stayed atop his horse longer, too fascinated with the appearance of the tribute collectors to break eye contact by dismounting. "They are not so different from us. Just look at the way they carry themselves."

"Have you lost your sight? They're strutting about like they're the lords of Spain. I don't stroll around like I've got a sword up my ass."

"Focus on the tree, and you will miss the forest, my friend. The Mexica came here today to gather tribute victims. They may take only one, they make take a dozen, or they may take dozens, but I saw not a shred of remorse on any of their faces. Each eye, dry as a desert. They carry out this killing business as efficiently and coldly as we do. We would be wise to fear them."

The tribute collectors disappeared into a large hut, and Cortés dismounted.

"Should we follow them?" Pedro asked.

"I'll have her follow them." Cortés beckoned to Doña Marina who still lagged behind. "Tether our horses. I'll help the lady dismount."

Pedro snorted but did as he was told. Cortés made his way to Doña Marina who was doing her utmost to stay balanced in her saddle.

He grabbed the bridle and led the horse at a more hurried pace. The Mexica must have begun conversing with the Totonacs and until Doña Marina stepped into the hut, he was deaf. He hastily tethered the horse near the others and motioned for Doña Marina to come down.

Doña Marina tried in vain to remove her foot from the stirrup. She shot him a pleading look. Cortés finished with the tether and clicked his tongue against his teeth. The horse recognized the signal and sat down on its haunches, much to Doña Marina's surprise. Cortés lifted her from the saddle before she could try to stand on her own. His hands slipped up to her breast, and the memory of their one night of passion, so long ago, came rushing back. A night like that could never again happen. At least, not until they completed the mission.

"Apologies for touching you that way. I did not mean to," Cortés said. She looked at him suspiciously, but she said nothing. He wondered if bondage had taught her to tolerate men who touched without permission.

"What are you needing me to do?"

Her voice was testy, but her awkward Spanish made him grin. She understood the language better than she could speak it. He had little doubt, however, that she would soon be fluent.

"I need you to go into the hut and tell me what they are saying. I want to know everything."

Doña Marina nodded. Without a word more, she made her way to the hut.

Pedro strode over to Cortés and stared as she passed by. "Can't tell you how many times I have thought about swiving her."

Cortés clenched his teeth and waited until she stepped inside the hut before he said anything. "Our campaign would suffer terribly if the main translator was looking after a baby. Keep your fantasies in check."

"Shame. So what now?"

"We wait for Doña Marina to bring us back news."

Cortés took a brush out of the saddle pockets and rubbed it along Arriero's hide. Pedro practiced his fencing, occasionally throwing in a kick or two for good measure.

"Pedro, about those officers…"

"What officers?"

"The officers who said they don't always want to be on horseback when meeting Indians. Since it gets in the way of using a sword properly and all."

Pedro swallowed. "What of it?"

"Tell them they shouldn't hide their opinions behind others. No matter how scared they are."

Pedro reddened and resumed his fencing practice. A bout of light rain descended upon the town, but still he said not a word. Cortés wondered if he would remain silent all day, but a nearby commotion put an end to that.

He looked to Pedro. His second in command was as confused as him. A stream of people poured out of the hut that Doña Marina had entered. Cortés and Pedro sprinted toward the hut, charging through puddles and thick mud. Cheers and screams rent the air, but he could make out none of the words flying through the air. Cortés unsheathed his sword just as Doña Marina emerged. Ashen-faced and glassy-eyed, she muttered something incoherent.

Cortés grabbed her by the shoulders. "Tell me everything from the beginning."

She nodded and cleared her throat. "It began nice. The Totonacs offered the Mexica chocolate and... bird. They accepted the food kindly and asked for more. But once they done, the Mexica let their anger loose. They abused the Totonacs greatly for giving comfort to your kind. They demanded Totonacs give them more tribute than ever. They demanded 20 more sacrifice victims as well as the normal tribute. The Totonacs agreed but then they bound and collared the Mexica right there! They only captured few, though. Many got away." Her eyes widened. "They will go back to Tenochtitlan. They will tell Motecuhzoma. He will come with army. They have started war!"

Cortés swore. Fat Chief, as his men had come to call the Cempoalteca leader, had not yet made good on his promise to give Cortés an army of thousands. He had no qualms about letting his warriors train with Cortés, but he had excuses aplenty about why they could not march on Tenochtitlan with Cortés. Now they could be at war soon, and his only ally had already proven himself unfaithful. The defenses for Fort Veracruz were nearly finished, but he doubted it could hold against the full might of the Mexica army.

Pedro threw his hands up. "This is what happens when you take savages for allies. They go and start a war while you have your britches down and your hand—"

"Be quiet," Cortés snapped. He racked his brain for a solution. He swiveled toward Doña Marina. "When the Mexica demanded the tribute, were the Totonacs upset?"

"No," she said. "No anger, no yelling. They agreed without question and then—"

"Thank God," Cortés said.

Pedro and Doña Marina both looked taken aback.

"I thought our allies had let their temper get the best of them," Cortés said. "All this—it was planned. They would've never agreed to the tribute payment if they thought they were actually going to have to suffer it. The Cempoalteca probably decided to arrest the Mexica long before today."

Pedro sneered. "Now why they would go and do something mad like that?"

"It's not mad at all. If Motecuhzoma marches and we agree to back Fat Chief in battle, the Cempoalteca get everything they want and more. They want us to battle the Mexica but never wanted us to march on Tenochtitlan. That would mean marching through unfamiliar territory with a foreign people to attack a city that has never been taken by force. No, they'd much rather do battle here where they know the terrain and can rally allies."

"The Cempoalteca get bent over the barrel if we don't agree to help them defend their territory," Pedro said. "It's like betting everything before looking at your own cards!"

Cortés ran his hand through his hair. "If we don't agree to back them, they'll blame us for everything. Doña Marina was in the hut, our army is scattered all throughout the town. They'll say we forced them to take the tribute collectors prisoners, and then the only battle will be Motecuhzoma hunting us down. The Cempoalteca are forcing our hand to see what kind of allies we will be."

Pedro's face screwed up as if he had stepped on a nail, but Doña Marina seemed too stunned to put any stock in his words. Cortés wished he could explain she did not need to fear for her safety, that he would protect her. For once, he wished Aguilar was nearby, if only so he could explain to her in the Indian tongue.

"You really think the Indians are that smart?" Pedro asked.

"I know they are," Cortés said. Unless Fat Chief was totally impotent as a leader, he must have had a hand in all this.

"And we should be glad our allies have placed us in such in a terrible position?" Pedro beckoned with his sword toward the hut. "The last thing we need is for the Indian king to attack us here. Even if we destroyed his army, we'd be dozens of leagues from the capital so we'd be dozens of leagues from his gold! And with only Cempoalteca for allies, I'm not sure we could win. An unfaithful ally is worse than a sworn enemy."

Cortés nodded and muttered to himself, his temper rising like a viper readying for a strike, bloodlust clouding his thoughts so he could think of nothing besides cutting down Fat Chief... and then clarity came. Cortés froze. His heavy countenance vanished and he locked eyes with Pedro.

"Come, we need to convince Fat Chief to let us guard some of the tribute collectors. War can still be prevented, but we have to hurry."

~ ~ ~

Caltentli stared at the *teotl* who had stepped into the hut. Not only had Caltentli been stripped of all clothing, he was also tethered and collared like some lowly sacrifice victim. When the Totonacs first seized him, it seemed a certainty that he, and all the other tribute collectors, would be put to death.

Much to his surprise, he was handed over to the *teteo*. For hours afterward, he sat in a dark hut alone, as naked and helpless as the day he entered the world. Now that he had a *teotl* for company, he had to wonder if he might soon be leaving this world.

Despite being in the same room as Caltentli, the *teotl* had yet to take an interest in his presence. Instead, he busied himself by checking the windows. Caltentli considered asking him about his strange behavior, but there was no sense in asking the *teotl* a question in a language he could not understand.

The *teotl* looked unlike any man he had ever seen. He was far taller than most, but even more striking than his height was his hair. Dirty yellow, flecked with bits of orange and red, the hair of the *teotl* could have rivaled the sun's radiance—if he washed it.

The *teotl* crouched down and stole toward him. Caltentli was still bound and could do nothing to move away. He held his breath as the *teotl* drew near and not just because of fear. The *teotl* stank worse than a tapir, as did so many of their kind. Their odor was even more distinctive than their complexion.

A chilling smile split the face of the *teotl,* exposing Caltentli to foul breath and stained teeth. Caltentli shuddered. The *teotl* slowly took out a knife unlike any he had ever seen. It was not made of flint or obsidian. Instead, it was made of some silvery material that winked and flashed in the light. The *teotl* drew closer and Caltentli tried to scoot away. The more he tried to move, the tighter the rope dug in.

The *teotl* raised the knife. Caltentli's eyes widened in fear. He had told himself he would be strong when this moment came, but he did not realize the memories of his family and his home would come rushing back with such strength. He pleaded with the *teotl* for mercy. The *teotl* held up a finger to his lips and made a shh sound. Caltentli did not recognize the gesture, but he stopped his begging.

The *teotl* wrapped his hands around the collar that bound him to the post. For some reason, the *teotl* was gentle about it. Even more odd, he set the knife to the ropes rather than Caltentli's flesh and started sawing through the rush fibers. The tension from the collar slowly lessened, as did the tension in Caltentli's body.

The *teotl* attempted to untie the knots that bound Caltentli's feet together, but he gave up and cut through them. The *teotl* took hold of the rope still dangling from Caltentli's neck and hurried toward the door. He motioned for him to follow.

Caltentli rubbed his throat. Nothing about today's events made sense. First, he had been taken captive by the Totonacs, normally servile and compliant, and now he was being freed by the *teteo*, normally brash and destructive.

The *teotl* tugged on the rope. The tug was too gentle to hurt but assertive enough to let Caltentli know he was not free yet. He followed the *teotl* out of the hut, passing two *teteo* stationed outside the hut. Much to his surprise, they did nothing to stop him.

Outside, Caltentli saw that a different *teotl* was digging a hole under the hut. No explanation was offered, but the *teotl* yanked the rope whenever he dawdled. The *teotl,* still in a crouch, led him downslope toward a dark thicket.

The fire-haired *teotl* paused before a thin curtain of foliage, glanced back one last time, and plunged forward. Caltentli took a deep breath and followed the *teotl* into the underbrush, unsure whether he was being led to sacrifice or liberation. They soon entered a small clearing where two other *teteo* were waiting. A woman also waited with them, but she was no *teotl*. Nahua, judging by her looks.

Caltentli studied the appearance of each *teteo*. One had wild eyes and fingernails chewed to a nub, but only the one who held the rope had the fiery hair. The other two had dark hair not so different in color from Caltentli's own hair. However, all the *teteo* had the striking pale skin so typical of their kind. One *teotl* had scars around his lips. The leader of the *teteo* was supposed to have scars like that.

A jaguar yowled in the distance. Most of the *teteo* turned in the direction of the sound, but the one with the scars did not take his eyes off Caltentli for a moment. He uttered something in a strange language. The woman then said in accented Nahuatl, "The *teotl* before you is Hernando Cortés." Caltentli's stomach tightened. He had heard much of Cortés' cruelty at Potonchan. "Cortés would like to know who you are and who you serve."

Caltentli furrowed his brow. The ignorance was surprising. It did not even seem possible. But he obliged and let her know he served the great and glorious Motecuhzoma, and that he had come to the Totonac lands to collect tribute. He let her know that the Mexica had collected tribute from the Totonacs for years, always without incident, but now that the *teteo* had made a home in Totonac lands, they had turned vicious. And he let her know that all those responsible for today's insurrection would pay dearly.

The woman passed on their words to the hairy, wild-eyed *teotl* who paled as he passed the words on. Cortés listened and responded almost immediately. Once again, his words had to pass through the woman and the hairy, wild-eyed *teotl*.

"Cortés would like you to know he had no part in the arrest. It happened despite his objections. He extends you his sincerest apologies for having to endure such unjustified Totonac aggression. He finds them uncouth, unrefined, and astoundingly thickheaded. He hates to see agents of the great Motecuhzoma, who Cortés considers incredibly generous and kind, treated so roughly. He cannot abide such treatment and will not tolerate it. He is releasing you."

Caltentli stared at the *teteo*, mouth agape and eyes wide.

The woman continued, "He says you must return to Tenochtitlan, and tell the Great Speaker all that has happened. You must let him know that the Totonacs arrested you and that we freed you. He understands your journey is a long one, but he will aid your return so that it is safe and quick. The *teteo* will smuggle you to the coast to help you escape Cempoala's reach. Do you understand?"

Caltentli nodded his enthusiastic understanding. He swayed on his feet as he realized he would be returning to his home and family. He heaped bountiful praise on Cortés for his kindness and promised to deliver Motecuhzoma a faithful retelling of events. Cortés smiled as word was relayed to him and shook his hand vigorously. Caltentli did not understand the gesture, but that did little to dampen his newfound joy.

"Cortés will have your other companions released soon. All of you will be returning home to your families in good time. Cortés places himself in great danger by enabling your escape, but he does so to please Motecuhzoma. He hopes to establish a strong friendship with the Great Speaker."

Caltentli swore he would not let Motecuhzoma forget Cortés' kindness and heaped praise on all the *teteo* for their selfless ways. Tears of joy brimmed in Caltentli's eyes as he followed the fire-haired *teotl* toward freedom.

Chapter 25

Tezoc studied the interior of the litter. After a week in confinement, his vision was still adjusting to natural light, but it was hard to overlook the fine upholstery, the jade-studded ceiling, the vibrant green feathers. Most difficult to overlook was Motecuhzoma, perched upon the seat across from him like an eagle on a branch, his gaze cold and imperious.

"Great Speaker, why didn't you have me killed?" Tezoc asked.

Being able to ask felt strange, like scratching at a scar that never should've healed. Instead of answering, Motecuhzoma stared out of the mesh screen to the world outside the litter. The silence was almost unbearable. It had been his primary companion during his week in the cell, and he had no interest in keeping silence around any longer than necessary.

At one point, he did have another companion. Tezoc's first introduction to this companion was an ear-splitting scream in the dead of the night. From then on, his companion at the other end of the hall did little besides sob. At first Tezoc pitied the man. But his cries were just a touch too obtrusive, a touch too haunting. Before long he hated the man. When he heard the man finally yell coherent words, Tezoc realized the man probably hated him too. His Huastec tongue was unmistakable, even at a distance.

Then the man stopped screaming, stopped making any sounds. That was even worse. The guards probably recognized the silence was torture because they hardly made any sounds, either. He never heard them talk at all save one night, when he heard snippets of hushed whispering, something about the tribute collectors being attacked by the Totonacs and freed by the *teteo*. They seemed just as confounded by the matter as he was, if not more.

"Milintica also asked me why I didn't have you killed," Motecuhzoma said. "He tells me I am setting a terrible precedent by not punishing you more severely. He suggested a flaying followed by an execution."

Tezoc's blood ran cold. "Milintica may have been speaking on his own desires."

"Be careful that his desires do not align with my interests, then."

Tezoc stared at his dirty feet. Motecuhzoma's feet were so clean they were practically shining. Tezoc swallowed down the rage building in his chest. No sense releasing it when he didn't know if he should be angry with Milintica, Motecuhzoma, or himself.

"How did you find out?" Tezoc once thought that Motecuhzoma trusted him over Milintica, or at least trusted him enough not to lock him in a cell without proof of wrongdoing, but he had some doubts now.

"Milintica told me that you approached him with a good plan to discover the intentions of the pale people. He was very effusive in his praise. I agreed it was a good plan and gave orders for the plan to be carried out. He came back the next day and opened his wrist right in front of me."

Tezoc's eyes widened.

"I was also confused," Motecuhzoma continued. "Milintica tried to explain, but he was faint, almost incoherent. He said something about being unfit for my service and falling for some evil trick of yours. Naturally, I was intrigued. When he regained consciousness, he gave me a full account of his meeting with you."

Tezoc shook his head. Milintica had risked his life just to make sure that Motecuhzoma took his account seriously.

"Give Milintica some credit," said Motecuhzoma. "He was quite adept in outmaneuvering you."

"I am not inclined to give Milintica any credit."

Motecuhzoma's face hardened. "Your current predicament is your own making."

The litter was lowered to the ground and Tezoc waited for Motecuhzoma to exit. Tezoc emerged from the litter afterward and discovered that Motecuhzoma had walked ahead instead of waiting for him. Tezoc trailed behind him, scanning his surroundings carefully. Motecuhzoma had taken him to the Great Skull Rack. The nearby plaza was empty of visitors, and Tezoc wondered if it was empty on Motecuhzoma's orders. The plaza was as good a spot as any to be executed, but he still had hope that fate might be avoided.

He studied the skulls peering down at him. Thousands upon thousands were hung from racks four men high in a feat of engineering that was just as impressive as it was morbid. Motecuhzoma stopped in front of the skulls, studying them the way a scholar would peruse sacred text.

A breeze passed through the courtyard and the grating of bone on wood made Tezoc shudder. "What will happen to me?"

"I am not going to execute you. But I have taken measures to ensure you never try to poison members of my inner circle again. Your servant has lost his ears. You will never be able to ask him to do foul again. And your son will never be allowed to serve in the military."

Tezoc's throat caught. There was simply no way to achieve meaningful rank in Mexica society without serving in the military. His son could never serve on the Council of Four or in any important policy position for that matter. From now on, his family would always be relegated to the outside circle.

He thought of how much worse his punishment would be if the Huastec had informed his tormentors of Tezoc's trysts with Chimalli. Tezoc owed him a great debt and he intended to make good on that debt—if given the chance.

"You are family to me," Motecuhzoma said. "It is the only reason I did not have you executed, even though you poisoned my cousin."

Motecuhzoma sounded more like a detached spectator than kin. It was jarring. While Tezoc had not been spared punishment, he had been allowed to keep his life. He assumed it was because Motecuhzoma still had affection for him. Now he was not so sure.

"You will continue to serve on the Council of Four," Motecuhzoma added. "I value your counsel still. Have you heard about the developments in Quiahuiztlan?"

Tezoc thought back to the conversation he had overheard in his cell. Or thought he overheard. It may not have happened and could have just been the invention of a fevered mind. That happened to men sometimes; nothing enabled the cruelty of the mind quite like captivity of the body. Tezoc released his breath. "I know the tribute collectors we sent to Quiahuiztlan were attacked by the Totonacs and released by the *teteo*."

Motecuhzoma smiled. "Even in captivity, you manage to stay aware of military affairs. Very impressive."

"Why aren't we deliberating as a council to discuss this?"

"Feuds are a dangerous thing to ignore. A bone must be set right and given time to heal, so I must keep you and Milintica apart for now."

Tezoc reached out to stroke one of the skulls. The near-petrified bone felt warmer than Motecuhzoma. "What did you plan to do before you learned that the pale people had freed the tribute collectors?"

"I was readying an army to march on the Totonac confederacy to crush every rebellious *altepetl*."

Tezoc did his best to hide his surprise. It had been many years since Motecuhzoma had committed himself to a massive military endeavor. "Since you know the pale people helped the tribute collectors escape, you now wonder if that would be wise?"

"None of our tribute collectors were killed. Word may have spread to other parts of our confederacy, but that word remains rumor for now. After the pale people give us the last tribute collectors, there will be no prisoners to substantiate the Totonac claims. But if I march on Cempoala…"

"You will breathe life into the rumors."

"Exactly. And absent a quick, decisive victory, we could get drawn into another prolonged conflict, like the one we already have with Tlaxcala."

Motecuhzoma took a seat on a nearby bench. Stacked before him were thousands of skulls yet his face betrayed no emotion.

"We can assemble the largest army in all the One World." Tezoc seated himself next to Motecuhzoma. "A quick, decisive victory is possible."

"Military campaigns succeed best when undertaken at opportune times against weak enemies. The rainy season has already started, and the Totonacs are not weak. The distance does not help either. Our supply lines would be stretched thinner than a corn husk. Every day of battle would weaken our hegemony." Motecuhzoma shook his head. "Rebellions are a tricky thing. Tamp one down in a far-off corner of the map, and two more spring up elsewhere."

"So, you are opposed to a military march?"

"If I were, I would not be discussing one with you," Motecuhzoma said.

Tezoc rubbed the nape of his neck. "Are the pale people still encamped in the Totonac lands?"

"They are, but they have offered to release the last three prisoners when it can be done safely."

"Interesting that no rift has formed between the Totonacs and the pale people. Surely, the Totonacs cannot approve of both the capture and the release of the tribute collectors."

"Rifts can be difficult to spot from a distance," Motecuhzoma replied.

"As is sleight of hand," Tezoc countered. "I think the Totonacs and the pale people still have a pact. Yes, it's hard to understand why the Totonacs would continue to ally themselves with the pale people after recent events, but tricks are not meant to be easily understood."

Motecuhzoma turned toward Tezoc. "You are an authority on deception, then?"

"If I were, I could explain exactly why the Totonacs and the pale people are still at peace. But I do not need to understand the method of the illusionist to understand that the illusionist has a method."

Motecuhzoma returned his gaze to the skulls.

"Do you think the pale people were acting in our interests when they released the tribute collectors?" Tezoc asked.

"I am still trying to learn the answer myself," Motecuhzoma said. "My cherished counselors all differ in opinion. The Givers tell me I would offend the gods by mistreating the pale people since they did so much to save the lives of our tribute collectors. They suggest I send a reward to the pale people and leave them be in their coastal settlement. Milintica goes even further and suggests we ally with them. He believes they have already proven to be supportive of our tribute collections and thinks we should combine forces to collect more."

Tezoc reared back. "An alliance!"

"We have formed alliances with powerful foreigners before and gained much for it. The Teotitlans are some of our best allies. Why should these foreigners be any different?"

"These foreigners are making bed with our enemies," Tezoc snarled. Tezoc half-expected a reprimand for his harsh tone, but the statuesque Motecuhzoma did not seem to notice his outburst.

"If the pale people become our allies, we would have much greater ability to influence their partnerships. And if they make bed with us, our enemies will want nothing to do with them."

"Unless they decide to dabble from more than one dish. It is not so impossible. They have already proved themselves unfaithful allies."

"Unfaithful allies to the Totonacs," Motecuhzoma countered. "The pale people have served us quite well. Why are you so adamant now that we march on them? You advised caution not too long ago."

"Our tribute collectors have been attacked—that demands a response. We may not know if the pale people are responsible for the attack, but we do know they made a pact with our enemies. They would not have done so unless they had sinister designs. The friend of my enemy is my enemy."

Motecuhzoma chuckled. "Remember, none of our allies would have offered aid to the pale people. We explicitly instructed them not to. We may have given them no choice but to make shelter with the Totonacs. Besides, the Totonacs are not our enemies. They are our vassals."

Tezoc turned his back on the Great Speaker. It would be dangerous to let his frustration get the best of him and he took short, measured breaths until his pulse slowed. "Milintica's idea of allying with the pale people pleases you, doesn't it?"

Motecuhzoma laid a hand on Tezoc's shoulder. The physical contact was startling. *Pilli* could be put to death just for touching Motecuhzoma. "Leadership is no easy burden. So many important decisions, so much conflicting counsel..." Motecuhzoma squeezed Tezoc's shoulder. "I do find Milintica's proposal appealing. Our confederacy is but a two-legged stool. We need tribute to preserve stability, to protect what we have built. If an alliance with the pale people will secure more resources for our people, I will happily forge a friendship with them. An alliance with the pale people could be the key to expanding our confederacy to new lands."

Tezoc thought about the future posited by an alliance with the *teteo*. It seemed dangerous more than advantageous. "Do you plan to invite them to Tenochtitlan?"

"The Givers believe I should reward them but do not think I should privilege them with an invitation to Tenochtitlan. Milintica urges me to not only invite them into Tenochtitlan, but to also guide them here. And you urge that I kill the pale people. It's as if you all conspired to pick the most irreconcilable positions."

Tezoc forced a small laugh. He turned back to the skull exhibit that fascinated so many. His father had tried, on numerous occasions, to count the amount displayed. The final tally spanned an entire day. He had returned with tears in his eyes, mumbling that there were too many.

"Great Speaker, why are we here? Why did you choose to come to this place?" Tezoc asked.

"For a reminder of the past. This here is all that remains of the conquered. Everything else ends up consumed by rage and fire. The texts perish, the people perish, the bones remain. This conquering business is a vicious cycle. Collections like these used to be made of our own ancestors. But now we are the conquerors, so we possess the bones. We have to do terrible, unspeakable things to remain the conquerors, but if we don't, this is all that will be left of us."

Tezoc looked over the bones with a new appreciation. Still grim but less haunting.

"May I return to my family, Great Speaker?"

"Of course. Treasure them while you still can."

Tezoc's stomach tightened. He could only hope that Motecuhzoma had not meant it as a threat. "If you decide to send another envoy to the pale people, I would advise against sending Tentlil."

"Why?" Motecuhzoma asked.

"He is opposed to going. Last time I spoke with him, he told me that the *teteo* plague his dreams."

"The imprisonment of the tribute collectors left him even more frightened," Motecuhzoma said, a dark look passed over his face. "He claimed it is unsafe for Mexica to go where *teteo* are. He refused to act as an intermediary from here on out."

Motecuhzoma said no more, his expression as cold as his tone. The mirth and warmth that once animated his face was gone, and Tezoc wondered if it would ever return.

"You put Tentlil in a cell, didn't you?" Tezoc asked.

Motecuhzoma huffed. "Dissent cannot be tolerated. I had him executed."

Tezoc sucked in his breath. Motecuhzoma's cool expression did not falter in the slightest. Tezoc took his leave, his heart thumping so hard no Giver could have held it in one hand. He wondered how Motecuhzoma had come to value his bone collection more highly than his attendants and tried not to think about what would happen when he stopped being valuable to Motecuhzoma.

~ ~ ~

Pedro studied each member of Motecuhzoma's delegation while Cortés and the translators went through the customary introductions. He saw some familiar faces in the delegation, but he did not see Tentlil. His absence was a little puzzling since Tentlil had always been a part of each envoy. They had rapport with him, albeit a limited one.

Nevertheless, it was hard to be too concerned about Tentlil's absence. There were more pressing concerns. If the Cempoalteca saw them returning the tribute collectors to the Mexica, Fat Chief would surely insist that the Spaniards vacate Totonac lands. None of the men had any wish to return to the marsh, so Cortés arranged for the handoff to happen far away from prying eyes.

Pedro felt subterfuge was unnecessary when it came to Indians, but most of the officers agreed with Cortés' caution. They were already on thin ice when it came to Fat Chief. After he discovered that the tribute collectors Cortés borrowed for interrogation had disappeared, Fat Chief flew into a rage and demanded explanation.

Fortunately, Cortés was no stranger to self-serving explanations and convinced their Totonac host that the tribute collectors had escaped through no fault of any Spaniard. He explained that the rain had made it easy to dig out of the hut, that cutting the ropes would not have been too difficult so long as they had something sharp nearby. The wily Cortés even convinced Fat Chief that Cempoalteca had to be partially responsible for their escape since Fat Chief had given orders to the attendants to clear the hut of sharp objects.

Fat Chief found it all plausible enough and reasoned that killing the other tribute collectors would be the most logical course of action. Cortés protested that doing so would violate natural law, an argument Pedro found a tad baffling, and insisted they be spared. Being able to interrogate them was very important, more so because of the escape, and Cortés threatened to stop training Totonac warriors if any harm came to them. He also reminded Fat

Chief that the Indians of Potonchan had once tried to defy Spanish might.

After much hemming and hawing, Fat Chief agreed to let the Spaniards keep custody of the other tribute collectors. It helped that Cortés explained it would be near impossible for the tribute collectors to escape if he put them in chains and locked them in a *carrack* brig. It also helped that Cortés did not explain he only put them onboard the ship so he could sail them out of reach of Cempoala before releasing them.

Grinning like a child, Pedro looked over the gifts the Mexica had brought. No jade, no feathers anywhere. Only gold. He fought the urge to laugh. When the scouts first sighted the Mexica delegation, many concluded that Cortés' ploy had failed and assumed the delegation was a war envoy. Pedro had momentarily succumbed to the same fear and had primed his musket in expectation of hostilities.

Now he had to wonder why he ever doubted Cortés. Not only had his machinations prevented war, they had succeeded in making the expedition even richer. He gazed at Cortés, almost awestruck. *Perhaps I am finally serving a man worthy of my talents.*

Cortés asked his translators if Motecuhzoma would now be willing to receive the Spaniards as guests in Tenochtitlan. The translators passed on Cortés' words to the Mexica delegation. Upon hearing the question, Pedro expected them to confer amongst each other to discuss an answer. Instead, the delegation leader responded almost immediately.

"Motecuhzoma still does not feel it wise for you to visit Tenochtitlan now, but he admits the future is open to many possibilities. If you feel that you must travel to our poor *altepetl*, Motecuhzoma beseeches you to travel slowly since he cannot entertain you for many weeks."

Cortés shot a smug glance toward Pedro. If they succeeded in getting to Tenochtitlan, the riches would be even more plentiful.

Cortés thanked the delegation for brightening their day with such joyous news and turned the last tribute collectors over to the delegation, hurling proclamations of gratitude at them even as they departed. As soon as they disappeared from sight, Cortés ordered the men to stow away the gold. News of the good fortune spread like word of Jesus' miracles and it was not long before every man in the company heard. Pedro was so taken with the infectious spirit that he threw his arms around Cortés and yelled, "We're going to be richer than all the nobles of Spain!"

Chapter 26

Cortés surveyed the village of Tizapantzinco from atop a hill as he waited for the cannons to be hauled into position. Once the cannons were ready, it wouldn't take long to raze the place. Assuming there was anything left—a group of Totonacs were already busy raiding it and did not seem inclined to stop.

His horse stirred beneath him. Cortés leaned forward to stroke Arriero, but kept his gaze fixed on the village. A group of Totonac raiders wrestled a child from a screaming villager. Closer still, raiders shoved a bedraggled man back and forth. Cortés frowned and studied the Cempoalteca positioned at the rear of his formation. They had marched with the Spaniards all the way from Fort Veracruz, an hours-long trek that had consumed most of the afternoon. Nonetheless, Cortés was not certain he could consider them his men, despite Fat Chief's promise that they were his to command.

He turned back toward the village, the screams and the cries coming back into focus. The Totonacs raiding Tizapantzinco were certainly not his men. He wondered what had brought them to the village and considered his own motivations for coming to Tizapantzinco.

He had come at the behest of Fat Chief. They had hardly spoken since the incident with the tribute collectors, so Cortés was surprised when Fat Chief approached him earlier in the day to request his aid. Apparently, an evil band of Mexica had attacked a Totonac village near Cempoala, and the village Tizapantzinco had to be punished for providing refuge to the garrison. Cortés had been skeptical when he first heard Fat Chief's account, but he agreed in order to do some investigating of his own. Now he had to wonder why he trusted him at all. No matter where Cortés looked, he saw no Mexica. Only a small village being raided by some wayward Totonacs.

Cortés called for Doña Marina. He liked the way her name rolled off his tongue, he liked even more how fast she came to his side.

"Doña Marina, can you hear those voices, the villagers, on the wind?"

She stilled, closing her eyes and inhaling slowly. "Yes."

"What are they saying?"

Her brow furrowed. "I no understand their words. They not speaking Nahuatl."

Cortés sighed. Doña Marina had the name of a proper Spanish lady, but she could not yet speak like one. He hoped her abilities would soon improve. There was so much he wished to speak with her about... he cleared his mind of those thoughts and focused on the matter at hand. "What language are they speaking?"

She stared at the ground. "I do not know."

Cortés turned around to study the country he had led the company through. It had taken hours to traverse the rolling hills and the meandering brooks, but he had seen nothing to indicate that any town had recently been attacked. Moreover, the simple village sprawled out before him seemed too small to garrison Mexica forces.

Cortés leaned forward to smack a mosquito that had landed on his horse. "Is this village loyal to Motecuhzoma?"

Doña Marina shifted her weight. "I not from here. Local allegiances unknown to me. But I think if the villagers loyal to Motecuhzoma, they would live closer to Tenochtitlan and would speak Nahuatl. I do not hear them speak any Nahuatl. They speak language similar to what Cempoalteca speak."

Cortés blinked. "It wouldn't make sense for a Mexica garrison to launch attacks from here."

"No, it would not," Doña Marina agreed. "If garrison so close to Cempoala and upset with Fat Chief, they would attack Cempoala."

Cortés bit back a smile. Never in his life had a woman seen fit to give him military advice. "Why do you think the Cempoalteca are raiding this village?"

She stiffened and looked at him suspiciously, perhaps confused he would solicit her opinion. "Because they know you coming. They want to grab valuables before you destroy village. They not part of army. Probably come from nearby town."

Cortés nodded. "Why does Fat Chief want us to destroy this village?"

"I think…" Doña Marina trailed off. "I think he want to know if you will fight people because he tell you they are loyal to Motecuhzoma. He want to prove to others you are his friends—and that you are powerful."

Cortés pursed his lips, wondering what offense the villagers may have committed. It didn't matter. Once again, Fat Chief had tried to make a fool of him. No Mexica forces were garrisoned in the village and none ever had been.

Rage bubbled up inside him, and he squeezed his hands into fists. He turned his gaze on the Cempoalteca that had marched with him. His stomach twisted. To think he had allowed them the honor of marching side by side with Spanish men. Not a single cannon had been set up in the proper position, all because the Cempoalteca had still not managed to pull them over the final crest. One of the groups struggling with a cannon was only thirty paces away. Cortés bid Pedro over and whispered commands to him. Surprise flashed across Pedro's face, but he offered no objection to Cortés' orders.

Cortés turned to Doña Marina. "Pay close attention to what I say next."

He spurred his horse into a gallop, heading directly for the nearest cannon. Nearly a dozen Cempoalteca were crowded around it, and they were so focused on pushing it up the hill they did not notice he was charging at them.

By the time they did, he was halfway to them. Panic spread through the group like a bolt of lightning, and men scattered in every direction. Some ran, some shouted, and some dived to the ground.

Cortés hugged himself closer to his horse and pulled back on the bridle. Arriero reared on his hind legs and smashed his front hooves onto a patch of ground previously occupied by a terrified porter. A stunned mass of Spaniards and Cempoalteca stared at him.

"Fat Chief said Mexica forces were garrisoned in this village," Cortés shouted. "Does he think we are fools?"

Cortés waited for Doña Marina to translate, his rage building like wind in a tropical storm. The Cempoalteca muttered amongst each other, but no one stepped forward to speak. Pedro and a group of Spaniards rushed toward the cannon and hurried to turn it around.

"Does he think I am a fool?" Cortés shouted.

The Cempoalteca warriors quieted. No one said a word. Cortés ripped his sword from the sheath and pointed it at the Cempoalteca. "Go back to Cempoala. Go back to Cempoala right now, or we will smite you like we did the Poton army."

His treacherous allies jeered and shouted as they stabbed their weapons into the air. Cortés looked back to Pedro who had finally turned the cannon and now directed it at the mass of angry, confused Cempoalteca.

Their bellicose spirit vanished, snuffed out like a candle in a strong wind. Cortés fought back a smile. He

242

had demonstrated the cannon too many times for the Cempoalteca to be ignorant of its deadly power. The Cempoalteca outnumbered the Spaniard at least two to one, but none of that mattered so long as he had the cannons and the muskets and the steel and they did not.

"Go back to Cempoala!" Cortés shouted.

He motioned to Pedro to hand him the priming stick. He tipped it toward the gun powder and looked back to the Cempoalteca. The Cempoalteca finally realized the sincerity of his threat and made a disorganized retreat. He sneered and threw the priming stick to the ground.

Cortés turned toward his soldiers, good honorable men who had served him faithfully and diligently. "Fat Chief has made trouble for us again! We will clean up his mess this one last time, but we will teach him not to cross us again."

He spurred his horse into a gallop, heading directly for the village center. His men would not arrive until well after him, but he would subdue the Totonac raiders by himself if he had to.

Fat Chief had crossed them one too many times. He needed to be taught a lesson. And he needed to lose something far more valuable than Mexica prisoners.

~ ~ ~

Vitale took off his helmet and heaved a deep sigh of relief. Even without the helmet, the heat could be dizzying. Fortunately, August was already halfway over so the worst of summer soon would be over.

He wiped sweat away from his brow, thankful he had not needed the helmet today. Just a few hours earlier, he had been convinced otherwise since orders had been given for a joint offensive against a nearby village. However, upon reaching the village, orders were given to defend the hapless villagers from Totonac raiders. Never mind the villagers had never done anything to help the Spaniards—the raid had to be stopped. Vitale didn't get much time to question his orders because the Totonac raiders fled for the horizon once they discovered the Spaniards intended to defend the village.

While the Totonac raiders probably disagreed, Vitale felt he had done some good today. Cortés certainly had. In addition to ending the raid, he forbade any future fighting between Totonac peoples. After finding a villager that could speak some Nahuatl, he declared that Tizapantzinco would forever be safe from Cempoalteca aggression and promised that all loot seized during the raid would be returned. The villagers cheered wildly when they heard the news. Many of them flocked to Cortés just to touch him and stroke his horse. They were so grateful that they agreed right then and there to become military allies.

Vitale picked his helmet off the ground to examine it better. It was a fine piece of craftsmanship, but he doubted he would be needing it anytime soon. Thanks to Cortés, the Tizapantzinco villagers loved the Spaniards like the Hebrews loved Moses. He put the helmet down again, leaned against a hut, and soon succumbed to drowsiness.

He woke as a shadow crossed over him and started when a sword pressed against his throat. He peered up but with the sun on the man's back, he could only see the outline of a dark figure.

"If I were Indian, I coulda bashed ye head in before ye coulda said prayers," the man said. The voice sounded familiar, but Vitale couldn't place it. He pressed the sword closer to Vitale's jugular. "Them cuts healin' up nice?"

Vitale realized the man standing over him was the same one who had goaded him into cutting his own face and tried to steal his mother's necklace. Vitale reached for his helmet. If he could get it, he could throw it at him. There was no guarantee it would help, but it seemed better

244

than letting the man with the sword make all the decisions.

Vitale arched his back, and the blade pressed deeper into his skin. He expected that though, planned it even. The more the man focused on Vitale's neck, the less he'd notice Vitale's creeping hand.

He hissed in pain once his probing fingers finally found the helmet, the surface almost scalding from sitting in the sun for so long. He gritted his teeth and grabbed it anyway.

"How much longer you gonna keep that sword there?" Vitale asked as he pulled the helmet toward him.

The man cocked his head to the side and surprised Vitale by sheathing his sword. He even reached out a hand to help him up. Everything about his hand was repulsive. His nails were yellow around the edges, his grimy fingers were slick with sweat, and his palm was covered in peeling calluses. The hand was as confusing as it was repulsive, and Vitale could think of no good reason why the man who had subjected him to so much abuse would now offer help.

Maybe he plans to push me back down? He looked up at the man's face, sure that his features would reflect his cruel nature. He saw no smirk or sneer, but he did see plenty evidence of cruelty in his features. Both his ears were clipped, a punishment that had probably been meted out by someone of higher station. If the man hadn't tried to steal his mother's necklace, he may have felt bad for him.

"No hard feelings, 'eh? Just tryin' to remind you to stay vigil. Gotta be careful out here. These savages cut you up and eat you for no reason."

Vitale raised himself up. The man withdrew his hand, looking confused and angry, even a bit wounded.

"What your name?" Vitale asked.

"Morla." He puffed out his chest. "Apologies never been my strong suit, but I can see you all boiled up. I'm headin' into that Indian house to grab some goods—how 'bout I bring you out some?"

Vitale loosened his grip on the helmet. "Perhaps some other time."

Morla gave a gruff nod and sauntered toward the house, whistling like nothing had happened. If not for the muffled screaming that followed his entrance, it might have seemed like he was walking into his own house.

A mosquito buzzed past Vitale's head, and he swatted at it. The mosquito buzzed even louder. Frustrated and indignant, he stuffed his head into the helmet. The buzzing stopped, and he felt safe again. He castigated himself for letting Morla walk away as if nothing had happened. Morla and his friends had goaded him into cutting his own cheek open, and he let them walk away. Morla had even tried to steal his mother's necklace, and he let him walk away. Now the same man had put a sword to his neck, threatened his life, and Vitale had let him walk away again.

He ripped out his knife, his hand shaking, and marched toward the house. He froze as Morla stepped out with a turkey in each hand. Vitale and Morla stared at each other across the short distance of a narrow walkway. Vitale wondered if the distance was short enough to rush. *Will Morla drop the turkeys and draw?* Probably not, it would take too long. But he had only light armor on so he could easily outrun Vitale. If he was fast.

"What's going on here?" Cortés asked.

Vitale almost dropped his knife in surprise. He tucked it away and turned toward the horse-mounted Cortés, relieved to see that the captain-general had focused his attentions on Morla.

Morla shrugged. "Just grabbin' me some turkey, sir."

246

Cortés straightened in his saddle. "I ordered an end to the Totonac raid less than an hour ago. Do you think I stopped it so you could personally resume the raid?"

"Just wanted some turkey," Morla said.

"Did you trade for it?" Cortés asked.

Morla flashed an impish smile. "The woman who gave me the turkey won't soon forget me. She gonna' remember for a long time." He chuckled. "Gave her something she probably been wanting for a long time now."

Cortés narrowed his eyes. "Men, seize the turkey thief!"

Men who had been ambling about just moments before suddenly turned into vicious dogs and pinned Morla to the ground in seconds. They hauled him back up to his feet.

"What now, Captain?" one of the men asked.

"Hang him," Cortés said.

Morla reacted like a cat dropped in water. He writhed and seethed and escaped for a moment, only to trip over the very same turkey he had tried stealing. The men grabbed him again and called for rope as they hauled him over to the nearest tree. Vitale followed without pause and watched as Morla was dragged toward the tree. The prospect of a hanging drew a crowd, and Vitale felt lucky to be at the front of it.

A man advanced toward the turkey thief with a rope in hand. It had already been fashioned into a noose, and he held it up as if he expected Morla to let him slip the noose on.

Morla tried to pull his head back but a punch to the gut doubled him over. Before Morla could so much as straighten his back, the noose was fastened around his neck.

Morla dropped to a knee, muttering curses. He was a sad sight, and many men seemed reluctant to carry out

247

such a harsh punishment against such a pitiful creature. They looked to Cortés for guidance. His cold face was answer enough. Five men yanked down on the rope and hoisted Morla up into the air.

Morla's eyes bulged out so far it looked like they were going to pop out of his skull. He swung like a fish on a line, kicking and jiggling as he clawed at the tight noose. A disturbing disquietude, punctuated only by haggard choking and straining rope, settled over the crowd as they watched their compatriot dangle and dance before them.

The uneasy calm seemed to last forever, but it was abruptly destroyed by Pedro. He charged toward Morla atop a galloping horse and slashed his sword through the taut rope. Morla crashed to the ground with a thud and drank down air so fast his entire frame shook.

Pedro did not waste time comforting him and made his way toward Cortés. "Sir, can we please speak somewhere privately?" Pedro asked.

Cortés bid his horse forward and motioned for Pedro to follow. Their departure was as unceremonious as it was abrupt. Unsure what do next, the crowd dispersed. Vitale overheard Pedro say something about needing every man.

He probably would have heard more if he had followed them, but it was impossible to tear his focus away from the gasping, crumpled figure on the ground. He studied the sad little thing the way a snake might study a half-dead mouse.

A bead of sweat rolled down his brow, and he closed his eyes. When he opened them, he realized that he was the only one still standing by Morla. He left, feeling awkward. But even more than that, he felt disappointed the hanging had ended so early.

Chapter 27

Malintze marveled at the mercurial temperament of the *teteo*. Just yesterday, Cortés and Pedro had discussed killing Fat Chief for his incessant duplicity, but neither of them seemed upset with him now that he was actually in their presence. Pedro stood nearby with his hand on his sword hilt, but that was nothing unusual; he always did that whenever he conferred with people not of his country.

Whereas Pedro had spent the past hour brooding, Cortés had been lecturing Fat Chief on the need to keep the peace with other Totonacs, cajoling and threatening in equal measure. Perhaps weary of the hectoring, the Speaker of Tizapantzinco and Fat Chief agreed to an informal peace pact. Upon achieving this objective, Cortés insisted they shake hands to prove their sincerity.

Now that the two had clasped hands, the part of the exchange that Malintze had been dreading all day had finally come. She groaned as the two released hands, and Cortés approached her.

"Do it just like we practiced," Cortés whispered.

She took a deep breath. It was comforting to know that if she translated wrong, none of the *teteo*—not Aguilar, not anyone—would know. She cleared her throat and began to speak in Nahuatl.

"The master *teotl* would now like to deliver his Holy… exposition of their Holy… Faith. He wants you to know he serves a great and glorious God. You can also serve this great and glorious God, but first you must give up your unholy practices and your old beliefs. He says you must do away with your foul practices of sodomy, your penchant for robbery, and your wretched practice of human sacrifice. He has been deceived by followers of the gods, but never by those who follow the One True God, so he insists you become… Kristuns."

Some of Fat Chief's attendants responded with nervous laughs, but most kept quiet as word percolated to them through the Totonac translator. In some ways, the muted response was a good sign. She had been afraid they would react with violence and warned Cortés of such. Not that he had taken heed of her warning.

"He says you will receive much if you serve his God," she continued. "If you do so, you will have a friendship with…" Malintze paused to remember the word. She knew that it began with some harsh sound, but the rest of the intonations escaped her. "Jezuz. Yes, you will have a friendship with Jezuz as well as the *teteo*. Refuse to accept Jezuz's friendship, and they can no longer be friends who will help you in the fight against the Mexica. He says you must decide to accept Jezuz now and forget the old gods forever—"

The outcry was immediate. She looked to Cortés for guidance and was surprised to see him brandishing a musket. He fired the weapon into the sky, and the ear-splitting crack hushed the crowd. Pedro, perhaps in an attempt to enforce the silence, aimed his musket at Fat Chief's retinue. The Spanish soldiers nearby, at least fifty in number, all unsheathed their swords in unison. Aguilar went slack jawed as he took in the alarming turn of events.

Fat Chief, seated in his sedan chair, bellowed something unintelligible and gestured frantically to a nearby attendant, who translated for Malintze. "The Speaker apologizes for anything he may have done to upset the *teteo*. He says the *teteo* ask too much. The Cempoalteca cannot forget their gods, but they can forget the *teteo* request so they can be friends just like before.

He wants the *teteo* to know he has a present waiting for them in Cempoala's central plaza."

Malintze contemplated what she should tell Cortés. If fighting broke out between Fat Chief's forces and the *teteo* forces, she would also be in danger. Perhaps more, since she had no shiny *teteo* armor.

"Fat Chief apologizes for deceiving you in the past," she told Aguilar. "He would like to make it up to you. He says a present awaits us in the central plaza of Cempoala."

Aguilar nervously eyed the Speaker as he passed on the words. Cortés responded that he was happy to hear Fat Chief admit wrongdoing and suggested they all head toward the central plaza to see the present.

"The master *teotl* is grateful for your apology and accepts it without reservation," she told the Totonac translator. "He would also like to pass on his apologies to you. He would be honored to walk with you to the central plaza to see this gift he is most eager to accept."

Fat Chief's retinue exchanged hushed words, but the walk to the city center was mostly quiet, their scowls and curses replacing the friendly words of earlier. Pedro, not content to ride alongside Cortés, circled around Fat Chief's retinue, jabbing his musket at them as if he were corralling turkey. The villagers of Tizapantzinco followed behind at a safe distance—but not so far back that she could not make out smirks. She wondered what outrages the Cempoalteca had forced upon the villagers to inspire such hate.

The Spaniards, the Cempoalteca, and the Tizapantzinco villagers soon arrived in the central plaza where a row of eight finely dressed Cempoalteca women awaited them, along with an anxious crowd of Cempoalteca.

Cortés nodded toward the women. "Does Fat Chief intend to sacrifice them?"

Malintze considered it unlikely, but passed the question on anyway. The translator informed her the women were intended as wives. Each woman was daughter to a prominent Cempoalteca family, and the Cempoalteca hoped they would bear many children for the *teteo* officers.

Malintze huffed. She looked at the daughters. They held their heads high, wore fine apparel, and had applied generous makeup to their features. She thought back to the day she had been given to the pale people. She possessed nothing more than a dirty skirt and cooking ware then. The women standing in front of her had probably not touched cooking ware in years. Highborn daughters of marrying age were too good for that.

She kept her eyes on the women as she translated and approached with some trepidation. Malintze searched the group for a woman that looked like her the day she had been given away. One with tears in her eyes or shame on her face. As far as she could tell, most of the women looked to be at peace. She puffed out her chest. It was little matter to her. Cortés had freed her from Puertocarrero, and no new wife could imperil her status now.

Cortés and Pedro studied the highborn daughters with undisguised interest. Whereas Cortés kept his distance and stayed atop his horse, Pedro dismounted and paced in front of the daughters to personally evaluate each. Now and then he paused to brush aside hair and examine breasts. The daughters might as well have been livestock.

Fat Chief spoke to her through a translator, and she passed on the words to Aguilar. "Fat Chief presides over the largest city in all the Totonac confederacy, the very beautiful Cempoala, and he hopes Cortés will take his daughter as a wife. She is the woman on the far left."

All eyes turned toward Fat Chief's daughter. She lacked her father's corpulence, but that did not seem to

252

count for much with the *teteo*. They regarded her as an abomination and spat out insults about the plain-faced, cross-eyed woman. One man pretended to vomit after taking in her appearance.

She looked at Cortés, but he wore the same inscrutable mask that he always donned whenever he conversed with dignitaries. With everyone watching, he dismounted and approached his new wife.

He lifted her hand and laid a small kiss on it. "I shall name her Catalina!"

The men erupted with hearty laughter. Malintze made her way to Aguilar. "Aguilar, why they think this name so funny?"

"Cortés has a wife in Cuba named Catalina."

"Cortés has woman?"

"Yeah. Governor of Cuba arranged the marriage years back. What does it matter to you?"

Malintze studied Cortés with new eyes, wondering if he ever would have told her. She realized with a startling certainty he never would have.

Pedro pointed to a short woman with plaited hair and fulsome breasts. "I want this one."

"Pick another," Cortés growled. "The prettiest one must go to Puertocarrero."

"Me?" Puertocarrero asked.

"Consider it a repayment for agreeing to release Doña Marina from your service. Friends of mine are always rewarded for sacrifice."

Puertocarrero straightened. "Well, I happily accept her." Puertocarrero said something to the other *teteo*, and they laughed heartily. The woman chosen for Puertocarrero offered a demure smile, but there was no hiding the confusion in her eyes.

Pedro jabbed his finger at a different woman. "I want this one then!"

"You have been a faithful friend and ally, Pedro. Of course, you can have this woman."

The *teteo* applauded on his behalf. Some even whistled, much to Pedro's amusement. Cortés called out the names of the other individuals deemed worthy of a new wife. Much to her surprise, the men not deemed worthy of a new wife did not erupt in outrage. For reasons she could not fathom, they seemed to understand and respect Cortés' marital politicking. The men denigrated the Cempoalteca for their polytheistic beliefs, but Cortés was lord to them just as much as the one in the heavens.

Cortés turned toward Malintze with a pleading expression that she almost mistook for a loving one. For a moment, she thought he needed her. Then she remembered he needed her linguistic talents.

He marched toward her and motioned to Pedro, who then began whispering to the other officers. "Doña Marina, please tell Fat Chief we happily accept these presents—but tell him that we cannot marry these women unless they are baptized as Christians."

Malintze groaned and turned back to Fat Chief's retinue. "The *teteo* would be honored to marry these women and would like to perform *teteo* rites with your daughters."

Fat Chief conferred amongst his attendants. He consented and admitted they would perform their own religious rites if they were the ones receiving wives. Malintze felt it best to translate only his agreement.

"Doña Marina, please translate for us once more," Cortés said. "Tell the chiefs they must give up their false beliefs, abandon their abominable practices, and remove all artwork dedicated to idols from their places of worship."

Malintze's breath stopped. Either Cortés did not know that he was inciting violence, or he did not care. Both were dangerous.

"The master *teotl*… kindly asks if you would do him the honor of removing the beautiful artwork you have placed in your temples just for tonight—"

Fat Chief slammed his fist on the armrest of his sedan chair and hurled words at his attendants with a vehemence that made her blood run cold. She tried to get them to calm so she could translate something coherent, but the frenzy of shouting and screaming drowned out her pleas.

Her heart hammering, she turned to Cortés and translated directly into Spanish. Trusting Aguilar with such a sensitive issue, relying on him to faithfully recount the urgency in her voice and the niceties in her speech, was as hopeless as it was foolish. "Cortés, they cannot," she yelled. "The Cempoalteca love their gods too much. They consider gods responsible for everything good— their harvests, their weather, even their lives! They fear world will end if they disrespect the gods the way you want them to."

Cortés nodded like he understood, but his words made it clear he did not. He ordered the Cempoalteca to remove the statues from any places of worship and threatened to desecrate them if they did not. Ashen-faced, she translated the statement to Fat Chief's retinue. They erupted into raucous bellowing before she could finish and an angry Cempoalteca shoved her so hard she fell to the ground.

Before she could even try to stand, Cortés pulled her up and unsheathed his sword. Fat Chief's men recoiled, but the weapon kept them at bay more than it pacified them.

A flash of lightning cut the sky. Malintze looked around, confused and scared. The sky had gone ominously dark, and the pregnant clouds looming overhead looked to be on the verge of release. Thunder rumbled in the distance, but the forces of nature could not drown out the bellowing of Fat Chief. This time it was not the Totonac translators who came to life when Fat Chief yelled, but the crowd of Cempoalteca that had gathered in the central plaza.

An armed mass of Cempoalteca rushed to the summit of a nearby pyramid, drew weapons, and assumed fighting stances. If the *teteo* wanted to march up their pyramid and destroy their statues, they would have to get past the warriors first.

"Men, take up positions across from the Indians," Cortés shouted. "Do not cut them down yet!"

Malintze's knees went watery, and Cortés rushed her toward his horse. Lightning flashed again. He shoved her up into the saddle and then clambered into the seat behind her. Without warning, he spurred the horse into a gallop, heading straight for the *teteo* army. The thunder crashed down on them louder than before, perhaps angry they had ignored all the signs of the brewing storm.

Rain poured down as if a giant dam had ruptured. Despite the deluge, Malintze could see that the *teteo* army was doing exactly as Cortés had commanded. Within seconds, they amassed into formation, swords and shields ready. There were only fifty *teteo* in the central plaza, but they were a formidable force with their armor and their weapons. The Cempoalteca warriors knew it well. If the Cempoalteca fought the *teteo*, few would live to tell the tale. But not a single one moved to let the *teteo* advance up the stairs to their sacred temple.

Cortés brought the horse to a halt once they reached the soldiers. He leaped off the saddle and helped Malintze dismount. He escorted her into the center of the *teteo* army, then vanished without a word.

Lightning flashed again and illuminated the gray sky in vivid detail. For a few fleeting moments, the individual figures of Fat Chief's retinue were superimposed against this awesome spectacle, and fear seized her in its vise-like grip. Fat Chief's men closed in on the rear guard of the

Spanish forces. Her *teteo* companions were surrounded on both sides. *And so am I.*

Fat Chief's men stopped an arm's length from the rear guard, and the Cempoalteca warriors maintained a similar distance from the forward guard. Unless the *teteo* were willing to use their weapons on their own allies, they could no longer go forward or backward. A jealous rumble of thunder briefly commanded attention.

The Cempoalteca chanted something unintelligible. Perhaps a promise of vengeance, perhaps a song about brotherhood; she had no way of knowing either way. The Spaniards wore their confusion openly, glancing toward one another for explanation that could not be provided.

Cortés waded through rank and file to reach Fat Chief's retinue. "I want to talk to Fat Chief!"

Malintze did not need to be prodded to know that she needed to translate. A duo of lightning bolts pierced the sky. The crowd of attendants parted to allow Fat Chief's sedan chair to come to the front.

The servants carrying the sedan chair stopped just five paces away from Cortés. Cortés responded by kicking the nearest servant in the groin. The bearer faltered, unbalancing the litter. Before anybody else could react, Cortés had whipped out his sword, and the servants holding the carriage bolted. The sedan chair crashed to the ground as the thunder roared. Fat Chief spilled to the ground, into the mud, and before he could gather his senses, Cortés had pointed a sword at his heart.

Cortés motioned for him to stand and then seized him by the elbow. He twisted his arm behind his back and pressed the sword against his throat. He bid him forward with sharp words and a forceful shove. Fat Chief understood no Spanish, but he obeyed just as dutifully as any of Cortés' troops would have. They made their way toward the front line of the Cempoalteca warriors.

Cortés yelled, but the lightning and thunder were happening in such quick succession that she could barely hear anything he said. She yelled for Aguilar's help. At first, she was answered only by Nature's wrath, and she worried that he might not be within earshot. But then Aguilar's gentle voice came to the rescue, carrying Cortés' harsh commands.

"Cortés says he will kill the chief and all the Cempoalteca who pay heed to the gods if his troops are not allowed to go up the steps of the pyramid," Aguilar said.

Malintze translated word for word. There was no sense in trying to soften Cortés' rhetoric anymore. She made her way to the front line to make sure her voice would carry. The hateful glares of the Cempoalteca gave her pause, but she could not hide from responsibility so she put her fear aside.

They weren't going to kill her, she assured herself. It wouldn't make any sense. Cortés had already won. Now they just had to swallow their pride. But she knew men well enough to know that did not happen easily. And with the villagers of Tizapantzinco still watching, it would be no small thing to humble themselves before the *teteo*.

The lightning flashed again. Like an animal closing in on prey, the thunder roared. And all the while, thick sheets of rain pummeled friend and foe.

Malintze wondered how much longer the Cempoalteca could keep their bows taut. One accidental slip—wet fingers, tired muscles—and an arrow would fly. She knew the steel armor would protect the *teteo*, but she also knew they would respond by slaughtering all the Cempoalteca warriors; they knew no other way to respond to danger.

The lightning flashed again, and Fat Chief raised his hand. The Cempoalteca recognized the signal: they were being ordered to move aside. They kept their muscles

258

tense even as they lowered their weapons, ready to snap them back up on the smallest signal. Receiving none, they cleared a way for the teteo. Thunder rumbled resignedly in the distance.

The *teteo* flew up the temple stairs as soon as the Cempoalteca stepped aside. Malintze remained behind with Cortés, Aguilar, and Pedro. Together so often, they were a unit of their own, but she did not take pride in the inclusion.

The *teteo* hooted and hollered like children as they raced up the rain-slickened stairs. Once they reached the top of the pyramid, the men gathered into groups to destroy the sculptures and statues.

The lightning and thunder retreated into the distance as the *teteo* rolled, pushed, and heaved the statues to the edge of the stairs. They kicked the stone statues down the long procession of stairs without even pausing for a breath.

The stone statues tumbled end over end. By the time they reached the ground, they were nothing more than ugly stumps. In a matter of seconds, the *teteo* had managed to destroy statues that artisans had labored over for years.

Cortés ordered the religious authorities to deface the statues, to scrub the life water from all the temples, to help build an altar in the temple of the pyramid, to reject all the trappings of their old beliefs. No matter what he said, she translated. That was her duty.

Pedro looked on with a bemused expression. "The Indians will always hate us for this."

Cortés shook his head. "The Cempoalteca will hate us for a time, but the Tizapantzinco villagers will always love us for humbling their former masters. Word will spread throughout the land that we have brought a tyrant to his knees. Oppressed people everywhere will flock to our cause. With tyrants for enemies, we will have friends aplenty."

Pedro laughed heartily, mentioned something about stupid Indians. Everywhere she looked it seemed like all the *teteo* were laughing.

The Cempoalteca must not have considered themselves privy to the joke because they wailed, screamed, and begged the gods for forgiveness. They even pleaded with the gods to make the *teteo* stop. But the gods did not, and the destruction continued.

Intuitively, she knew she should pity them, but her heart was too cold for that. The Cempoalteca were learning what she herself had learned years ago: the concept of a higher power, whether one god or many gods, was nothing more than a comforting lie.

When she was first taken, she had also begged the gods for mercy. She had been answered by indifference and silence so she swore to never again put stock in spiritual matters. From then on, she swore to concern herself only with power that could actually make a difference in her own life. Looking at the destruction her Spanish compatriots had wrought, she knew without a doubt she was no longer a weak girl.

Chapter 28

Aguilar closed his eyes and pinched the bridge of his nose. His head was swimming from the alcohol, and he gave thanks the soldiers weren't around. If they were, they might have forced him to give Malinche language lessons. Not that she needed him anyway. Malinche had her head buried in a book and seemed to be learning well enough on her own.

Aguilar rolled onto his side. Another roll, and he would fall off the makeshift bed. His muscles ached from lying on top of the crates for so long, but he was not ready to stand yet. "Why don't you..." Aguilar trailed off. He ran his hand along a crate, trying to remember when they had been moved into Malinche's tent. A stray splinter embedded itself in his palm and he withdrew his arm. "Why don't you hate us?"

Malinche kept her head buried in her book. Aguilar considered asking the question again, but it was too much effort. The events of the day—first the altercation with Fat Chief, then the sighting of an unfamiliar *caravel* in the harbor of Fort Veracruz—had robbed him of energy. The latter had been especially exhausting. Aguilar had been standing next to Cortés when a scout reported that a *caravel* had been sighted in the bay, anchored alongside Cortés' own fleet.

Seeing the worry that flashed across Cortés' face had forced Aguilar to imagine what a future without the captain might hold. After all, it was an open secret that Governor Velázquez wanted Cortés arrested.

Despite the personal risk, Cortés rode into Fort Veracruz to investigate. Once he discovered more about the ship, he proclaimed it a godsend. As was later explained to Aguilar, the ship was part of Cortés' original fleet and had been separated from the others in the rush to leave Cuba. Cortés hailed the reunion as divine providence and wasted no time unloading valuables off the ship. The ship had brought food stores, sixty more soldiers, new provisions, and twelve more horses. In a matter of minutes, Cortés' cavalry had nearly doubled.

Almost as important as the horses was the information Saucedo brought: Velázquez had been awarded a royal charter to settle the New World. Upon hearing this, Cortés ordered the men to load all the treasure onto a ship intended for Spain. The men balked and objected as loudly as the Cempoalteca when they destroyed the temple, but, much like the Cempoalteca, their protestations fell on deaf ears. So long as Velázquez was armed with royal support and Cortés was not, none of the winnings would be secure. While many of the men would have preferred not to send all the loot, they also preferred to earn the support of court officials before the campaign was concluded.

Some of the men wagered that a larger treasure had never been put to sea. If the ship capsized, if pirates attacked the ship, the gold would be lost forever. Aguilar did not care. Malinche was the main translator now, and he did not expect to receive a large share of the riches.

He looked again at Malinche, still absorbed in her book. She was probably made privy to the important decisions. Because she was important. "What are you reading?"

She flashed him a kind smile. "I am looking at some pictures in the Bible. I hope one day I know how to read it. You *teteo* did not bring many other books."

Aguilar hated her smile. It was enigmatic, like her. He hated it, and he hated her. She should have reciprocated the hatred, but she didn't, which confused him and made him hate her more.

He sat up from the bed and reached for the cassava bread. The stale taste almost made him gag, but he swallowed it down anyway. His stomach roiled, and he drank some water. It was almost as if his stomach had forgotten how to digest anything besides alcohol.

"Are we bad Christians, in your expert opinion?"

He asked the question in Yoko Ochoko. That was still the easiest way to communicate with her—for now.

She closed the book. She looked small sitting on her stool. "Why would you be bad Kristuns?"

"Christians," he corrected.

"Kristuns."

He sighed, and she went back to reading.

"Because of what we did at the temple.

"God would be upset about this?"

Aguilar let the question hang in the air before answering. "Maybe," he said. "God is... kind. We were not."

"The God I learn about is an angry and jealous God. What you *teteo* did at the temple is the same as what Joshua did at Jericho. You *teteo* were gentle toward the idolaters compared to the other *teteo* I read in the stories."

Aguilar nodded and lay back down on the bed, too tired to sit up straight anymore. "That's the Old Testament," Aguilar said. He rolled onto his side so he could see Malinche. Anytime they were in a room together she made sure to sit far away from him. It used to hurt. Now it was just normal. "The soldiers, they focus on the old writings. But the Bible changes as you read more. There's love, kindness. The ending is different than... the beginning."

She flashed him another enigmatic smile. "That's the way it should always be."

Aguilar closed his eyes and rolled onto his back. "Why don't you hate us?"

"Why would I hate you?" she asked in a soft voice.

"We were not kind... at the temple."

"None of that was directed at me. I have no reason to hate *teteo*."

"But the Totonacs are your people," he demurred.

"No, they are not."

"They're Indian."

She laughed. "What is this Indian you speak of? I have not heard it anywhere until I met you *teteo*. I am Painallan, not Indian."

Aguilar shook his head. "No, no... you are Indian. Anyone from the New World is an Indian. Anyone from the West Indies... is an Indian. Anyone not from the Old World is... Indian."

Silence settled over the room. For a moment, Aguilar thought he had finally won her over with reason.

"Are all the people of the Old World kin? I hear much talk of Moors and heathens in your Old World. When Moors and heathens are treated roughly, do you hate the abusers? I hear talk of *altepetl* outside your beloved Spain, places like Florence and Sicily, and I wonder would your Spain feel hurt if these cities ever came under attack?"

"Those people aren't our kin. They aren't even Spanish."

"And the Cempoalteca are not Painallan. They do not have the same customs as my people and they do not speak the same language as my people. They are not me. Only you *teteo* come here and think all the people here are the same."

Aguilar rubbed his temple. "I am very drunk... explain to me again what Painallan means... please." His head lolled as his energy failed him again.

"It means I am from the *altepetl* Painalla."

"What country do you come from?"

"I am Painallan before all else. That is where I am from, that is who I am. Anyone who is not from Painallan is a foreigner to me. Cempoalteca think same way. So do Tenocha."

Aguilar nodded. If he were sober, he would have chided her for being ridiculous and left by now. A proper priest would have reminded her that all idolaters are the same. But the alcohol that had robbed him of his balance had also awakened his curiosity. "Do you miss your people?"

She stiffened. "Do you know why I hate Motecuhzoma? Why I disdain Tenocha?" Her voice, usually soft, had gone cold.

Aguilar snorted. "Didn't know you hated him."

"I am helping you *teteo* for many reasons. I am helping you because Cortés promises me rewards, and he is giving me freedom, but there is another reason more important than all the rest: I hate Motecuhzoma."

Aguilar arched his brow. "What'd that *tl...*" He tried to think of their Nahuatl word for king, but the alcohol had scrubbed his mind clean of torments like knowledge and memory. "What'd that king ever do to you?"

"Motecuhzoma is Great Speaker, so he soars up high. From there, he sees all the *altepetl* of the One World. He must see that his is the biggest and the strongest, but this does not content him so he swoops down and takes from many *altepetl*. He attacks everybody and spreads war throughout the One World."

Aguilar nodded like he understood, but his distrusting nature made it hard to sympathize. "You would have your heart cut out... if Motecuhzoma had attacked your village."

"My heart," she said fondly, like she was recalling a distant memory. "My heart is still here." She patted her chest. "But it's a crushed little thing. Crushed because my

265

own family sold me into slavery!" She threw the Bible to the ground. "Motecuhzoma always wanted more from our *altepetl*, harvests were getting smaller... and traders pay well for little girls. Sometimes they pay enough to make up for crop shortfalls."

Malintze stilled. All her warmth and emotion sloughed away, like water down the side of a hill, leaving behind an expression so devoid of emotion that Aguilar wondered if he was staring at stone.

"I can still remember when the traders took me. Maybe if I had run faster, I could have gotten away, but my legs were so small then. I screamed and screamed for help, and they told me to be quiet, and I screamed more so they took away my power. They took my power for hours, over and over. I swore I would never let anyone ever take my power again. And then the same thing happened the next day."

She talked about it like it had happened to somebody else, and Aguilar suspected there were more tears in his eyes than in hers. He cleared his throat. "Has Cortés... ever taken your power?"

Malintze narrowed her eyes. "Always so curious, Aguilar. I learned many things at Potonchan. You have to when you are used that young. I learned not to cry, I learned to stay quiet, and I learned that a man does not share a woman he cares for. So, I learned how to make a man care. And now Cortés cares about me."

Aguilar cleared his throat again. He had never met a woman so jaded. He wondered what she had been like before.

"I think I'm going to need another drink now." Aguilar pushed himself up and let his feet dangle above the ground. Once the room stopped spinning, he would stand up.

"Why are the men not here to stop you?" she asked, a hint of concern in her voice.

Aguilar massaged his temple. "They are loading gold onto the ships so that Montejo and Puertocarrero can take it to the king. Earn his favor, just like Cortés wants." Aguilar giggled like a little boy. "If that gold gets to Spain, Spaniards will come pouring into the New World like Noah's flood."

Malinche approached with some trepidation. "And if more Spaniards come, it will be easier to crush Motecuhzoma?"

Aguilar dabbed at the drool trickling down his chin and gazed at the beautiful woman standing before him. "Give Cortés enough men, and … Motecuhzoma will never fly again."

Malinche nodded and made her way to the door.

"Where are you going?"

"To help Cortés load the ship."

Without a word more, she stepped outside to help destroy the man who had helped destroy her.

Chapter 29

Vitale fought the urge to wipe away the bead of sweat trickling down his cheek. He eyed the setting sun. Half shrouded from view, but still relief was hard to come by. The heat never went away here. It was always lurking nearby, slowly regaining strength to exact revenge on the forgetful.

Another reminder why he needed to leave. And tonight, for the first time, he had a way of leaving. Cortés had overestimated the strength of his men. Watching the ship sail for home with the gold, making preparations for an inland march—it was too much. If everything went according to plan tonight, Vitale and a handful of other men would steal a ship tonight and sail to Cuba.

Vitale took a deep breath. Had it not been for an accident a few days earlier, he never would have learned of the plot. Off in search of fish for Solomon, Vitale had happened upon a small group huddled together in discussion. From afar, he had recognized León, nephew to Governor Velázquez and former Cortés dissident, which had piqued his curiosity. He snuck closer and by the time they caught him, he knew far too much to let him go, so they grudgingly welcomed him into the fold. It helped that he shared some of their misgivings about life in the New World. It also helped that they couldn't kill him without arousing suspicion.

They told him of their plans to gather supplies for the journey, to steal a vessel from the bay, to intercept the treasure ship, and return to Cuba. Vitale hoped they wouldn't have to kill anybody when they seized the ship, but he saw little difference between cutting down a Spaniard and an Indian.

The bloodshed didn't bother him so much as the danger did. The treasure ship had departed at the end of July, almost two months past the ideal sailing window, and they would be embarking even later. And if they were caught trying to escape, mercy would be out of the question.

Despite everything, Vitale was more concerned with leaving Solomon behind than the danger involved with leaving. Vitale had searched for him nearly the entire day only to discover that Solomon, along with a group of other slaves, had been picked to help secure lumber and would not return to the fort before dark.

Vitale had stuffed his knapsack with the important provisions—a rusty compass, some fletches of bacon, his mother's necklace—but he felt strangely unprepared. Leaving without Solomon seemed an awful mistake. Vitale thought of nothing else all day, besides the punishment he would surely suffer if caught trying to escape.

He unsheathed his knife and threw it at the ground. The blade burrowed into the sand effortlessly, and the handle jutted out at such a perfect angle that it looked like a sundial. He almost felt proud. Having taken a seat on a large block of driftwood, all he had to do was lean forward to pluck the knife out of the ground. He weighed the knife in the palm of his hand and threw it down again to see if he could get it to land the same way. Somehow, he did.

"Did the sand offend you?" Cortés asked.

Vitale jumped to his feet as he realized he was no longer alone. Off to his right, just half a pike's length away, stood his captain-general. *Was he spying on me?* He bit his lip and tried to calm his nerves.

Vitale, suppressing the urge to run, sat back down on the driftwood. "Sand makes for good target practice. It don't strike back."

Cortés huffed and took a seat next to him. Vitale shuddered. He had never sat so close to Cortés before. Snakes were intriguing at a distance, but they could be downright terrifying up close. "It's getting dark out. Should we head back to Fort Veracruz?" Vitale asked.

"Oh, I think we'll be fine. Every now and then, we have to take time to admire our spoils, no?" Cortés flashed him a winning smile and gestured to the beach, the trees, and the ocean with a grand wave of his hand.

"Can men really claim ocean?" Vitale asked.

"Seems a lot more practical than claiming land. No inhabitants to bother about." Cortés turned his gaze toward him. "Son, what brings you here?"

"Beach is peaceful. I like it."

Again Cortés grinned, but it seemed more forced this time. "No, I mean what brings you here to the New World?"

Vitale thought carefully about his answer, but it was hard to concentrate with Cortés boring his eyes into him. He turned toward the waves. "Came here for gold."

"Must've been sad to see the gold go, then."

Vitale stiffened. The conversation, which hadn't felt all that friendly to begin with, was beginning to feel an awful lot like an interrogation. "I'm sure if I stick with you long enough, there's gonna be more."

Cortés huffed. "Good answer." He laid a hand on Vitale's shoulder. Vitale recoiled and hoped the flush creeping up his neck was hidden from view. "So edgy! And so fixated on staring into the distance. Is there something out there I can't see? Wait, you see Mexica warriors in the distance, don't you?"

Cortés bobbed his head back and forth like a hungry snake as he scanned the horizon. Vitale could not tell if he was being teased or ridiculed.

Cortés frowned. "I can't see them." He shaded his eyes. "Perhaps you have better vision than me."

Vitale kept silent, squeezing his hands together to prevent them from shaking.

"With those sharp eyes of yours, do you see something on my face?" Cortés asked playfully. "Do tell me if you do."

Vitale turned to look at Cortés. His heart was hammering so hard he was sure Cortés could hear it. "No. Why?"

He held his captain-general's stare and pretended he had nothing to hide.

"It feels as if you don't want to look me in the eye," Cortés said. "Is there something about my appearance you find displeasing?"

Vitale moved back a fraction. "Sorry, sir. Sometimes I lose sight of the important things." Vitale looked down at the ground, his ears burning. "And then I just get to staring off. My ma hated it. Clapped me over the ears for it all the time. Said I was the most absent-minded son that ever lived."

Vitale smiled like he was thinking of a happy memory and returned his gaze to Cortés. The predatory glean in Cortés' eyes faded.

"You seem square in the head to me. What's your mother's name?"

Vitale opened his mouth, but stopped himself before answering. He thought of all the different times that Cortés had convened mass, all the times he spoke about the greatness of Christ, the way he spoke about those that did not accept Jesus into their heart. Speaking his mother's true name aloud did not seem wise. A halfwit would know the name was Jewish and Cortés was no

271

halfwit. He racked his brain for an answer and said the first name that popped into his head.

"Catalina."

"A good Christian name. But it almost looked as if you were going to say something else for a moment."

"The absent mindedness again."

Cortés narrowed his eyes. "Son, I feel like you're hiding something from me."

"I haven't done nothing wrong, sir."

Cortés nodded. His roving eyes pored over Vitale's face, traveled down his person, and surveyed the ground next to Vitale. For a moment, they snagged on the knife, but then they found something of genuine interest: Vitale's knapsack.

Cortés reached for the knapsack. Vitale considered snatching it away, but the battle was already lost. All he could do was hope that Cortés did not find the knapsack too suspicious.

His commander opened the knapsack and searched inside. Vitale tried to think of an excuse for the contents of the bag. Stuffed inside were victuals, his water canteen, a dirty compass he had managed to snatch, and the necklace from his mother. It was the only piece of physical evidence he had to prove she'd existed and was more important than anything else in the bag. More important than any possession he had ever owned.

Cortés finished with his search and let the bag sit idle on his lap so he could stare Vitale in the eyes. "Looks like you have quite the journey ahead of you, son. Care to explain?"

Vitale gulped, his heart in his throat. "It's for an Indian woman, sir."

"Explain what you mean."

"I meet with an Indian woman sometimes. I give her trinkets like them ones in the knapsack so I can take liberties with her. I come all the way out here so we can meet in private. I don't want the other men knowing—"

"That you're with an Indian woman?"

Vitale cast his gaze down.

"There's nothing wrong with loving an Indian woman, son. They make as fine a wife as any Spanish lady."

"Not sure all the men agree with you on that one, sir."

"I know. I've heard the jeers. Some of our countrymen act as if the Indians belong to a different species! Unbelievable how many of them were opposed to an alliance with the Totonacs. The Indians really aren't that different from us, and there's no reason to treat them different than any other people. Be good to them if you can, and be rough with them if you have to. Not sure all our countrymen would agree, though. But always a few bad apples, right?"

Cortés nudged him in the ribs. Vitale managed a weak laugh and said, "We've roughed them plenty. If you think so good of the Indians, why we preparing to march on those ones behind the mountains?"

"Because that's what gets us the gold." He answered like it was the simplest thing in the world.

"Sir?"

"Yes?"

"Do we really got to do all this? The marching and the searching and all?"

Cortés chuckled. "Have you ever been to Medellin?"

"I haven't."

"No great loss. Rural little town in Extremadura. None too big, smaller than Cempoala, actually. I was born there, and even I don't love the place. For a place with so much open space, it's hard for a man to breath out there. I thought things would be different once I left, but the weight on my chest never really went away no matter where I went in Spain. My father was a poor *hidalgo*, one that fought on the wrong side in some battles, so my opportunities in life were always a bit limited." Cortés took a deep breath. "My family secured me work as a notary to correct this, but a passing knowledge of law can do only so much. I had two choices if I stayed: be the tail of a lion or the head of a mouse. I have never had much interest in either. I wanted something more. So, I sailed west, went to the West Indies. But that weight was still there. Less burdensome, but still there. Do you know the burden I'm talking about?"

"I'm no stranger to crushing burdens," Vitale said. It was the most honest thing he had said in their entire conversation.

"Well, I trust you understand what I mean then. Some men would simply be content to suffer that burden, but I was never that type. I've always wanted more, something I could give my children. I wanted to do better than those that came before me. So, when Velázquez offered the chance to explore the New World, I jumped at it. You see, a man has room to breathe out here, reinvent himself, even climb the ladder a bit. I think you know the reason as well as I."

Vitale nodded. "Because there's gold out here."

"Exactly!" Cortés thrust his fist into the sky as if he were aiming for the heavens themselves. "That curious rock that weighs so heavy in the hand, but makes you light as a feather when you climb the ladder, is right beyond those mountains. It's ours for the taking so long as we can muster the strength for a simple march."

"I hear that the king beyond the mountains already took it." Vitale meant it as a joke, but Cortés did not seem to take it as such.

"We earn our bread by taking it. Riches belong only to the strong. That king beyond the mountains used his strength to seize gold from others, and now we will use our strength to take it from him. But a gold seeker like you already knows that, right?"

"Of course," Vitale stammered.

Cortés did not look convinced. "Son, I pray you know we all do things we're not proud of. All of us have made mistakes we deeply regret." Cortés laughed drily and shook his head. "Well it's just like you said, we lose sight of the important things. Now as captain-general, it's my duty to protect my men. Not just from Indians, but from themselves. I couldn't be a good commander, if I let my men do things I knew they would regret later."

"You a great commander, sir."

"I try my best." Cortés sighed. "I pray you understand I'll have to take your knapsack now."

Vitale's heart skipped a beat. "Why is that?"

"Prevent you from doing anything you might regret later. Don't worry, I'm not going to keep the knapsack."

Vitale stood up. "Then what you gonna do with it?"

"I'm going to hold on to it for a little while. That way you have time to get your head on straight, think about what you really want. Should you decide you need the bag, feel free to come collect it from me later—so long as you are willing to confess your true intentions. I won't be angry, I won't be vengeful, I'll be merciful. Just like a father."

Cortés stood up, smiled one last time, and made his way back to Fort Veracruz with the knapsack. Vitale's heart sank lower and lower with Cortés every footstep. He knew he should retrieve the necklace, even if it meant trapping himself in the New World, but a part of him wondered if family was worth that kind of sacrifice.

Chapter 30

Pedro ran a hand through his hair. "Do you need any more mutineers arrested?"

"I think not," Cortés said, bent over his makeshift desk as he composed a letter. "Every mutineer of consequence has already been captured. A good thing we caught on to their plan when we did. A little later, and they may have succeeded in stealing a ship."

Pedro nodded. Before Cortés had brought him a list of the mutineers to arrest just a few hours prior, he had not even heard of the treacherous plot.

"Escudero was the ringleader, then?"

"Indeed." Cortés took a moment to check his penmanship and sprinkled some gum sandarac on the parchment to help dry the ink.

"If Montejo were still here, we probably would've needed to clap irons on him also. Good thing you sent him with the gold. I'm surprised León was not the ringleader, though."

"From what I understand, he preferred a peripheral role."

"How do you know they're guilty?"

Cortés shot him a self-assured look. "Back to doubting me again?"

"Course not, Captain." Pedro took a seat on the nearest stool. He studied the interior of Cortés' tent. It was a cramped space, with maps strewn along all the walls and crates stacked high as a man, and pitched so low Pedro had to stoop when entering. Despite all this, Cortés had somehow transformed the meager tent into a base of operations that was both feared and respected.

Cortés huffed and returned to his writing. "Give them more time in the brig. They'll all start confessing soon enough—they just need to get past their anger. Pride can be harder to swallow than a bitter draught."

"I can torture them if they take too long."

Cortés' writing stylus stopped. "Always so thoughtful, Pedro. They will confess without." Cortés resumed his scrawling.

Pedro grunted and rubbed his ear lobe. "What are you writing?"

"A letter to our dear king on our journeys, our battles, and our achievements. We must please the king for him to confer blessings on our colony."

"Doesn't seem wise to tell the king everything. I'm not sure he would approve of all that we have done."

Cortés dipped the stylus in ink. "Worry not. Trust me, I am writing solely to please. When the king reads everything I have written, he will want to knight us himself. The unpleasant details have been reworked."

"Might not be a good idea to lie to a king."

"You think that is what I am doing?"

"I was never one for politics. Dishonesty and deception always seemed like the same thing to me."

"To think that I am lying is a very simple way of looking at things. Pedro, if only you could understand!" Cortés turned around to face him. "I am making names easier to pronounce, I am making battles fiercer, I am making our enemies seem Moorish—"

"Why would you want to make anything seem Moorish?" Pedro asked. Cortés stared at him coldly. "Sorry I cut you off, Captain."

"Do not do it again," Cortés said. "I am making the Indians seem Moorish because there is no comparison court officials would find less favorable. When I am done with these letters, when we have brought Mexico under our yoke, we will be as great as the heroes of the *Reconquista*."

"A place among the rich matters far more to me than a place in history," Pedro said.

"Why pick just one?"

Pedro chuckled. He cracked his knuckles and rolled his wrists as he waited for Cortés to finish writing. A suffocating silence descended upon the tent, punctuated only by the scratching of the stylus across parchment. By the time Cortés turned around to face him, Pedro was sure that half an hour must have passed.

"Done already?" Pedro asked.

"I will continue it later. A letter to the king is not written in one day."

Pedro shrugged and scratched at a stain on his shirt.

"I get the distinct feeling you did not come here to discuss letters," Cortés added.

"You know me too well. I came to discuss the arrests."

"Go on."

"I don't doubt their guilt," Pedro said. "I've learned to trust you in these matters. I know you have more of a mind for these things. But sometimes you get carried away and you come up with punishments that are overly…"

"Severe?"

Pedro stabbed his finger into the air as if he had been struck by divine revelation. "Aye, that's the word for it."

"You counsel mercy then?"

"Aye. I know you probably want to hang 'em all. But we're short on men, and we can't go around killing every single one for being stupid. Won't have much of an army if we do that. And if you're merciful, it will help you keep your good standing with the men. I mean, we arrested a priest—we have to be merciful with him. The men won't like it if he's taken to the gallows."

"Would not want to cast a pall over our mission." Cortés tugged at his beard, burying his fingers in the curls of his hair. "I pray you know I take no pleasure in killing. Sometimes I think it would be better not to know how to write. Then one would not have to sign death sentences."

Pedro let Cortés ruminate in silence. He hoped it meant Cortés was giving his suggestion serious thought.

"Good for morale, you say?" Cortés asked.

"Very good."

The corner of Cortés' lip curled upwards. "First you want to save Morla, now the deserters—you are becoming quite soft-hearted toward your countrymen."

Pedro barked with laughter. "Oh please, Cortés. Save the deception for Don Carlos. If we had more men to spare, I'd suggest burning each plotter at the stake. But our fighting force is small right now. Even if we win some allies among the Indians, we can't trust them the same way. Godless Indians just don't have the same..."

"Priorities," Cortés finished.

"Exactly. We only got half a thousand countrymen fighting with us, not including the sailors. We oughta keep as many alive as possible."

"Very important, I admit. But I'd rather my men come down with fever than desert. They won't rush to join the dead, but they will rush to join the deserters if they think they can get away with it. Our whole march will fail. Better for a few Velázquez loyalists to die than let the whole army think I tolerate desertion."

Pedro wondered whether he might get a larger share of the treasure if some of the other officers met tragic fates, but he dismissed the thought. "I agree some of the men need to die. Just not all of them."

"I'm not sentencing them all to hanging. One of the sailors will only be receiving a few lashes."

"How many lashings exactly?"

"Two hundred."

"All at once?"

"Sends a better message that way," Cortés said.

"A man can't survive that much."

"Is that so?"

"Did it to one of my own slaves in Cuba. Barely made it past one hundred fifty." Pedro checked his fingernails as he spoke and started picking at the dark grime trapped under his nails.

"Fine." Cortés waved dismissively. "One hundred fifty lashes spread out over some weeks. I suppose I shouldn't cut off Umbria's feet either—he might not survive the blood loss. He is a valuable pilot. I'll just have to settle for the toes."

"Very wise. I'll carry out the order for Umbria right now if you'd like."

"Leave the maiming to somebody else for once," Cortés said. "Not all of the deserters will be as lucky as Umbria. Bodies will swing from the gallows. We must send a stern message to avoid these things in the future."

Pedro frowned, remembering how outraged Cortés had been when he learned about Pedro's unauthorized attack on the Cozumel Indians. *Did he consider hanging me to send a stern message?* He cleared his throat. "I agree. But one body can still send quite the message."

"If only one hangs, it will be Escudero. He was the chief instigator and completely unrepentant when I spoke with him."

"What did he say?"

"Oh, he reminded me how once—many years ago—he had me in chains and could have taken me to the hangman. He said I should think about that if I sent him to the gallows."

Cortés spoke about his brush with the gallows as if it were no more troubling than a bad dream.

"What'd you say back to him?" asked Pedro.

Cortés tucked his tongue in his cheek. "I reminded him that we are different men, and that I finish what I start."

Pedro scratched his scalp. "What'd you do to almost get taken to the gallows? I can't remember anymore."

"I was arrested on trumped up charges of pissing off Governor Velázquez," Cortés said. "Listen, Pedro. I'm agreeing to your suggestion because I'm a reasonable man. You gave me good counsel on Morla, so I'll listen to you again. Tell the officers you changed my mind, and that they should also come to me with counsel. And let them know I expect them to be more vigilant. An officer should have brought word of this escape plan to me. None did."

"I'll go speak with the officers now." Pedro stood up and gave a quick salute. He brushed aside the tent flap, but he stopped before he stepped out. "Cortés, how did you find out about the plan to desert?"

"Young soldier named Vitale. Caught him with a knapsack full of rations earlier today. I confiscated it and told him I would return the knapsack once he confessed his true intentions. I assumed that he had made plans to run off into the jungle. Much to my surprise, he barges in here and confesses to mutiny and desertion."

Pedro furrowed his brow. Vitale? He could not put a face to the name. "Did you have him arrested as well?"

"He's sitting in his tent right now with his precious knapsack, free as a bird. I'm not a tyrant."

Pedro almost responded that he was glad to hear it. Instead, he gave Cortés a curt nod and stepped out. He made a note to himself to meet this Vitale at some point. The way Cortés told it, the young soldier had saved the entire mission without even knowing it.

~ ~ ~

Fort Veracruz hadn't been the same since Cortés hanged Escudero. Solomon was just a slave so he was largely ignorant to the political machinations of Fort Veracruz, but even he noticed the change. The men glanced over their shoulders more and hushed whenever the officers came around.

Walking toward the beach with everyone else, Solomon wondered if camp would soon change again. Half an hour earlier, Cortés had given orders for every man—sailors, soldiers, and slaves—to assemble on the beach for an important announcement. It was obvious he needed labor, considerable labor since he saw fit to gather everybody, but the why was less obvious. Looking around Veracruz, Solomon saw little they could work on.

Already the fort had a marketplace, a granary, a gallows, and all those other constructs so essential to social upkeep. But perhaps most important, the extensive defenses had been completed. Surrounded by siege walls and defense towers, the fortress would not be easily taken by a hostile army and unless Cortés was commissioning a moat, there didn't seem to be a good reason for him to assemble so much labor.

Solomon looked around for Vitale. He had not seen him much after the botched escape. He knew he was alive, which was a great relief, but knew little otherwise.

"Men! I have disheartening news." The crowd grew silent as Cortés' bellowing voice rang out. "I had the ship hulls surveyed, and it's become clear that our ships have been compromised. Some have been weakened by storms, some by surf. Others have fallen victim to a more nefarious enemy: worms. I fear they may no longer be seaworthy."

The crowd gasped in surprise.

"I am just as heartbroken as all of you," Cortés continued. "But we must act fast before it's too late. There is a great deal of important, usable material onboard the ship. We need to strip the ships of everything lest they sink and we lose it all. We need to salvage the sails, the cordage, the navigational equipment, the nails—everything."

Solomon looked to the ships floating in the placid harbor. Cortés was right not to consider them seaworthy. Interestingly, none of the great beasts that had conquered so many oceans looked compromised yesterday. Now they looked to be in their final death throes, and many were listing to the side. Solomon knew enough from his seafaring days to know that kind of damage did not just materialize overnight unless it was brought about by human hand.

"Speak with your officers. They will provide specific instructions as to salvaging."

The officers gave their commands to the subordinates, slave and free, and every able-bodied soul was soon preoccupied with disabling the only means of escape. Solomon made his way to the nearest ship, his feet heavy as slag.

He pored over the features of everyone he passed with the same urgency and despair of a condemned man. Never again would desertion be viable for anyone in the company. Even the most disgruntled soldier preferred the company of uncouth countrymen to the untamed jungle. His chest tightened. Cortés wasn't just putting his own life on the line now. Every person involved with the expedition—the mending women, the slaves, the soldiers, the pilots, the porters—would die if he failed.

A quick glance was all it took to know that many others shared his somber assessment of the future. Few commands were given, and the work was carried out in silence. A few of the free men sat down and began to cry. Were he less inured to misfortune, Solomon may have also given in to misery.

He looked back at the land they were now stranded in. There was no denying its beauty. He was a well-traveled man, and even he found the sights breathtaking. Yet for all the beauty of the land, Solomon did not want to die here. His eyes misted as he realized he might never see Mecca again.

The salvaged materials were gathered on the beach for all to see. The mighty ships had exhausted their purpose and would have nothing left in remembrance except a pitiable pile of the redeemable materials.

Seeing the salvage work done, Cortés gave his next order: scuttling the ships. As far as Solomon could tell, the order did not elicit much surprise. Cortés was not one to leave a job half-done. None of the ships were seaworthy and now that they had been stripped, they could not even be steered. But trusting his men to not set sail with gutted ships was leaving too much to chance for Cortés, so it was none surprising he wanted the ships scuttled. He was willing to gamble his own life on the success of the mission, but he would be damned before he left anything in the mission up to chance. Laughter seemed just as appropriate as sorrow.

As a group, soldiers and slaves set about putting the nails in their own coffins; the ships that still clung to life were run aground and the ones too weary for that final surge of energy were unceremoniously sunk. One by one, ships succumbed to the watery clutches of the bay. Solomon kept an eye out for Vitale. He hoped the boy could now see Cortés' dangerous nature.

Cortés shouted, "No commander could ask for a finer fighting force! History will tremble before our might— the soldiers that crossed the Rubicon with Caesar aren't half as brave as those assembled upon this beach."

Solomon did not think brave the apt word. The men that crossed risked their reputation, even their lives, but they had still allowed themselves a means of escape. *Cortes would deny his men even that, all for glory and riches.*

Solomon studied the man who imprisoned and executed his opponents on personal discretion alone, the man who cut down his enemies on the battlefield with brutal efficiency. This was now the man responsible for saving all their lives and winning the mission. No longer could the mission be considered a simple search for gold. It was now a military campaign. They would either win the land or die in the attempt.

The long-awaited march to Tenochtitlan had finally begun.

Note to readers

Deciding to publish through Black Acorn Literary Press was not a decision I made lightly. Mainstream publishing offers a host of benefits that are hard to find elsewhere. Being able to count on the assistance of industry veterans in manuscript editing, promotion, and distribution goes a long way when it comes to finding an audience. Despite all the benefits of going the traditional route, BALP offered me something I found hard to find elsewhere: complete creative freedom. To be fair, the Big Five can be very good about offering this to established authors, but to do so for an unknown commodity is simply not the norm in the industry. Complete creative freedom can have drawbacks of course, but I personally found it to be very appealing because it meant I was never pressured to use terms like Aztec in place of Mexica, I was never pressured to add any pointless love triangles, and I was never pressured to remove the foreign words from my novel.

In addition to this, I was allowed to take a great many narrative risks and give priority to the academic understanding of the Spanish-Mexica war, as opposed to the popular understanding of this event which is so often, and problematically, referred to as the Conquest of Mexico. Prophecies involving returning gods have an understandable appeal, but I opted not to include a storyline like this because I generally believe the plot for a historical novel ought to mainly include references to events that could have happened, or better yet, events that we know happened. Omitting this storyline does come with some risk, the most popular novels on the Spanish-Mexica war tend to include very prominent references to the Quetzalcoatl myth, but I worried that including it would diminish my work. Ultimately, readers will decide the value of *The Serpent and the Eagle,* and I humbly ask that any who enjoyed my work leave a written review online on Amazon or Goodreads. Even if you did not enjoy it, please leave a review anyway. Not every author can count on agents and publicists to promote their work, so every review matters when it comes to finding the right audience.

Historical note

One of the most difficult aspects of studying history is that one event lends itself to multiple interpretations. Thomas' *Conquest* tells a very different version of the Spanish-Mexica war than Levy's *Conquistador* and Townsend's *Malintzin's Choices* tells a very different version also, not to mention the countless other books written on the subject. *The Serpent and the Eagle* is in many respects an amalgam of many different historical accounts, but it does give priority to the secondary sources that have been published recently.

In terms of researching *The Serpent and the Eagle*, the secondary sources I found most helpful were Townsend's *Malintzin's Choices*, Restall's *Seven Myths of the Spanish Conquest*, Aguilar-Moreno's *Handbook to Life in the Aztec World*, Levy's *Conquistador*, Thomas' *Conquest*, Rojas' *Tenochtitlan*, the 2007 University of Oklahoma Press' *Indian Conquistadors*, Greenblatt's *New World Encounters*, Kamen's *Empire*, Schwaller and Nader's *The First Letter from New Spain,* and Hassig's *Mexico and the Spanish Conquest*.

In terms of primary sources, I found the 2010 Stanford English translation of Chimalpahin's *Conquest*, Díaz's *True History of the Conquest of New Spain*, Padgen's annotated *Letters from Mexico*, Vaca's *La Relacion*, Siepel's *Conquistador Voices*, Casas' *In Defense of the Indians*, León-Portilla's *The Broken Spears*, *Codex Azcatitlan*, *Codex Borgia*, *Codex Mendoza*, and *Florentine Codex* to be the most useful.

In terms of articles, blurbs, and videos, I found Kimball's "Aztec Homosexuality: The Textual Evidence," The Economist's "On the Trail of Hernan Cortés," Daniel's "Tactical Factors in the Spanish Conquest of the Aztecs," Brooks' "Marriage, Legitimacy, and Intersectional Identities in Sixteenth-Century

Edward Rickford

Spanish Empire," Townsend's "Burying the White Gods: New Perspectives on the Conquest of Mexico," Cummings' "Moctezuma: Aztec Ruler," Totopec's "The Bow and Arrow," NPS's "Cabrillo," Graulich's "Aztec Human Sacrifice as Expiation," Dodds' "Cortés and Montezuma: The Conquering of Tenochtitlan," Zhang's "The Genetic Legacy of the Spanish Inquisition," Minster's "Hernan Cortés' Conquistador Army," Ashton's "How Hernán Cortés' Sexual Appetite Affected the Course of History," Tuck's "Jeronimo de Aguilar: the Marooned Priest Who Speeded the Conquest," Argote's "Location Through Ert Geophysical Method Of The North-western Corner Of The Wall Surrounding The Pre-hispanic City Of Mexico-Tenochtitlan," Sîmbeteanu's "Warrior Jaguar - Elite of the Aztec Empire Army," Minster's "Timeline of Hernan Cortés' Conquest of the Aztecs," NativLang's "How Interpreters Helped Conquer the Aztec Empire," Invicta's "Tenochtitlan - The Venice of Mesoamerica," the History Channel's "History Specials: Coroner's Report - Aztec Sacrifice," Science Magazine's "Feeding the gods: Hundreds of skulls reveal massive scale of human sacrifice in Aztec capital," and National Geographic's "The Aztecs Empire Documentary" to be the most helpful.

For those interested in traveling to Mexico to visit these sites in person, I would recommend using private bus companies to travel between cities as there are many good, cheap options. Long distance trains may be an option worth considering, but I have not taken any within Mexico, so I cannot personally recommend any. The Templo Mayor Museum and the National Museum of Anthropology were my favorite sites in Mexico, but those more interested in nature would probably prefer Quiahuiztlan and Cempoala. Playa Villa Rica is beautiful, and very close to the ruins of Villa Rica de la Veracruz, but it is a little hard to reach. Anyone who takes a tour of Lake Xochimilco ought to avoid the lettuce.

In the interests of making sure readers don't come away with bad information, I feel compelled to mention which parts of *The Serpent and The Eagle* conflict most significantly with respected historical accounts. The scene where Cortés discusses the strategy for attacking Potonchan ends with him ordering Pedro de Alvarado to lead the flanking contingent. Most sources, however, indicate he sent Alonso de Ávila, but I gave Pedro this task for narrative reasons. In the showdown between Montejo, León, and Cortés, I wrote the scene in a way that suggests Montejo was illiterate, but this was probably not the case.

It is also worth noting that the backstory for Malintze in *The Serpent and the Eagle* conflicts with testimony provided by the conquistadors. A number of scholars have noticed, however, that the account provided by the Spaniards bears some suspicious similarity to the Biblical story of Joseph. Keeping in mind the highly stratified nature of Renaissance Spain, it isn't especially hard to believe that the Spaniards wanted to think they were being helped by a woman of noble birth as opposed to a common woman. Considering all this, I felt it appropriate to give her a backstory that helps explain some of her later actions in the Spanish-Mexica war.

While little is known about the exact battle tactics the conquistadors used when they attacked Potonchan, it is unlikely they would have used a maneuver like the Testudo square. The Testudo square is a tactic that requires a great deal of intense training and coordination which, to be frank, was more typical of the ancient Roman armies than 16th-century conquistadors. However, owing to the interesting parallels between these fighting forces, I felt it would be appropriate to use the term Testudo to encourage a juxtaposition. In addition to this,

I should also mention the Spanish would not have called themselves Spanish at this time because the country was not a united kingdom yet. Instead, there were three main kingdoms that were loosely bound but relatively autonomous.

The term *pilli* is used all throughout the book so it seems important to mention that *pilli* would have been used in a plural sense and that *pipitlin* would have been used to refer to a single person from the *pilli* class. I decided to use terms like *pilli* and Spain, even when it was not technically appropriate, because *The Serpent and the Eagle* has numerous foreign terms that many might consider confusing, and I wanted to reduce confusion when possible.

When it comes to spelling, some degree of confusion may be inevitable because there is so much disagreement amongst sources. I opted to rely mainly on academic accounts and historical sites, like the Templo Mayor, for spelling guidance and I would encourage readers to keep this in mind when reading about the Spanish-Mexica war. In some instances, I did invent names for the sake of the reader, though.

For example, Milintica is based upon a real person. However, sources disagree as to the name of the person who held his position. Most of the names I came across would be difficult to comprehend for non-Nahuatl speakers so I opted to use a Nahuatl name with an intuitive pronunciation and a meaningful translation. My hope is readers will understand why I made this decision and will read many other books on this same topic to gain a rich understanding of this fascinating historical event.

Acknowledgements

I owe a great thanks to many individuals and if I listed them all, I would have an acknowledgement equal in length to my novel. In the interests of keeping the list short but still acknowledging the help I have received, I feel obligated to mention the individuals that were most supportive of my writing endeavors. First and foremost, I should thank my mother, my siblings, and my extended family for doing so much to support me in my ambitions. I would like to give a special thanks to Mustafa, Mr. Arbegast, and Alex for reading my early work and I would also like to apologize for letting you do so. My early work is nothing to be proud of. *The Serpent and the Eagle* has gone through many different iterations and I owe thanks to Casey, Marcy, Kara, Louis, Matthew, Ben, Brittany, Armand, Michael, Abigail, Margaret Dalton, Mitchell, Pat, and Cyrus for reading those early versions.

I also owe thanks to Alamtwaha for assistance with the cover illustrations. The painting, *Arrival of Cortés in Vera Cruz*, on the front cover comes from the Kislak collection. Additionally, I owe thanks to Anna Kerr-Carpenter for the help with the map, to Annie for making me more mindful of grammar matters, to the FHS English department for making me more appreciative of literary symbolism, the GWU history department for providing me so many research tools, and to Mariana Nieto for assisting so much with my most recent visit to Mexico. Most of all, I would like to thank Ms. Patterson, one of the many heroes involved in public education. I stopped being able to keep track of the many hours she dedicated to improving my abilities as a writer, speaker, and student but I know I will always be grateful.

www.ingramcontent.com/pod-product-compliance
Lightning Source LLC
Chambersburg PA
CBHW071537110726
47908CB00007B/1922